A HARVEY ROSS COASTAL MYSTERY

Book 1

MURDER MOST FOUL

THEO HARRIS

ALEMAR
PUBLICATIONS

Also by Theo Harris

DC Kendra March - 'Summary Justice' series

PREQUEL (FREE): TRIAL RUN

BOOK 1 - AN EYE FOR AN EYE

BOOK 2 - FAGIN'S FOLLY

BOOK 3 - ROAD TRIP

BOOK 4 - LONDON'S BURNING

BOOK 5 - NOTHING TO LOSE

BOOK 6 - JUSTICE

BOOK 7 - BORN TO KILL

———

BOXSET 1 - BOOKS 1 TO 3

BOXSET 2 - BOOKS 4 TO 6

BOXSET 3 - BOOKS 1 TO 6

———

Think you've gotten away with it? Think again!

PROLOGUE

Beeston Hills, Sheringham, Norfolk, November 1957

The storm pounded the cliff mercilessly as Percy crouched over, holding on to his flimsy jacket tightly in the vain hope that it could ward off the fierce wind, lashing rain, and bitter cold as he made slow progress back to the safety of his home. He had greatly misread the signs, not expecting the storm to be as fierce as it now was, and it had put him in grave danger. Despite this, he had no regrets; venturing out into the storm in its infancy had been a calculated gamble that, despite his current predicament, had paid off. He had succeeded in his mission to hide the family treasures and keep them away from his stepfather—the man who was slowly killing him and his frail mother.

Percy and his mother had both been feeling unwell for several months now, but the doctor had been unable to accurately diagnose the problem. When his mother had started feeling unwell initially, a few weeks before Percy, it was thought to have been caused by depression; the pain of losing her childhood sweetheart—and later husband—at the end of the war had been too much for her ailing heart to cope with. When Percy had started developing similar symptoms, the doctor could not give the same diagnosis and was stumped as to the cause. A fellow doctor had guessed it could be psychological and the equivalent to 'sympathy pains', as Percy was very close to his mother, especially after losing his father at such an early age.

Percy had never liked his stepfather, whom his mother, Dorothy, had married—after many failed proposals—two years earlier. Although she had rebuffed Robert Franklin many times, she was eventually persuaded that having a husband would be far more beneficial than being a widow. Franklin, who was a cousin to her dead husband, was also a widower and had a son two years younger than Percy. Despite the younger age, his son, Bradley, was a bully, and as such, the sons had a fractious relationship.

When the pains in his stomach had started, Percy finally realised the pains were like his mother's, leading him to suspect foul play and, after some thought, believe that Robert was responsible. Without proof, there was nothing he could do, until the previous evening when he had the good fortune of being in the right place at the right time. Having helped his weak mother to the table, Percy and Bradley had sat and waited for Robert to bring out the rest of the food for their dinner. It was only by good fortune that Percy had left the table to go to the lavatory, and it was that decision that finally led him to the proof that he needed. As he passed by the kitchen, he saw Robert place something in the bin. It wasn't done casually but furtively, whereby he put his hand in and hid whatever it was underneath the rubbish. Fortunately, he hadn't seen Percy as he walked by.

Later that night, when everyone was asleep, Percy crept

downstairs into the kitchen and searched for whatever it was that Robert had concealed. He first felt before he pulled out a small glass bottle, and it was then that it hit him that he was indeed in trouble.

'Arsenic', he whispered as he stared at the small, brown, and now-empty bottle with the skull and crossbones printed on the cream-coloured label, above the name of the contents, *ARSENIC TRIOXIDE*, and the warning in slightly larger letters—*POISON*.

He had heard about the poison and about how chronic poisoning could not be reversed, whilst also causing long-term damage, but, in many cases, could be fatal.

'Mum,' he whispered. 'Oh, poor Mum,' he whimpered, before realising that he needed to get back upstairs before anyone saw him. He wrapped the small bottle in an empty paper bag from the bin and crept back upstairs.

When he finally laid back down on his bed and thought of the consequences of the poison, along with the reasons why it was happening, it became all too clear. Robert Franklin had always been jealous of his older cousin, Percy's father—jealous of his stature in the community as a wealthy landowner, and, in turn, jealous that he had neither a good standing nor wealth of any kind. When Percy's father, Captain James Flynn, had been declared dead in 1944, the announcement had a devastating effect on Percy's mother and on five-year-old Percy. Now, as he approached his seventeenth birthday, and having made the devastating discovery of the poison, Percy suddenly recounted several occasions when he'd seen Robert admiring many things in the Flynn household: paintings, family heirlooms, the family silver, that sort of thing. By marrying his mother and ridding them both, he would finally have the wealth and standing that he had so fervently wished for—without having to share it with anyone. With Dorothy and Percy dead and out of the way, nothing could stop Robert Franklin from becoming the rich landowner.

Percy knew that he had a chance of surviving the poison if he went to the doctor and asked for help, but before he did so, he would try and stop Franklin from succeeding in his devious plan.

He would take most of what Franklin yearned for, and hide it.

THE FOLLOWING MORNING, after Robert Franklin had left for an appointment and fourteen-year-old Bradley had gone to play with his friends, Percy went upstairs to see his ailing mother. When he saw that she was asleep in her favourite chair by the window, where she could see the sea, he decided to leave any explanations until later and crack on with his plan before either of the Franklins returned home.

The first thing Percy did was take a leather satchel, one that his father had cherished, from the wardrobe where he knew his mother had kept it. Inside the satchel were the deeds to the house they lived in—Cambourne House—that had been in the Flynn family for three generations, along with other deeds for the land and properties owned by his father in the Sheringham area, which included extensive farmland and farmer's cottages. There were also several letters and proclamations dating back to the early 1800s that showed provenance and titles to the land that had been bestowed upon the Flynn family due to heroism on the part of an ancestor during the Napoleonic Wars. He then retrieved his father's prized campaign medals from the war, including the Victoria Cross that he had been awarded posthumously after his gallantry in saving twelve men at the Battle of Arnhem during Operation Market Garden, before unfortunately succumbing to injuries and being declared dead. His mother was distraught that his body had not been returned and was buried in an unknown grave somewhere in the Netherlands.

Using one of his mother's pillowcases, Percy then took her two jewellery boxes, along with the pendant from her bedside table—one that held a picture of them as a family before James's death—along with a lock of his hair, which he remembered was cut on the day the pendant was given to his mother. He also took his father's prized pocket watch that had been passed down to him from his great-grandfather.

'It's for the best, Mum, I'm so sorry,' he whispered, his voice sounding helpless and desolate.

Moving quickly downstairs, Percy took two canvas sacks from the pantry, previously used for storing potatoes, and headed for the study. He removed two small paintings from the wall that he knew were prized greatly by his father: a small Turner landscape and a John Constable study of a plate of fruit and a glass of wine. He remembered watching his father smile as he looked at them from time to time, and although both were small paintings, he knew they had some value. He retrieved an engraved tin that his father had brought back from a trip to Cornwall and had kept his calligraphy pens and brushes in. He placed the medals, pocket watch, and pendant in the tin, along with an envelope that he took from his pocket, and placed them into one of the sacks along with the leather satchel. The two paintings were placed carefully into the other sack.

Percy looked around one last time before heading for the door. As he stepped outside, he saw that the wind had picked up and he guessed that it would start to rain later. He grabbed a trowel from the flower bed as he left the front garden and headed up the hill towards the nearby Beeston Hills. He knew exactly where to hide the treasures, and he didn't have much time.

———

THE STORM WAS merciless as Percy made his way slowly back home, having achieved what he'd set out to do, now returning empty-handed. This was after one last task that needed to be done before his return, a change of plan due to the ferocious storm, in case something was to go wrong—something he'd hope to correct later, certainly after the storm had passed. He was expecting all hell to break loose when he walked through the front door, knowing that the Franklins would both have returned. He would face up to his accusers and accuse Robert Franklin of trying to kill him and his mother both.

Beeston Hills were very exposed, and at times, the wind was so strong that Percy felt he would be blown over. The rain lashed at him almost at right angles; such was the ferocity of the gales. He was still some way from home when he realised that he was in deep trouble. He felt his already-diminished strength fading further, his pace slowing as a result. It was only his fierce determination and the thought of protecting his mother that drove him on.

He was just a hundred yards from his house, so close to the path that led to the Hills, when Percy finally succumbed to the elements. He fell to his knees, disorientated, exhausted, and crestfallen. His hand, shivering from the cold, went to his inside jacket pocket and pulled out a small, grainy photograph of his childhood sweetheart: the girl that he'd planned to elope and spend a life with... his beloved girlfriend.

He fell forward onto the sodden ground and laid there, his life ebbing away. He barely had the strength to say his final word as the wind took the precious photo from his hand.

'Millie.'

1

THE COTTAGE

The cottage, Beeston Common, Sheringham, Norfolk –
Present day

Harvey stood by the side of the road and looked
fondly at the cottage that he'd spent so many happy summers
in all those years ago. He smiled as he looked around at the
large field, a grass common that was popular with dog walkers, and was pleased that the land had never been developed.
There were plenty of decent walks in the area and he was
now about to live with them on his front doorstep, something
he was looking forward to. He closed his eyes and took a deep
breath of the fresh air; it was so different to London's. The
proximity of the sea, just a five-minute walk away, meant that
it was another thing he would enjoy as a result of the move.

The two-storey, three-bedroom cottage was clad in tradi-
tional Norfolk flint, with red bricks around the wooden-framed
windows and the traditionally styled wooden front door that
was painted in a pleasant pastel green. His aunt had spent much
of her book earnings on keeping it well-maintained, and it
showed: it was immaculate. The cottage was semi-detached,

with a generous front garden that was separated from the neighbours by a low, flint-built wall that was still visible despite the tall, well-trimmed hedge that grew in front of it. There was a side gate that led to a small back garden that Harvey remembered being mainly paved with raised beds on each side and the end, each hosting a plethora of fragrant herbs and other plants, with jasmine and honeysuckle growing either side of the back door.

He looked down at Max, the Patterdale Terrier that he'd agreed to look after for a month or so while his now ex-wife was on a cruise to get over their divorce, and patted him on the head.

'Well, Max, this is now home for me, and you too, for a while. Let's go and see what the inside is like, okay?' he said. 'Maybe you can claim one of the bedrooms, eh?'

He opened the front door to a well-lit, spacious living area, the carpeted staircase straight ahead for the first floor. The lounge was freshly painted in a neutral colour, as was the rest of the cottage, and led to glazed doors that opened into an open-plan kitchen and dining area, with modern appliances installed.

'Wow, Aunt Agatha, you didn't mess about, did you?'

The place was spotless, just as he remembered it, although with much newer furniture. He opened the back door to the small garden that made him smile instantly. The raised beds were full and vibrant with colour from the herbs and other plants that his aunt had lovingly tended for so many years. He sat on one of the wooden garden chairs that surrounded an ornate, wrought iron table and took in the smells and sounds that came from this wonderful space.

'I think we're going to like it here, Max,' he proclaimed, patting the dog on the head. It was a feel-good space, and he smiled at the thought of sitting outside without a care in the world.

IT WAS ONLY when he went back inside that Harvey noticed the letter propped up against the microwave, his name neatly written on the envelope. He let Max off the lead and picked the letter up, taking his time to open it. The letter was handwritten in his aunt's famous flowing handwriting—something she was very proud of.

Dearest Harvey,

I need to start off by apologising for the suddenness of my departure. I made the decision not to bother anyone and just fade away as nature intended, which is why I kept it from you. I hope you understand.

Anyway, on to other things. I hope you don't mind being lumbered with the cottage. I remember how much you loved being here and thought that you should be the one to look after it. I made sure everything is nice and tidy for you, freshly decorated and everything serviced, so you can start using it whenever you need to. Hopefully, you'll get to use it frequently. I'm sure Becky and the girls will enjoy it as well. I don't know whether you managed to read any of my poetry books, but I do remember that you loved H.G. Wells, J.R.R. Tolkien, and Jules Verne, amongst others, so I hope you enjoy my book collection as much as I did.

There's also a manuscript that I wrote and which I intended to send to my publisher, a sort of real-life crime anthology that I adored writing, involving some local landmarks and old legends. You should have a read and see if it inspires you to engage with the area more. Linked to some of the manuscript is a box of souvenirs and memories that I have left in the loft, and which I have entrusted to you to do with as you see fit—I trust you to do the right thing by them. It will give you a better idea of my life and hopefully answer some questions.

Finally, I've left a list in the kitchen drawer that has everything you need to know: who the neighbours are, when to put the bins out, that sort of thing, along with spare keys. There's also one last surprise for you which you probably have no idea about, a car I bought around fifteen years ago, which I called Archie. I had Archie restored a few years ago and have kept him nice and dry in a nearby garage. I only drove him in nice weather, but what you do with him now is up to you, as it is part of my bequest to you. You'll love him, I'm sure, he's marvellous!

I missed having you here after you grew up, Harvey, but it was always wonderful to hear from you each year on my birthday and at Christmas. I know how busy you were, so the fact that you remembered me meant a great deal to me. I hope that you remember me as fondly. I hope that you have a wonderful life filled with joy, Harvey. It is what I wish for you and your loved ones.

All my love,
Your aunt Agatha xx

HARVEY SMILED and wiped a tear away. He folded the letter and put it back in its envelope, taking it with him into the kitchen. He opened a couple of drawers before he found the one his aunt had mentioned in the letter. There was a plastic container that had a number of keys in it, all labelled; there were several spare front door keys—two each for the side gate and the back door, as well as several smaller keys for the window locks. There was another envelope, which contained a list of everything to do with the cottage, including contact and account numbers for the utilities, names of a few of the neighbours, including one to avoid, that sort of thing. Finally, there was a black leather pouch that Harvey picked up and untied. Inside were two old-fashioned, brown, leather key fobs, each with two keys, which he assumed were for the car and the garage. He looked at the list and saw on the last page an entry:

Archie's Garage—next to number 57—paid up until the end of next year, see Brenda McNeil at 57 when you want to renew.

'LET'S SEE WHO, exactly, Archie is, Max,' he nodded to the dog that was eagerly wagging his tail beside him.

He put the lead back on Max and they left the cottage, walking towards the end of the row of cottages that faced the common. The last cottage was number 57, some hundred metres from Agatha's cottage, and there was a detached garage alongside it. Like the cottage, it was well-maintained. The garage doors had been painted recently, the green matching that of the cottage. The twin wooden doors had a Chubb lock that Harvey assumed matched the key in his hand. He tentatively put it in the lock and turned it. The faint click assured him that, like everything else of Aunt Agatha's, it worked very well. He pulled the first door open, and then the second, after lifting the bolt on the inside. The garage was spacious enough for the car and for him to walk either side of it without any obstructions. There was a work-bench at the end with a tool rack, the tools neatly arrayed in size order. The car was covered with a modern, grey cover, designed to keep the car dust-free as well as waterproofing it.

Harvey pulled the sheet from the car, revealing a well-polished work of art, a red 1969 MGB Roadster with wire wheels and a black soft-top.

'Wow! What a beauty, eh, Max?' Harvey exclaimed, running his hand across the front wing.

The car was immaculate, recently restored just as Agatha had explained. The chrome trim and grille gleamed in the dim light, and the black leather interior was pristine. He opened the driver's door and sat in the car, noticing that the mileage was low for its age and nodding in appreciation.

'You are certainly full of surprises, Aunt Agatha,' he stated in disbelief, running his hands over the steering wheel. 'God bless you.'

After locking the garage up, he walked back with Max to the cottage and made himself a cup of tea. He walked to the bookcase in the lounge, a dark antique oak with glass doors partially hiding the treasures within. Harvey's eyes widened once he saw the books inside: first editions of many classics in great condition, some of them worth thousands. He whistled in appreciation before noticing the anomaly in the collection: a large, black, leather-bound manuscript with nothing written on the spine. He pulled it out and saw that it was a relatively modern spring back binder, used for loose-leaf binding. When he opened it, he was amazed to see that it was filled with handwritten pages, all in his aunt's handwriting. Many of the pages had sketches or hand-drawn maps as references, which Harvey found fascinating. He sat down with the binder and flipped to the start, which was when he saw the index that Aunt Agatha had written. It was titled *Unsolved Mysteries by the Sea*.

'More surprises,' he muttered out loud as he turned the pages to see names, locations, dates, lists of unanswered questions, and lists of evidence. It went on and on and surprised the hell out of Harvey. What he read in the binder was of a high quality and what a seasoned detective would be capable of, and here he was, admiring something written by an elderly aunt who had just passed away.

The former detective inspector sat back and pondered on his situation. The thoughts of what he was going to do now that he was officially retired had been vague and uncertain, but the binder and the generosity of his late aunt had given him something to cling on to, and possibly work with.

'Maybe retirement won't be all that bad, eh, Max?'

2

REVELATION

Three weeks later

Harvey stood in front of the cottage and stared at it, something he had done regularly since moving in, a half-filled shopping bag in one hand and Max on a lead in the other, thinking on memories when he had visited as a child. It had only been three weeks since he had moved in, and it still hadn't sunk in that he was now retired and living at Beeston Common in the Norfolk town of Sheringham, in a cottage that his aunt had recently left him in her will. He was no longer a crazily busy, successful detective inspector in London working on cold cases that nobody else had solved, with the busy work schedule leaving little time for anything... or anyone else.

He looked down at Max and smiled. The friendly dog wagged his tail excitedly, making Harvey laugh out loud.

'Back home again, Max,' he said to the panting dog. 'What do you want to do next?'

It had taken him just three weeks to start feeling the boredom that he'd so feared would hit him when he arrived in the popular seaside town. Having moved his few belongings into the immaculately kept cottage, all that remained was for him to get to know the area again and settle into his new life. Aunt Agatha had modernised the cottage and maintained it as well as humanly possible, so there was no DIY needed, no gardening needed, and nothing even to clean when he had moved in. Even Archie, her beloved red MGB Roadster that she had also willed to Harvey, had been lovingly and meticulously restored and needed no work on it. There was very little, or nothing much, for him to do but explore the area and try and engage with the neighbours. As he stood looking at Max, knowing that there would be no response, one of the neighbours hailed him.

'Morning, Mr Ross, how are you settling in?' asked Alan Hudson from the adjoining cottage.

'Just fine, thank you, Alan, and please, it's Harvey,' he replied.

'That's good to know, Harvey. Just knock on the door if you need anything, but I'm sure it won't take you long to get to know the place,' Alan offered with a smile.

'Thank you, that's very good of you. And please thank Jamila for the cookies, they were delicious,' Harvey grinned.

'I will, but expect more; she would bake for England and win gold medals if it were a sport,' Alan laughed.

'One thing, Alan, my aunt Agatha left me some books and letters relating to the history of Sheringham which I've started to read. It's all fascinating stuff, but is there anywhere else or anyone you know who could help me if I had any questions?'

'To be honest, the best place you could probably ask is the Sheringham Museum; the team there are extremely helpful, especially Lisa and Ken, so between them, they'll know pretty much all there is to know or where you can find the answers,' Alan replied.

'That's great, thanks. I may visit tomorrow.'

'Well, have a good day, and pop in anytime for a cuppa if you fancy some company,' Alan said, waving as he walked back indoors.

Harvey keyed himself into the cottage and let Max off the lead. The terrier ran to the water bowl to slake his thirst. He emptied the contents of the carrier bag into the fridge and took a cold bottle of lemonade out, before sitting in the comfortable armchair opposite the television that he hadn't yet switched on. It was one of the things he was determined to avoid, watching television when there was a world to discover out there.

But still, he was bored.

He remembered the binder that his aunt had left him, along with a wonderful selection of first edition books, so he walked to the antique oak bookcase to retrieve it. He opened the glass doors and pulled out the large, black, leather-bound spring back binder, nodding again in appreciation at the array of valuable books that Aunt Agatha had so lovingly collected over decades.

Sitting back into the armchair, Harvey opened the binder to the title page and smiled when he saw the title: *Unsolved Mysteries by the Sea*. In her letter to him, Agatha had mentioned the manuscript as being a labour of love that she had intended to send to her publisher but had never quite managed it. Her success as a poet had emboldened her to write something new and different, and the real-life crime anthology based on local stories, legends, and folklore had inspired her to jot down notes about her discoveries and research over many years.

As he flicked through the manuscript filled with hand-written pages, newspaper clippings, sketches, and maps, Harvey again nodded his head in amazement... and with great respect at the detail that his aunt had included, almost detective-like, if not better. There were copious notes on the Duchess of Leith, a cabin cruiser that was found abandoned just off the coast, going round and round in circles before eventually being stopped. There were also the cases of April Fabb, a nine-year-old girl that had vanished in 1969; the tragic death of Dorothy Flynn, a mother at her son's inquest where his death had been ruled as suspicious; a Polish trawler that was suspected of being a Soviet spy ship that had ran aground in the 1950s, and many more. Harvey decided that when the time was right, he'd continue his aunt's research and maybe complete her labour of love.

It was then that he remembered something else his aunt had mentioned in her letter: a box of souvenirs and memories linked to the manuscript that she had put in the loft. Looking at Max, now lying next to him on the floor, he got up.

'Now's as good a time as any,' he told the dog, making his way up the stairs to retrieve the box.

He used the stowing pole to open and pull down the loft hatch before lowering the ladder. Seconds later, he was in the loft, which, when he switched the light on, he saw was surprisingly spacious and well-lit. It was fully insulated and boarded, and the boxes and furniture up there had been carefully arranged and stored. Harvey scratched his head, not knowing where to start. On one side were a dozen or more large wooden crates, which he saw were labelled. Most were filled with neatly folded clothing, with dates on the labels, which Harvey found strange. They were separated into decades, starting from the 1960s with two or three per decade up to the 2000s.

Other boxes contained multiple copies of her poetry books along with other books that she had stored there. Along the other side were two antique ottoman storage boxes and one vintage dressing table missing its mirror. Even in the loft, Harvey could see that Aunt Agatha had kept the place meticulously clean; there was no dust or dirt to be found anywhere. Next to the dressing table was an upholstered stool, which Harvey imagined his aunt sitting in whilst looking through her memories that were no doubt stored up there.

The first ottoman contained a large number of cloth-bound notebooks on one side, each with a neatly scribed year on the front, also going back to the 1960s, along with a stack of folders on the other side, which Harvey assumed were paperwork that Agatha had kept for some reason.

The second ottoman contained smaller storage boxes of different sizes, some wooden, some plastic, and one that was made from a dull metal of some kind, possibly pewter, that Harvey was immediately drawn to due to the engravings that covered it. The box itself measured approximately twelve inches long by nine wide and four deep, and the engravings were crude and depicted wartime scenes including a Spitfire plane, a tank, a warship, and six soldiers. Harvey recalled that his aunt's father had served during the Second World War and that this had probably been his.

When opening the box, which was heavy for its size, Harvey saw that it contained a number of small boxes, each containing a medal that Harvey assumed had been given to Aunt Agatha's father for his service. There were also several large envelopes that were addressed to A. Ross, again whom

Harvey assumed to be his aunt's father. He opened one of them and found that it contained a certificate that had accompanied each of the medals. Harvey was about to replace the certificate when he did a double take and saw that it had, in fact, been awarded to Agatha Ross.

'What?' he blurted out in astoundment, opening the rest of the envelopes to find that they had all been awarded to his aunt.

'Aunt Agatha, what secrets have you been keeping from us all?' he laughed out loud.

One of the certificates and medals awarded was the George Cross, awarded in 1971 for gallantry, diligence, and fortitude in assisting in the prevention of an attack on the royal family by foreign agents. There was a Director's Honur Award from the United States Secret Service, for her contribution and collaboration to the same—that had Harvey shaking his head in amazement. Another was the Meritorious Service Medal, dated 1966 to 1996, for long service and good conduct that had been awarded by the Royal Navy. The last was an award presented to her by MI5 for long service and good conduct for the same years, 1966 to 1996.

Harvey gasped when he realised what he had found. His beloved aunt, with whom he had stayed with during many summers in his youth, had been a serving officer in the Royal Navy and an MI5 operative for at least thirty years, and nobody was aware of it.

'Bloody hell. Aunt Agatha was a spy!'

3

DISCOVERY

I t took some time before Harvey emerged from the loft and made his way to the kitchen table. He was armed with a box containing some of the clothbound notebooks, a handful of the folders, a small black book of contact names and numbers, the pewter box containing Aunt Agatha's medals, and a small bundle of letters that had also been in the pewter box.

'Things just got a little more exciting, Max, eh?' he stated in excitement, patting the terrier on the head.

He laid everything out on the table so that he could start looking through everything to make more sense of it all. He'd grabbed six of the notebooks and picked one of them up, dated 1973, and started reading.

The first entry was dated January 2nd, 1973. Written in his aunt's distinctive style, was a short entry that made him raise his eyebrows.

*Made visual contact with Agent 215 at northern
perimeter fence Lakenheath.
Agent 215 took discrete photos of Phantom F4D
taking off.
Reported to main office.*

Harvey was stunned. This short entry basically explained
that she had covertly spied on a foreign agent that was taking
photos of U.S. Air Force planes at RAF Lakenheath, where
they were based. He imagined her crouching behind a tree,
or even hiding up high in the branches, and laughed out loud
at the thought of his beloved aunt being involved in something like this. He turned the page to read another entry
made on January 23rd, 1973.

*Followed Agent 332 to 16 Canterbury Way,
Thetford.
Driving maroon Morris Minor TTU 445J.
Used key to enter end terrace house.
Reported to main office.*

Harvey read on and saw that there were similar entries
throughout this one notebook for 1973. Agatha had sent
reports to her office for each entry but had made these
shorter entries for her own record.

He checked the folders he had brought down and found
they contained more handwritten notes on individuals that
she had been watching. Each folder was a dossier of a foreign
agent and included black-and-white photographs along with
the notes that she'd made for each of them. Again, it seemed

that Agatha had duplicated what she had sent to the main office and kept her own diligent records. They were meticulous.

Most entries were of Russian individuals, with a smattering of Polish and German suspected agents, and a surprising number of British individuals that had clearly preferred the communist way of life—a worrying development at the time.

Based on the number of notebooks, he surmised that his aunt had been very busy during her years as a covert agent, and her main job was keeping an eye on Russian agents that were spying on U.S. and British bases.

'Max, my old aunt was a hero and not one person knows about it. How sad is that, eh?' he lamented, stroking the terrier's head as it sat alongside him. 'Let's see what other surprises she kept from us.'

He untied the string that held the bundle of letters together and saw that they were addressed to her. He took out the first letter in the bundle, written on typical 1970s blue letter paper, and opened it. It was dated December 19th, 1972.

My Dearest Agatha,

I hope this letter finds you safe and well. It is one of the most painful that I have written in all my years, and I am finding it incredibly difficult keeping my emotions in check.

The day has come, my darling, the day that we have both dreaded and talked about on those solemn occasions. As Christmas approaches, my posting has come to an end and my plane leaves tonight for New York. It pains me to say this, but it is unlikely that I will ever return.

The past eighteen months, since that first incredible day that we met, have been some of the happiest days of my life, even knowing that they would not last long. You changed my life and made me realise that it was one very much worth living, my beautiful English rose, and I will forever be grateful to you.

Parting ways yesterday was one of the toughest things I have ever had to do, and I no doubt made an ass of myself, for which I apologise profusely. It is the reason I am sending this last letter, now that my head is clearer, despite my sadness, to tell you how I feel.

I pray that you have a wonderful life, Agatha Ross, and that you remember me fondly, for I shall never forget you.

Lovingly yours,
Robbie xx

HARVEY PUT the letter back in its envelope and sat back in the chair, mesmerised by what he had learnt this past half hour or so.

'I need a drink,' was all he could say to sum it up.

HARVEY'S BOREDOM was completely forgotten, the revelations about his aunt now playing havoc with his mind. The fact that nobody was aware of her secret life was astonishing and made Harvey realise that she must have been an operative of the highest calibre. He vowed to investigate his aunt's life in much more detail, almost as a way of thanking her for her incredible service and keeping her memory and accomplishments alive.

'Thirty years, Max. Thirty years and nobody had a clue. How good is that?' he marvelled.

It would take some time to go through all the notebooks and folders, as well as the letters and contacts book. He smiled as he automatically thought of ways that he'd structure the 'investigation', with it being second nature to him and all.

'Maybe life here won't be as boring as I thought it would be,' he affirmed, leaning back in his chair and pondering all the possibilities of where to begin, happy that there was at least this unexpected but interesting new development to keep him occupied.

His thoughts were interrupted by his phone ringing, and he looked down at the screen with a smile before answering.

'Well, if it isn't defective Sergeant Steve McGarry, finally remembering his old boss. And before you say anything, yes, I did mean defective,' he drawled. 'Have things gone badly wrong in my absence yet?'

'That's not remotely funny, none of it,' Steve shot back. 'And actually, things have improved dramatically since you *abandoned* us.'

'Well, that's good to hear if it is, in fact, true,' Harvey laughed.

'No, it's not true. The new DI is a bit dim, to be honest. He's just left us all to it and doesn't really get involved. I suppose we should be grateful after the last slave-driving boss.'

'That's very good, thank you,' Harvey replied, refraining from rolling his eyes. 'Now, tell me why you're bothering me on such a lovely day here by the sea.'

'I guess, like you, I was tired of waiting for a call, so I thought I'd check in and see if you've started sleeping all day yet or ordered your first Zimmer frame... you know, typical retirement activities like that.'

'You should work on that humour of yours, Steve, it hasn't changed at all, despite all the suggestions everybody makes,' Harvey quipped.

'Yeah, sorry about that, I find it hard not to take it up a notch now that you're not my boss anymore. Seriously, though, just checking in to see how you are,' Steve replied.

'Well, I was starting to get a little bored, but things have picked up today and I think I'm going to be alright here. It's a lovely town; the people are great, and the drives around the countryside visiting all the pubs I've been recommended have been pretty cool. The MG is a great little car for that,' he effused.

'So, you've taken up drink-driving, after all these years of keeping it at bay?' Steve tutted, his tone obviously teasing.

Harvey chuckled. 'They're pretty surprised when I ask for a diet cola, that's for sure.'

'Well, now that I know you're safe and well, I can rest easy,' Steve mused. 'And maybe one day soon we'll pop over and visit one of those pubs with you.'

'You're more than welcome, I have plenty of room if you want to stay for a bit. It's a tad different from London, so brace yourself for clean air and friendly people.'

'Londoners are friendly, they're just... misunderstood. Anyway, catch you later, Boss,' Steve countered before hanging up the phone.

Being addressed as *boss* again made Harvey smile, knowing that it was an affectation that he would happily live with. He got up and made his way to the kitchen, picking up Max's lead on the way and attaching it just as the dog immediately came running, knowing that a walk was about to start.

'Sorry to have kept you waiting, boy, I'll make it up to you with a long walk along the beach. What do you say to that, eh?'

Max barked; he loved the beach and understood that's where they were heading. His tail was working overtime as he looked at Harvey longingly, hoping they would leave right that moment.

Harvey obliged and was soon outside, locking the front door. In the few weeks he had been back in Sheringham, the man had wandered around, learning new walks for Max, as well as revisiting places from his childhood. He soon found that the town had changed a fair amount since he was last here, with many new housing developments on the outskirts along with renovations to old haunts. Alan, his neighbour, had told him that the past ten years had been particularly difficult as more and more houses were bought by out-of-towners as holiday homes, which meant that for much of the year they sat empty, especially in the winter.

'The community has changed as a result,' Alan had explained, 'but it's starting to rebound now, and things are getting better. It was voted one of the best places to live in the UK, so it can't be that bad, can it?'

Harvey turned right out of the cottage and walked along Curtis Lane, under the railway bridge and through the narrow lane leading to Nelson Road. He turned left there and was soon walking down the slope to the promenade, where the colourful beach huts were lined up, facing the sea in their spectacular multi-coloured hues. Harvey turned right and walked along the shorter part of the promenade before going down the steps to the sandy beach now the tide was out. He looked around and smiled at the wonderful view; the spotless, sandy beaches went on for many miles, devoid of humans except for the occasional dog walker or couple out for a pleasant walk before the tide came in. He let Max off the lead and watched as the dog bounded away excitedly, stopping to sniff occasionally when he came across something new.

Walking towards West Runton, Harvey could see the attraction of living in the area. Not just because of the fresh air and empty beaches, but because of nature at its finest. As he crossed over the groynes that separated the beaches, he could see the wind farms a few miles out into the North Sea on one side, and the impressive sandy cliffs of Beeston Hills, now commonly known as Beeston Bump. He walked close to the cliffs and could see remnants of recent collapses where the rainwater runoff inland had caused erosion and the subsequent collapse of some of the cliffs into the sea below.

He walked towards one recent collapse from two nights earlier where a storm had led to a fresh collapse. As it was so new, the sea hadn't yet washed it away, so it was there for all to see. The sandy collapse had formed a barrier almost thirty metres long, so some of the beach area that people walked along was blocked. Max ran towards the pile of sand and started sniffing away. Harvey walked around it, crossing back through the old coastal defences that had been left to nature and onto the unaffected area of the beach. As he was about to circumnavigate the collapse, he turned to see Max digging feverishly at an area nearest to the sea, where it was shallower than the rest. The terrier barked as he continued to dig away.

'What have you found there, Max?' Harvey walked back to see what the commotion was about.

When he reached Max, he saw that the dog had dug a hole a foot deep and slightly more than a foot wide. Harvey saw that there were several large, broken sections of fabricated concrete scattered nearby and wondered whether a small structure had collapsed in the fall—maybe an old pillbox from the Second World War or an abandoned storage shed. He grabbed Max's collar and pulled him back gently.

'What is it, boy? What have you found?' he asked, peering into the hole.

He leaned closer and saw something poking a couple of inches out of the sand. Leaning in, he grabbed it and started to pull. It moved slightly and Harvey could see that it was something made of leather. As he continued to pull, the object emerged slowly, and it became clear, when it was halfway out of the sand, that what Max had found was an old leather satchel.

Harvey brushed away some of the wet sand and shook off the rest as he looked at it closely. It had some weight to it so there was something inside, but the clasps had rusted shut and so he couldn't open it.

'Sorry, Max, but this is too tempting to continue your

walk. Let's get home and see what's inside, eh? I'll make it up to you on the next walk, I promise.'

Before turning around, Harvey took some pictures with his phone of the location so he could match it with any known landmarks on a map, just in case. He then turned and started to walk back towards the promenade and back towards home, wondering what was in the mysterious satchel.

'Today has most definitely not been boring,' he reasoned out loud.

4

THE CONTENTS

Back at the cottage, Harvey made room on the kitchen table and laid down some old newspaper before placing the satchel face up. He sprayed some WD40 lubricant on the clasps to free them from the rust and gave the satchel a wipe down to remove all the remaining sand and mould. The condition of the satchel made Harvey believe that it was decades old, but until he had access to the contents inside, it would be impossible to tell. While he waited for the WD40 to take effect, he made himself a mug of tea and gave Max a treat for his efforts in finding the satchel.

Having given it enough time, Harvey attempted to release the clasps, but the effort to release them failed, so he realised he had no choice but to cut the straps. He fetched a pair of scissors from a nearby drawer.

'Damn shame to do this, but it's the only way,' he sighed before cutting into the first strap. It took some effort, but eventually the scissors won, and he managed to slice through both straps.

'The moment of truth, Max,' he mimicked a drumroll in the air before lifting the flap on the satchel.

He peered inside before reaching in and pulling out a brown leather folder tied together with string, much like it was done many decades earlier. Putting it on the table, he then pulled out a hardback book, sopping wet, but with a legible title: *Fun with Science*. He put that down and picked up the leather folder again. It was also sodden, so Harvey didn't think that the contents would be in good shape. He put it to one side and reached in to remove an ornate metal box with engravings on the top that depicted a landscape. Harvey could make out the name engraved at the bottom:

St. Just, Cornwall.

The box had survived the elements, and despite it being wet and dirty in places, appeared in very good shape, giving Harvey hope for the contents inside.

After some effort, he was able to prise open the lid and was relieved to see that the interior was bone-dry and the contents unaffected. He whistled when he saw what they were. There were several medals; one was a Victoria Cross, the highest and most prestigious decoration of the honours system, one that was rarely given and only to those that were worthy because of valour in the presence of the enemy. Turning it over, Harvey saw the date engraved on the rear of the medal, on the suspension bar:

19TH SEPTEMBER 1944
No. 35/182776 CPT. J. FLYNN,
3RD BN, PARA RGT

Putting them to one side, he picked up a heavy, gold-embossed pocket watch. He flipped the case open to see an engraving inside:

A. Flynn, 1881

Harvey nodded slowly, realising that these were significant clues to finding the original owner of the satchel, giving him hope that he could somehow return these valuables to the rightful owner, despite the time that had lapsed.

There were three other items in the box. One was a gold pendant on a chain, which when Harvey opened it revealed a photograph of a family of three smiling happily, the child being a toddler. The second item was a small, brown, empty bottle with the skull and crossbones printed on the cream-coloured label, above the name of the contents, *ARSENIC TRIOXIDE*, and a warning in larger letters – *POISON*.

Finally, there was a cream envelope with the name and address written by hand on the front.

Miss Millicent Dalglish
24 Holts Road
Sheringham

Feeling somewhat guilty, he took out the folded sheet of paper inside and saw that folded within it was a piece of tracing paper with several random dots on it, along with some short dashes at right angles, which meant nothing to him. The sheet of paper was a letter that he began to read.

Darling Millie,

It seems our plans may have to be delayed for some time, for I fear that my mother and I are in grave danger. I must therefore take immediate action to prevent anything further from harming us. I think we have been poisoned, and the foul man responsible is getting away with murder.

I have written this quickly in case I cannot see you as normal on Saturday afternoon, so please do not fret, as I will endeavour to see you as soon as I have resolved this. My intentions are to hide our family heirlooms and report the matter to Constable Waring tomorrow.

We can revisit our plans when we next meet, I promise you, darling.

With all my love,
Percy xxx

HARVEY NODDED AGAIN—ANOTHER name, another potential owner, and a possible police report. This was likely to assist in narrowing down the date of the letter, and therefore the satchel. One thing troubled Harvey though: why was the letter in the box? It had clearly not been posted, so had something happened to Percy before he had a chance to deliver it? More importantly, had the poison done its job and ended his life before he had a chance to deliver it? Harvey sat down and looked up at the ceiling, thinking hard as he was so used to doing when he was a busy DI.

He came to his shocking conclusion very quickly, much like what had happened on many occasions during his time on the Specialist Casework Team in London.

That the person that had written this letter had been murdered.

AFTER A FEW MINUTES pondering on what he had read, Harvey carefully snipped the string that was tied around the brown leather folder that he had pulled out of the satchel. He opened the folder and took out a number of card folders, each containing documents that he recognised as deeds to properties and land. The documents were wet, and much of the text had faded or run as a result, making it difficult to decipher in places. There was enough for him to identify locations and people involved, so he laid out the documents and took photographs of each one.

One of the folders was bound in blue leather with a gold crown embossed on the front and was also tied with string, which he carefully untied and opened. The folder was triple-sided, and so the documents within were better protected than most of the others. He saw that one of the documents was a proclamation that related to land that had been bestowed to the Flynn family by the Crown because of the heroic service of an ancestor from the early 1800s. Harvey nodded respectfully and took photographs of everything within, along with the folder itself.

Harvey took photographs of everything else that he had found and made detailed notes in a blank notebook. He knew what needed to be done but had a hunch that some-how, nothing would be investigated by the police due to the time that had passed. His mind was working overtime as he planned on how to deal with the likely ramifications of a filed investigation.

'Stuff that, I'll make sure to find out who wrote that letter if they don't,' he reassured himself.

5

LOST AND FOUND

W hen he was satisfied that he had made a record of everything, Harvey put everything back in the satchel, as he had found it, and put it into a plastic carrier bag before leaving the cottage with Max in tow. His destination was the police station at North Walsham, the nearest that he was aware of that had a front counter; somewhere he could report his find. Turning left out of the cottage, he walked to the end of the terrace and to the garage that Aunt Agatha had been renting from the owner for many years. A few minutes later, he managed to reverse Archie, the 1969 bright red MGB Roadster, out of the garage and onto the road. Before driving off, he made sure the garage was locked, and that Max was securely fastened into the front passenger seat.

'You ready, boy? Let's take Archie for a run, shall we?'

The drive was a pleasant one, and only took thirty minutes via the picturesque Brittons Lane, a narrow, winding, tree-lined road that the sports car stuck to like glue, and then several B-roads through the villages of Felbrigg, Roughton,

and Thorpe Market before arriving at the station in North
Walsham. Harvey smiled as he had visions of his old aunt
driving along with the roof down, waving to people she knew
and having the time of her life in the small roadster. He
parked the car in one of the few available bays and
approached the relatively modern, but not unattractive, two-
storey station that had been built in late 2017. He opened the
glass door and strolled to the front counter that was manned
by a civilian member of staff, with Max alongside him on the
lead, happily wagging his tail in the new environment.

'Good afternoon, sir, how can I help you?' the young man
welcomed.

'Good afternoon to you too, Devon,' Harvey replied,
having noticed the badge on his chest. 'I found something on
the beach this morning and thought I'd bring it here for you
to log in the property found book, if that's okay?'

He took the still-wet satchel out of the carrier bag and
placed it on top of the bag on the counter. He then took out
the box.

'Certainly, sir. Please give me a minute while I fetch an
evidence bag,' Devon informed.

Harvey looked around the reception area and saw that it
had been built relatively recently. It was very different to what
he had been used to back in London, but he appreciated the
location and that the types of crime in this part of England
were very different to that of the capital.

Devon returned with several large, clear evidence bags
that would hold the satchel and contents, before logging on
to the computer on the counter.

'Can I start with your details, sir?' he asked.

Harvey obliged, giving his full name, address, phone
number, and email address.

'I'll need to itemise everything, sir, so please bear with me,' Devon explained as he took out each item and laid it to one side before making a record, muttering each item as he logged it.

Harvey shook his head imperceptibly when Devon logged the medals.

'Three vintage medals,' he had muttered to himself, not recognising the importance of the Victoria Cross in particular.

'I took pictures of everything, just in case,' Harvey said, pausing before speaking once more. 'What do you think is likely to happen with them?'

'Well, sir, our policy is that if nobody claims the contents in the next twenty-eight days, then we'll call you and you can come pick them up as yours,' Devon replied.

'Fair enough,' Harvey shrugged. Just as he had antici- pated, it was unlikely that anyone would investigate anything to do with the find. And because of that, he thought it best to keep his thoughts to himself, particularly about the value of the Victoria Cross, the pocket watch, and the documentation he had found. He would make it his job to find the rightful owners and return them if he was indeed able to keep them after twenty-eight days.

'That's all done, sir,' Devon notified the man as he tied off the last evidence bag with a numbered zip tie. 'I'll just print off the record for you to keep, please give me a second.'

He returned a few moments later with two printouts of everything that Harvey had brought in.

'If you can just sign here, please, sir,' he requested, before passing Harvey one of the copies. 'That's your copy, please hold onto it as we'll need it if you return to claim everything.'

'Thank you, Devon, that's very efficient of you,' Harvey

said, before folding and putting his copy in his pocket. 'Come on, Max, let's get home, shall we?'

The drive home was just as pleasant, with a minor diversion to the petrol station to pick up some milk. Harvey's mind was still in overdrive as he continued to calculate the different lines of enquiry that he'd need to take to identify the owners of the satchel, the recipients of the medals, the family in the photo, and the girlfriend, Millie.

'Lots of work to do and much to figure out, Max,' Harvey resounded as he patted the happy terrier's head.

ON THE WAY BACK HOME, Harvey's thoughts drifted to the contents of the satchel and what the next step for him was going to be. One thing for sure was the need to identify the victim, Percy. There were several clues that would help with that, including the name on the Victoria Cross, on the gold watch, and the documents found—all were in the surname of Flynn. He'd been in Sheringham long enough to know that there were people who would most certainly be able to help, notably those guardians of all the local history at the Sheringham Museum, and also the records likely kept at the Sheringham Library.

Harvey deliberated his course of action as he took Max for a walk after parking the car and decided that he'd make a start the next day. Upon their return from a brisk forty-minute walk around Beeston Bump, he made notes for the following day.

Sheringham Museum - check addresses on deeds/Flynn mentioned?

Sheringham Library - microfiche records? Local newspapers?

Dates - start 1930s onwards.

Millicent Dalglish - 24 Holts Road. Check current occupant.

Land Registry - check re. deeds and ownership.

Tracing paper?

'That's a good amount of work to be starting with, eh, Max?' he reckoned as Max snored loudly by his feet.

As he sat in what was now his favourite chair in the lounge, Harvey found himself thinking of his police colleagues and the camaraderie that he was now missing. He realised that that was what he was missing the most: like-minded colleagues and friends, someone to talk to regularly... basically his friends. He looked over at the sleeping Max and realised that the dog was who he had spoken the most to since he'd arrived in the town. Shaking his head and smirking at the realisation, he made another decision, something that he would start tomorrow with his list of things to do.

He would make new friends.

6

SHERINGHAM MUSEUM

The following morning, Harvey was up earlier than usual, eager to get started on his new venture. After first letting Max out into the garden and then feeding him, Harvey sat with a tea and his notepad as he went over the list again, scheduling the day as he had so frequently done in the past back in London. A walk across the Common followed before leaving Max and heading off towards the first of his many stops for the day.

SHERINGHAM MUSEUM

Harvey walked the short distance to the museum, a modern build with a resplendent glass tower prominently situated on the promenade next to the sea wall, overlooking the sea. He had called ahead and was told that he would be met by Lisa, the museum manager, who would assist in his investigation, which he had earlier claimed was research for a novel that he was writing about local families and their involvement in the world wars.

'Thank you for seeing me so promptly,' he told her as they shook hands. 'I was lucky to find some correspondence that led to me writing the novel and was told you would be able to help.'

'It's our pleasure; we have helped a few authors with their research, it's always nice to meet a new one,' the manager said warmly. 'We've set out some materials for you to look through, hopefully it's what you're looking for and can help with your research.'

She led Harvey to an upstairs room filled with filing cabinets along all four walls. There was a large table in the middle of the room with four shallow plastic boxes, their lids off, waiting for him to inspect. Harvey was introduced to Lynne and Ken who worked with Lisa at the museum.

'Each of the boxes contains a decade's worth of material, starting with the 1930s up to the 1960s, like you asked,' Lisa explained, showing him the contents of one and picking up a small brochure about Sheringham from 1956. 'I'll leave you to it, but if you need anything, just ask Lynne or Ken, who are well-versed in local history. I'll be next door.'

'Before you go, does the name Flynn ring a bell? I'm trying to find out what happened to a Captain J. Flynn who was awarded a Victoria Cross in 1944. Does that ring a bell to you?' Harvey asked.

'No, it doesn't, but that doesn't mean we don't have anything here. I'll search our online records and see if anything comes up,' she replied, walking into the next room.

Harvey sat and started looking through the records, looking for any reference to the name Flynn. There was more material than he expected, with maps and records of all types from each of the decades mentioned. A gold mine for researchers, along with the knowledge that those who worked at the museum had. Lynne and Ken regaled Harvey with local folklore and legends, which he found fascinating in light of his Aunt Agatha's manuscript and vowed to return many times to pick their brains as he sought answers to Agatha's mysteries.

As he continued to make his notes, Lisa walked back into the room, and Harvey could see from the grin on her face that she'd found something.

'That was quick... what did you find?' he asked.

'I found a record in our newspaper archives about a Captain James Flynn, a Sheringham landowner who was posthumously awarded the Victoria Cross for his bravery in saving twelve men at the Battle of Arnhem in September 1944,' she stated, handing him a piece of paper, her grin unwavering.

'What's this?' he questioned.

'It's the address of where he lived, Cambourne House, at the top of Cliff Road, a five-minute walk from here.'

'That's fantastic, Lisa, it's a good place to start,' Harvey praised as he took the paper.

'I'm not finished; there's something else you need to see, but it's on our old microfiche system in the next room,' the manager disclosed, leading the way. She sat down in front of the bulky device and pointed. 'I got the address from another record that showed Captain James Flynn posing in his uniform with a local councillor before he went off to war. It gave his address as Cambourne House and mentioned his wife, Dorothy, and son, Percival.'

'Percy...' Harvey trailed off, the pieces of the puzzle

coming together in his head. 'So, it's linked to a letter written by Percy to his sweetheart, Millie.'

'There's no mention of a Millie in what I've found so far, but there is this,' she informed him, pointing to another article that she brought up.

Harvey leaned forward for a better look.

'Is it possible to print this off or copy it in some way?' he requested.

'Yes, believe it or not, we still have the key that allows us to print on this film here,' Lisa remarked with a smile, pointing to a small printer below the machine. She aligned the screen and zoomed in to the article, focusing so it was clear to read. She hit the print button, and the device made some strange sounds before spitting out the page below. She handed it to Harvey who read it again.

'It's a sad story, isn't it?' she shook her head regretfully with her words.

'It certainly is,' Harvey replied, his words a murmur.

The newspaper article was dated *November 17th, 1957*.

Tragedy at inquest

Tragedy struck at the inquest of 17-year-old Percival Flynn yesterday when his sickly mother, Dorothy Franklin, who had attended with husband Robert, collapsed in court and was pronounced dead shortly after. They had been attending the inquest into the recent death of her only son when, shortly after an open verdict was announced, Mrs Franklin collapsed into the arms of her husband as she stood to leave.

This is not the first time that the Flynn family has suffered heartbreak. Percival's father, Mrs Franklin's first husband, Captain James Flynn, was lost and pronounced dead in September 1944 during Operation Market Garden at the Battle of Arnhem, where he had heroically rescued twelve of his men before succumbing to his injuries. Captain Flynn had been posthumously awarded the Victoria Cross for his heroism.

Harvey read on and then folded the paper in half, putting it in his pocket so that he could revert to it later.

'That was a very unlucky family, wasn't it?' he expressed, shaking his head sadly.

'It is. Such a shame, too,' Lisa replied.

'One thing that's a little strange though... Percival's inquest returned an open verdict, which means that it wasn't clear what he had died from. Do you know if there are any records about that anywhere?' he asked.

'I'll have another look later, if that helps, but it may be prudent to check with the council records office, they should have more information,' she replied.

'Thanks, I may do that.'

Ken was waiting for the exchange to finish before he gestured for Harvey's attention.

'I know there isn't a formal record of it anywhere, but some local folklore is passed down by word of mouth or handwritten in local parish registers. For example, I found one yesterday about the body of an unknown man that was found on the beach at Beeston Regis in October 1955. I come across these every now and again when I check the older records. I remembered another story that was going around in the late fifties or early sixties about the Flynn family and their missing treasure,' he imparted.

Harvey was intrigued.

'Missing treasure? What can you remember about it?'

'Not a lot, sadly... only that word got around after the family had died that their family heirlooms and valuables went missing. There were various rumours that they'd been burgled, or the widow had sold them before she died to pay debts off... something like that,' Ken replied.

'Can you recall what type of valuables?'

'I think there was a few paintings, some gold jewellery, that sort of thing. They were a wealthy family, so the rumours went on for a few years. At one point, we had treasure hunters digging holes all over the place, looking for the mysterious treasure,' Ken explained.

'That's very interesting and good to know, thanks, Ken. You've all been a wonderful help, thank you,' Harvey expressed, shaking their hands in turn. 'Can I pop back again if I need to delve into the records a little more?'

'Of course, just give us a little notice next time, and we can prepare a little better for you,' Lisa replied.

Harvey left the museum buoyed by the discoveries and smiled as he walked back along the promenade.

Things were looking up.

HARVEY WAS BUZZING; knowing that he had found a name and address of the victim was a good starting point. He would check with Land Registry and find out the sale history when he got the chance, but for now, as it was on his way back home, he would have a look for himself. He walked along the promenade, taking in the sea breeze as he passed the colourful array of beach huts along the way. When he reached The Wee Retreat, a converted toilet block that was now one of the best-placed holiday rentals in Sheringham with outstanding views over the sea, he walked up the steps and along the slope towards Cliff Road.

At the end of the slope, instead of turning right and then into Nelson Road to go home, he turned left and walked along the track alongside the pitch and putt course, where he immediately caught sight of Cambourne House, directly opposite the course. The large Victorian house had been converted to a bed and breakfast, and Harvey could see from the car park that it was a popular one; just a stone's throw from the sea, and in an ideal location to explore the town. He looked to the left and saw the path leading up to what was now popularly known as Beeston Bump, or officially known as Beeston Hills.

Walking through the car park towards the house, Harvey could see that the three-storey house had been well-maintained over the years. Thinking back to the 1950s when the Flynns had lived here, he guessed that they were a wealthy family to have lived in such a grand house in such a prominent and exceptional location.

'So, the head of the household is killed during the war. His sole heir is seemingly murdered, and the mother dies at the inquest,' he prompted out loud. 'That sounds decidedly dodgy to me, and it doesn't take much to figure out who benefitted from that, does it?'

All fingers pointed to the stepfather, Dorothy's second husband—Robert Franklin.

'I guess that's where I start looking next.'

7

MILLIE

Harvey took to the task, as he had done for so many years in the Met. He started by conducting a search on the internet for a Robert Franklin in the Sheringham area. There were no social media accounts, nothing of note, and other than what he had read in the newspaper, there was very little about a Robert Franklin from Sheringham, which Harvey found odd. Appreciating that Franklin was likely deceased and not around during the advent of social media, he concluded that the open-source route would likely be a dead end for him. He decided on a different tact and picked up his phone, calling someone who he knew could help.

'Well, well... that didn't take long, did it?' Steve McGarry needled, laughing over the phone. 'Do you miss us that much?'

'Put a sock in it, McGarry, I can still make your life uncomfortable; I have a lot of friends in high places, remember?' Harvey jested, grinning. 'I'm calling to ask for a favour, if you can be bothered?'

'I'm sure I can spare a minute or two. What do you need, Boss?' Steve remarked.

'I'm trying to locate someone who lived in the Sheringham area in 1957... a chap named Robert Franklin. He's a suspect in an unsolved murder that I'm trying to prove,' Harvey responded.

There was a long pause.

'Sorry, Harvey, can you say that again? I thought I heard you say you're investigating a murder from the 1950s.'

'That is, in fact, what I said, Steve. From 1957, to be exact, like I said,' Harvey declared.

'Have I missed something? Have you joined the Norfolk Constabulary without telling us or something?' Steve interrogated.

'Nope. I stumbled across something and I'm keen to follow up on it, that's all. It's keeping me interested and busy, so I figured, why not?'

'Okay, well, that didn't take long either, did it? Bored so quickly that you've decided to start work again, but for no pay. Good one, Boss,' Steve chuckled.

'Double up on that sock, will you? Can you help me, or not?'

'I'll have a look. You know they're a bit anal with data protection nowadays, so I'll have to come up with something constructive to search, but leave it with me. Do you have anything else other than the name... a date of birth or an address?' Steve quizzed.

'No date of birth, just an address that he lived at, which is Cambourne House, Cliff Road, Sheringham, NR26. He was married to a Dorothy Flynn, whose son, Percival Flynn, died in the same year. Anything you can find on all three would be greatly appreciated, especially if there is a police record on

Percival Flynn's death,' Harvey rejoined. 'The inquest returned an open verdict, which suggests there was some suspicion, so I'm hoping there's a record somewhere in the Norfolk Constabulary archives.'

'Leave it with me, Boss. I'll call you if I find anything,' Steve replied.

'Thanks, Steve. And stop calling me boss, I don't tell you what to do anymore, do I?' he laughed.

'Don't you? Anyway, it doesn't matter, you'll always be the boss,' Steve commented with a smirk before hanging up.

Harvey grinned and shook his head.

'Damn, I miss the team.'

HARVEY REMEMBERED the book that he had pulled out from the satchel, *Fun with Science*, and decided to check online to see if he could find any information about it. Checking his phone for the photo that he had taken of the front and back covers, he searched online for an identical copy. It took some time after searches on eBay and other sites, but eventually, he found one on AbeBooks, a specialist directory of rare and antiquarian books.

'Voila!' he exclaimed, making Max jump, startling him awake from his sleep. 'Sorry, boy, didn't mean to scare you,' Harvey chuckled.

There were three copies available, so he chose one, paid twenty-five pounds for it, plus another ten pounds for expedited, next-day delivery, and sat back, satisfied that he had mentally ticked another job off the list.

'We're making some progress, eh, Max?' he asserted.

He picked up his notebook and looked back at what he

had written. He then picked up his phone and brought up a local map of Sheringham, making a mental note of where he was and how long it would take to get to an address at the other side of the town. Nodding, he made his mind up before looking over at Max.

'Fancy a walk, Max?'

WITH REGULAR STOPS for Max to stop and sniff, along with the terrier's occasional... *deposit*, they took almost half an hour to get to Holts Road, specifically to the vicinity of number 24, the address that was on the envelope that Harvey had found, addressed to Millicent Dalglish. The part of the road they were in was a quiet, well-kept residential road with mainly large, detached houses. Number 24 was no exception, sitting back from the road with a landscaped garden and a newly mowed lawn, with mature trees and shrubs along its borders and a small, detached garage to one side. The house was well-kept, the windows freshly painted, and the gravel drive swept clean. As he stood watching from across the road, he saw an elderly lady being helped from the house via the front door by another younger, middle-aged woman, who led them to a small, silver hatchback parked on the drive. The middle-aged woman opened the passenger door and took the cane from her senior as she waited patiently for her to get in the car.

The elderly woman looked up before getting into the car, locking eyes with Harvey, who was still watching from across the road with Max sitting patiently alongside him. He saw the younger woman say something and then also look towards Harvey when she received a reply. Leaving her charge behind, the middle-aged woman walked towards the pavement and stood directly opposite Harvey.

'Can I help you, sir?' she queried.

'I'm sorry, madam, I must look like a weird stalker type to you both, I didn't mean to cause any concern. I'm doing some historical research, and this house was mentioned,' he clarified. 'I was toying with the ideas of knocking when you came out.'

'Historical research? How far back? I don't think this house is more than a hundred years old,' the woman replied.

Harvey could see that the woman was in her late sixties or early seventies and assumed that she was a carer for the elderly lady that had walked out with her.

'Not that far back,' Harvey returned. 'Around seventy years or so, specifically 1957,' he explained.

'Well then, you'd better come and speak to the owner,' the woman dictated, looking back to the lady who was still leaning against the car door, watching them. 'She was living here in 1957.'

Harvey was stunned, not expecting to hear that.

'I'm sorry, what? Did you say she was living here nearly seventy years ago?' Harvey blurted out.

'Yes, that's exactly what I said.'

'What is the lady's name, if you don't mind me asking?' Harvey implored.

'I don't mind at all, it's not a secret. Her name is Millicent Parry,' the woman stated.

Harvey was gobsmacked, and his mouth suddenly became dry—a sensation he hadn't experienced for many years—with surprise and shock taking over in a matter of seconds.

'Was... was she ever called Millie Dalglish?' he questioned.

'Why yes, how on earth did you know that?' the woman gasped, looking just as surprised as Harvey.

THE ELDERLY LADY was still standing by the car when they approached. She looked down at Max, whose tail was wagging furiously as they reached her, and he edged ahead to sniff the lady's outstretched hand.

'This is Harvey Ross; he is doing some historical research about the area in 1957 and says that your house was mentioned,' the carer introduced when they stopped. 'This is Millie Parry, Mr Ross, formerly Millie Dalglish.'

'1957? That was a lifetime ago, young man, why are you interested in my house?' the lady queried.

Now that he was close, Harvey saw that she was an elegantly dressed lady, likely in her eighties, and from the tone of her voice, had a strength belying her age.

'It is lovely to meet you, madam, and I apologise for any inconvenience my tardy appearance may have caused,' Harvey replied. 'As your lovely carer told you, my name is Harvey Ross, and I am an ex-detective inspector in the Metropolitan Police in London. I have just moved to the area and came across a mystery that I can't help but try to solve. I'm hoping you can assist with some information I came across, involving a Percival Flynn. I believe you were friends when you were previously Millie Dalglish?'

Millie's expression changed at the mention of Percy's name, but she quickly recovered, confirming Harvey's assumption that she was, indeed, shrewd and very much in control.

'Goodness, I haven't heard my maiden name mentioned in decades,' she reminisced, smiling. 'What information is it that you are talking about?'

'It's quite sensitive, is it possible to sit somewhere so I can show you? Do you have time?' Harvey asked.

'We can sit on the patio,' Millie explained. 'I don't know you well enough to let you inside my house just yet, young man,' she laughed. 'Evelyn, be a dear and open the gate, will you? Mr Ross here can escort me to the patio, I'm sure.'

'Please, call me Harvey,' he insisted, offering the crook of his arm.

They walked slowly to the side of the house and through the now-open side gate that Evelyn had opened. Evelyn was waiting by the white, ornate, wrought iron garden table and it's six chairs, where the three of them sat.

'Evelyn, dear, would you bring Harvey a cup of tea and some biscuits? Or would you prefer a cold drink?' Millie asked.

'Please, nothing for me, I won't keep you long, but there is something you need to see,' Harvey returned. 'I don't have the original with me... I never expected to see anyone today, but I can bring it round later,' he continued, unlocking his phone and scrolling through the photos he'd taken recently. When he found the one that he was looking for, he showed it to Millie.

'This is a letter I found that was meant for you, from Percy Flynn,' he spoke softly. 'He never got a chance to post it.'

Millie took the phone, and Harvey noticed her expression change and her eyes water as she read the short note.

'Poor Percy,' she trailed off mournfully as she read the

note. 'I was devastated when he died—we were planning to elope. I had a feeling that there was foul play involved, but there was never any proof.'

'I'm very sorry for your loss, Millie,' Harvey apologised regretfully.

Evelyn leaned over and squeezed her arm gently in support.

'Where did you find this?' Millie beseeched.

'It was actually Max that found it,' Harvey replied, patting his faithful hound on the head. 'We were on a walk along the beach when he sniffed out a leather satchel with several things in it, one of which was this letter. Luckily, it was in a tin, so it didn't get ruined.'

Millie smiled softly as she glanced at Max.

'Even after all these years, to read this is somewhat emotional, I hope you understand,' she explained, wiping away a tear.

'I'm very sorry for your loss,' he replied, his voice sorrowful.

'So, what is it that you are researching?' Millie questioned. 'Have I ruined your search now?'

'No, not at all. In fact, I'm delighted to have found you. I had no expectation of ever finding anyone connected to you or Percy after such a long time. This is a wonderful bonus,' Harvey expressed.

'You haven't answered my question, Harvey,' she retorted.

Harvey paused for a few seconds, trying to think of the right words to use.

'Percy knew that he and his mother were being poisoned, Millie, so his death was murder, and I'm sure I know who was responsible.'

8

1957

'I'm sorry, Harvey, can you say that again?' Millie faltered. Her expression had changed again, and this time, not so subtly. Harvey could see a hint of anger that he hadn't expected. Millie was certainly full of surprises.

'I'm pretty sure that I know who murdered Percy, Millie. The evidence I found suggests that he was poisoned with arsenic over a period, and it didn't show up in the post-mortem,' Harvey explained his theory.

'What evidence, Harvey? How do you know all of this?'

Harvey scrolled through his photos again and showed Millie a picture of the small, brown bottle that had once contained arsenic.

'This was in the satchel along with your letter and some other items,' he uttered softly.

'So, it's true,' she whispered. 'He'd hinted that he had some suspicions at home that things weren't as they should be, but he could never prove it. And now, after all these years, we find that when he finally found the proof, it was too late.'

'It seems so, yes,' Harvey affirmed, his voice low.

'I wanted to go to the police, but we couldn't, because the local policeman was a cousin of Robert Franklin's, and he would have told on us. I'm guessing that's who you also believe is the killer?'

'Yes, I do,' Harvey agreed. He thought about how difficult that must have been for her, believing that someone had murdered the love of her life, but not being able to report it because the local policeman was a relative of the killer. He would remember that during the course of his investigation. After a brief pause, he spoke once more.

'Millie, there was one other thing in the letter that I can't figure out. There was some tracing paper with a few random dots and other marks on it. Does that ring a bell to you?' he prompted.

He scrolled again and showed Millie a photo of the tracing paper.

'That's so like Percy,' she whispered, smiling at his memory. 'We used to send each other love notes in secret using code. Sometimes using lemon juice, which was like invisible ink... that sort of thing. These dots mark spots on a map; we used them to show each other where we were going to meet next.'

Harvey was startled at this revelation before remembering something else from the satchel.

'There was a copy of a science book in the satchel that was ruined, did you use tricks from there?' he questioned.

'Why yes, there were all sorts of tricks in there that helped us during our courtship. Times were different back then, you must understand, and I knew that we'd both be in severe trouble if we were ever caught.'

'I don't blame you for being so secretive then,' he hummed in agreement.

'I wonder...' Millie began.

'What's that, Millie?' Harvey prodded.

Millie turned to Evelyn.

'Darling, can you get me the old, blue biscuit tin from my bedroom wardrobe? It's on the top shelf underneath some old shoeboxes,' Millie told her carer.

'Of course, give me a minute,' Evelyn gave a gentle nod and smile in response.

'What is it, Millie?' Harvey asked.

'See the dashes on the tracing paper?' she trailed off, smiling confidently. 'They are at right angles and indicate corner markings.'

'What of it?'

'That's how you line up the tracing paper as a reference, to show the exact locations on the map,' she clarified.

'Oh, I see, that's very clever. It's a shame we haven't a clue what the map is; there wasn't one in the satchel.'

'That's because we had one each... the same identical maps in the same identical booklets,' she grinned excitedly.

'Millie, are you saying...'

'Yes, I still have that booklet,' she exclaimed just as Evelyn returned with the biscuit tin, which she handed over to Millie.

When Millie opened the tin, Harvey saw that it contained a bundle of letters, some dried flowers, some post-cards, two plastic toy rings, and a small, seven-by-five-inch booklet with its title *Sheringham* and '1956' on the perfectly-bound spine. The cover showed a picture of Sheringham and its sandy beaches on a glorious summer's day. Millie picked it up and opened it, looking fondly at the black-and-white images and words within. There were adverts for local businesses along with information about local places of interests; it was a booklet highlighting the town and its offerings. Towards the back of the booklet was a folded map that Millie opened.

'Here you are,' she beamed, showing Harvey a map of the area. It was triple the size of the booklet, of which one-third were adverts for two local guesthouses. The other two-thirds were the map of the town and its orientation with the North Sea.

'See the corners?' Millie pointed to the outline of the map and the corners of the border. 'That's what you line the tracing paper up with, and it will show you the locations that Percy marked.'

Harvey nodded appreciatively. 'Wow, that is impressive,' he hummed, nodding once again in amazement.

'You can come back with the letter and tracing paper tomorrow and we can figure out what he marked,' Millie nodded with a grin.

'You'll get no argument from me, Millie. I think that's more than enough excitement for today, and I don't want you to be late for your appointment,' Harvey responded, standing. 'I think it's time for us to walk back home, Max.'

Before he could leave, Millie grabbed his arm, showing again a strength that belied her stature.

'Harvey, thank you so much for bringing this to me. I can't tell you how much it means to me after all this time,' she thanked Harvey with a genuine smile.

'Thank you, Millie. I hope I can get to the bottom of this, officially. It would be good to have some justice after all this time, wouldn't it?'

'It most certainly would, Harvey. Evelyn, please see this lovely gentleman out, will you? I think I'll sit and look through some of these letters again.'

Evelyn smiled and gestured for Harvey to follow her back to the gate.

'I think you've made a friend for life there, Mr Ross,' Evelyn stated, shaking his hand.

'I hope so, Evelyn,' Harvey agreed.

As they made their way back to the cottage, Harvey smiled inwardly, recognising that at least one of his objectives had already been met.

'I've made friends, Max.'

———

ON THE WALK back to the cottage Harvey thought back to the conversation and made a mental note of everything that had been discussed with Millie. Max trotted alongside, panting occasionally and, of course, wagging his tail.

'You're a happy little chappy, aren't you?' Harvey laughed.

Max barked, his wagging tail increasing in speed.

'It's been an interesting couple of days, hasn't it, Max? We've handed the loot in to the police, got some great information from the museum, have managed to get Steve checking on the people involved, and now not only have we found the surviving girlfriend, but also the way to translate those mystery dots into something more tangible. If I was back in the Met, I'd be giving doughnuts out to the team for their efforts,' he spoke cheerfully.

The first job upon their return was to feed Max and make sure he drank his fill of water. Harvey then sat down and made notes on the day's events, nodding to himself as he saw things aligning and making more sense.

'Hopefully, tomorrow we'll have more answers,' he muttered.

9

THE PLOT THICKENS

Harvey was woken early in the morning by a knock on the door. He scrambled downstairs in his pyjamas, wondering who would be knocking at 7.30 in the morning.

'Morning, sir, you have a special delivery,' the postman greeted, handing him a box and answering Harvey's internal question.

'Thank you,' Harvey signed for the package, wondering what it was.

He strolled to the kitchen and put the kettle on before opening the box.

'Ah, of course, *Fun with Science!*' he exclaimed, having forgotten that he'd ordered the book by expedited post.

He skimmed through the pages, smiling at some of the old tricks that he remembered as a child, thinking about all the fun that the modern generation of children would miss out on, not having a clue about how much fun some of the science experiments and tricks in this book were. He remembered some of them, like the bicarbonate of soda and vinegar volcano fizzy eruptions in the kitchen, growing crystals using salt and water, using lemon juice to write secret messages to his friends, making silly putty using cornstarch, and many more.

Placing everything he had on the table and referring to his notes, he remembered that there was one other call he needed to make. He searched for the number of the Norfolk Record Office and dialled it.

'Norfolk Records Office, this is Abigail speaking, how can I help you?'

'Hello, Abigail, my name is Harvey Ross. I'm trying to get a copy of an inquest that took place in Sheringham on November 17th, 1957, and was hoping you could help me?'

'I'm sorry, Mr Ross, Coroner's inquests are on restricted access for 75 years after the last date on file. So, an inquest from 1957 is not currently available to the public until December 2032.'

'Oh, really? I had no idea. Would you know if there are any other records from that time period that may assist in some research?' Harvey queried. 'It relates to an open verdict that alluded to potential foul play in the death of a teenager.'

'I'm sorry, sir, I can't help you. Maybe you can try contacting the coroner's office direct, or consider Norfolk Constabulary.'

'Okay, thank you, Abigail, have a nice day,' he trailed off, ending the call.

Harvey was finding out that being a civilian meant that he had limited access to information that would be profoundly useful in an investigation.

'I guess I have to find other means...' he mumbled out loud.

ONE OF THOSE *means* called later as Harvey was just finishing his lunch.

'You know I'm retired now, right, Steve? You know what they say about calling old people after midday—it isn't acceptable,' he greeted after answering the phone.

'You can blame yourself for that, boss. And it's good you remember that you're retired, maybe you'll consider giving less orders,' Steve McGarry quipped.

'I don't think that'll ever happen, Detective Sergeant.'

'I know, I know. Anyway, I have some information for you. It took me a little longer than normal as I had to call in a favour to check some old archives and Norfolk Constabulary records. You may want to grab a pen and paper for this as I don't have anything to send you,' Steve replied.

'Fire away,' Harvey gave him the go-ahead after grabbing his trusty notebook and vintage Special Branch pen.

'Okay, I'll start with Robert Franklin. He was a nasty piece of work; arrested half a dozen times for various assaults but never convicted. He beat someone badly each time, too. All the arrests came between early 1958 and late 1959, so he was obviously going through a bad patch during that time. I'll come to that later. Next is Dorothy Flynn, mother of Percival, widow of Captain James Flynn, later married to our friend Robert Franklin. Her family name was Brownlow. As you know, she collapsed and died at her son's inquest when an open verdict was given. Her inquest concluded that she had died of heart failure. Apparently, there was a genetic heart defect that ran in her side of the family. The coroner mentioned a possible catalyst that may have sped up the heart failure, but his autopsy was inconclusive, so despite some questions, the heart failure was given as the definite cause. My guess is that arsenic was the catalyst with her also.'

'But there's no mention of it or anything else anywhere?' Harvey implored.

'Nothing, sadly, other than what I told you. I also checked further and found there was no criminal record, nothing in the archives other than that she was the daughter of Woodrow Brownlow, a previously wealthy landowner who fell on hard times after the First World War, and who later sold his land to the Flynn family, with the proceeds going to pay his significant business debts. As such, there was no inheritance of note, so his daughter marrying a Flynn was a lifesaver for him and his family.'

'So, her wealth came from the Flynn side of the family, right?' Harvey clarified.

'Yes, and I managed to acquire James Flynn's will. It confirmed that Percival Flynn was the sole heir to his estate, subject to provisions made for his mother. In the event that she outlived him, then the estate would be passed on to her,' Steve confirmed.

'So, her new husband would assume that he would be next in line for that if they were both deceased?'

'You would assume that, yes. That never happened though,' Steve said.

'How do you know?'

'Once I read the background on these, I went digging into Land Registry records to see what happened to the land and property, when it was sold, who bought it, that kind of thing,' Steve explained.

'That's very inspired of you, Sergeant, what did you find?'

'It's *Detective* Sergeant, if you don't mind. Anyway, that's where things get very interesting. What I found was that nothing has been sold since 1957,' Steve replied.

'What? How can that be?' Harvey wondered aloud.

'Well, one reason is the proclamation that you found, bestowing some land and properties to the Flynn family. That document was very clear that nothing could be sold when the family line came to an end. If a sale was attempted, then it would flag up and be stopped before being checked for validity.'

'So, are you saying that the land and properties are still in the name of James Flynn, who died eighty years ago?' Harvey probed.

'That's exactly what I'm saying.'

'Will you jump to it and tell me what the hell is going on, Steve?' Harvey exclaimed. This was getting beyond confusing.

'I have a theory. If Robert Franklin was indeed the murderer of both Percy and Dorothy Flynn, his aim was to acquire the Flynn family wealth. When he looked into selling the land and property off, his solicitor would have conducted the standard checks and then informed him of the proclamation, and that was the likely cause of his heavy drinking and arrests,' Steve added.

'It's strange that there were no convictions... six times, did you say?'

'Yes, but I know why. I looked at the arrest reports and they were all made by different officers, but dealt with by the same custody sergeant, one sergeant Thomas Waring.'

'Waring? Where do I know that name from?' Harvey muttered. 'Give me a sec, will you?'

He flicked through the photos on his phone and read Percy's letter to Millie.

'Well, what do you know... Percy mentions a Constable Waring in his letter to his girlfriend, so I'm guessing he got promoted soon after,' Harvey nodded to himself, his initial thought correct.

'That would explain a lot, because I also found that Thomas Waring was godfather to Franklin's son, Bradley. He and Robert were probably best friends.'

'The plot thickens,' Harvey murmured.

'There's more, boss. You've opened a real can of worms with this one,' Steve laughed.

'Go on.'

I checked the voters registry and found Bradley Franklin. Born in 1941, still alive and living in Sheringham,' Steve confirmed.

'What? Seriously?'

'Yep, and guess which address he is registered to vote from?'

'I have no idea.'

'Cambourne House, the Flynn family home.'

10

ALIGNMENT

Harvey sat and looked at his notes, nodding as the pieces began to fall into place. There were still many holes, but with the way he was going with it, the confidence was very much there that he would solve this mystery. He picked up the tracing paper and placed it in an envelope in between the pages of the *Fun with Science* book, intending to go and see Millie Parry again in the afternoon, as he had promised.

'What do you reckon, Max? Fancy another walk so we can go and see our new friends?'

Max barked in acknowledgement.

They set off for Millie's house, with Harvey using the time to think over what he had learnt so far today. He beamed to himself when the realisation dawned upon him that he was no longer bored, and if anything, his new life was starting to become very interesting and exciting. He went over the list of things to do in his head, as he had always done, making sure that nothing was missed. By the time he got to Millie's house, he had also remembered what he had heard at the Sheringham Museum and the legend of the missing Flynn treasure that Ken had remembered. That led to the exciting possibility that there was, indeed, some sort of treasure to be found. He had found some of it himself at the beach, so who's to say there wasn't more?

'Interesting and exciting, indeed,' he stated out loud.

———

'PLEASE, COME IN, HARVEY.'

'Thanks, Evelyn, I hope this is a good time?' Harvey replied.

'Yes, she's been expecting you. I haven't seen her smile like this for a long time; you've brought some very fond memories to the surface with her, young man,' Evelyn beamed tenderly at the thought. 'Please, come this way.'

She led him into a spacious hallway that was well-lit and pleasantly furnished, with a narrow sideboard and antique chair to one side and an ornate hat stand on the other. A large wood-framed painting of a sunrise hung over the sideboard. They entered a large lounge, its double doors wide open, letting the sunshine and birdsong in. Millie sat in a comfortable-looking lounger facing the large garden. She gave a gentle smile when Harvey came in and started to stand, using her cane.

'Please, don't get up, Millie,' Harvey said, 'I'll try not to take up too much of your time.'

'My time is precious, Harvey, but I will tell you that I have been looking forward to your visit very much. Please, sit here next to me,' she indicated to a nearby chair, separated from Millie by a small table.

On the table was the Sheringham booklet that he had seen the previous day.

'Now, did you bring it?' Millie requested, putting her hands together excitedly.

'Yes, I did,' Harvey confirmed, taking out the tracing paper from his inside pocket. He unfolded it and placed it next to the booklet. 'May I?'

'Absolutely,' Millie consented without hesitation. Evelyn stood nearby watching, fascinated by the entire episode.

Harvey opened the booklet and turned to the map, which he opened out and lay flat on the table. He took the tracing paper and lined up the corner markings with the map borders. There were three dots on the tracing paper that Harvey hoped would mark the spots and give him an idea as to what Percy was trying to indicate.

'That's strange,' he muttered once the corners were aligned.

'What's that?' Millie asked with a raised eyebrow.

'Only two of the three dots are marking something on the map. The third dot doesn't,' he replied, pointing to the solitary dot to the right of the map, some way off the nearest location shown.

'What do you think that means?' Millie contemplated the possibilities.

'I'm not sure. I have a suspicion that these dots mark the places where Percy hid some valuables, but it's weird that one of the places isn't on the map that he shared with you. Do you know where this could be?' he questioned.

Millie peered at the map again and turned to Evelyn.

'Evelyn, be a dear and get me the Cromer and Sheringham map, will you? It's next to the telephone,' she requested. 'I keep it for visitors who aren't familiar with the town... it's very handy, you know.'

Harvey smiled warmly and nodded.

'I have my suspicions on what that third dot marks, but I want to wait until I see it with my own eyes,' she added.

Evelyn returned with a folded map that she opened and laid on the table. Millie looked at it and smiled, her eyes suddenly tearful.

'Are you okay?' Evelyn soothed, leaning alongside her and holding her hand.

'Yes, I'm fine, thank you. It's all flooding back to me now,' Millie reflected.

'Are you sure? I can come back another time...' Harvey started.

'Not at all. Look here,' Millie interrupted, pointing to the first dot, in the southeast of the map. 'That is the Beeston Regis Priory, a very old ruin that dates back to the thirteenth century, I think. The second dot marks a spot on Beeston Hills that I think shows a pillbox from the Second World War.'

'I think that's the one that collapsed to the beach, where I found the satchel,' Harvey shared.

'That sounds about right, that pillbox wasn't safe and was fenced off for decades to keep kids away. It was dangerous.'

'What do you think this third dot marks, Millie? It looks like it's the camping grounds next to the church,' he claimed, pondering the possibilities.

Millie shook her head and smiled before reaching over and gently grabbing Harvey's hand.

'It's marking All Saints Church. It's where Percy told me that we'd get married, the day he proposed to me in secret,' she reminisced aloud, a tear rolling gently down her cheek.

11

THE PRIORY

Harvey's mind was abuzz with excitement on the walk back to the cottage. If he was right, then the mystery and myth surrounding the missing Flynn treasure could come true. He already knew that some of that treasure was sitting in a police station's lost-and-found cupboard, which he would remember to claim in a few weeks. What intrigued him was what it was that he would likely find at the other two locations: the ruined Beeston Regis Priory and All Saints Church. Ken had mentioned paintings and gold jewellery, so if the stories were, indeed, true, then young Percy would have gone to great lengths to hide them somewhere safe and easily accessible at a later date. Sadly, it just wasn't to be accessed again by him.

When he got back, he sat and deliberated his next moves. One of them would be to try and speak with the suspected murderer's surviving son, Bradley Franklin. Steve had checked on him also and found that he had a record going back to his youth. Nothing major or excessive, just the occasional drunk and disorderly arrest and some allegations of harassment and bullying that were made by women and neighbours, but nothing that had led to any convictions. It seems that his police sergeant godfather had a persuasive charm about him, ensuring that his godson's name wasn't smeared in any way. Harvey would visit Cambourne House again and see if Bradley did, indeed, live there or not.

'It seems we have a treasure hunt on our hands, Max. It looks like you're going to get plenty of walks over the next few days!'

HARVEY PREPPED Max for another walk and they soon set off, aiming for Beeston Regis Priory, as it was now commonly and locally known as. Its formal name was the Priory of St Mary in the Meadow, Beeston Regis. The deserted monastery was close to the cottage and seemed the obvious choice to look at first, rather than St Mary's Church.

It took just five minutes to walk along Beeston Common until they reached the gate that led to the northern end of the ruins. They followed the grass footpath towards the western entrance of the priory, where Harvey stopped to read the notice that had been conveniently placed there for visitors.

He could see that the ruins were many centuries old and only the exterior walks remained partially intact. There was no roof or anything else resembling a building, other than the surviving ancient walls. They walked through the entrance into the nave, which led straight ahead to the chancel with the north transept and chapel to the left, and the south transept and chapter house to the right. Harvey imagined life being very tough here in the thirteenth century for its small community of canons, the ordained priests who lived according to the rule of St. Augustine. The monastery had been stripped and abandoned in the sixteenth century by Henry VIII, along with many others around the country, so the fact there was still some semblance of a building was testament to the skill of its solid construction.

They walked around the interior slowly, with Harvey checking to see any obvious place where something could be hidden, before exiting and checking the exterior. He tried to imagine whether it was any different back in 1957 when Percy had come here, but he couldn't think of anything that would have changed since then.

'Where would a seventeen-year-old hide his family's valuables in a ruined monastery, eh Max?' he muttered to his partner as they made their way around it again.

After an hour of asking that same question over and over while they continued to search, Harvey decided that he wasn't likely to make any progress and was prepared to leave. He took plenty of photos of the site, including the information board for reference, as it had a useful map, before they headed back home.

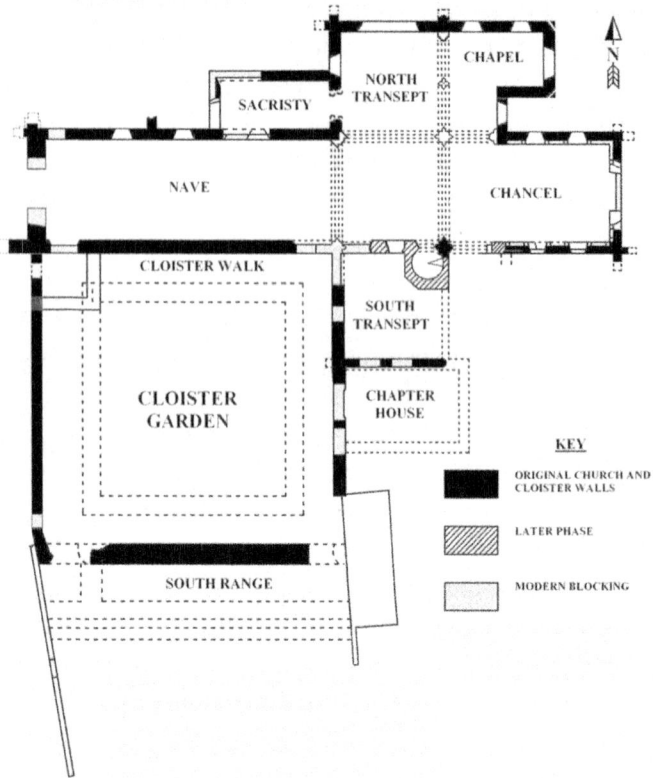

UPON THEIR RETURN, Harvey printed off the map and laid it alongside everything else he had on the table, looking over it all and attempting to fill in the blanks. Realising that he hadn't prepared much for the visit to the Priory, he decided not to make the same mistake again with All Saints Parish Church. He sat and searched the internet for all the information he could find about it. He saw that it stood next to a popular holiday park, hosting several hundred static caravans that were so prevalent in the area. The holiday park was nestled between the railway line that ran between Sheringham and West Runton and the cliffs that overlooked the North Sea. The church, built in the fourteenth century, was surrounded by a wall that encompassed its cemetery and was nestled just on the boundary of the southeast corner of the park, with a large, empty field to its south. It looked like there was only one access road from Cromer Road to both the church and holiday park, although there appeared to be a dirt track accessible from the east.

Harvey searched and found that it was still a functioning church and very much open to the public, so he knew that he could go along and have a good look around it when he needed.

'I may have to leave you behind for that one, Max,' he told the terrier as he patted his head.

Although it was a lengthy walk, Harvey judged that it would be prudent to drive there and use the time gained to have a proper look around. Glimpsing at his watch, he decided to leave that until tomorrow and take the rest of the day to relax. He made himself a coffee and sat with his tablet at the table, browsing the news and sports sites. As part of his long-term routine, he found this the best way to keep up to date with current affairs and his favourite sports. After satisfying his daily quota of knowledge, he decided on a whim to search his Aunt Agatha online to see if she had much of a presence there.

He knew that she had written and had published almost twenty poetry books, but hadn't realised they were so publicly available. They weren't bestsellers or massively popular by any stretch, but she had received wonderful reviews and had won a few county awards for contribution to local heritage. Harvey shook his head sadly, realising that other than himself, she had no family to share it with. He imagined that she would have shared much more with him, especially about her previous life as a government agent, had he not been a stupidly busy police detective with a life very much farther away than hers. He vowed to make an effort and read more, if not all, the poetry books, recognising it would bring him closer to her, and again shook his head guiltily, wishing he'd done more while she was still alive.

'Rest in peace, Auntie,' he muttered, 'and thank you for this precious gift,' he added, looking around the lovely cottage.

He went over to the bookcase and picked one of the poetry books, sitting in the armchair with a drink, ready to make good on his promise.

12

BRADLEY

The next morning felt like it had done all those years ago during his time as a busy police detective. Up early, a quick breakfast, a walk around the common with Max, all the while thinking and planning the day ahead. Harvey felt invigorated and raring to go, all thoughts of boredom and fear of the future now firmly banished from his mind.

The first port of call was just an eight-minute walk away, so he grabbed his notebook and pen and set off on foot, leaving Max behind with his belly full and sleeping off the brisk walk. Cambourne House was his destination, where Harvey hoped to find Bradley Franklin. He had many questions and considered how he would be phrasing them when he eventually caught up with the man, who was most likely going to be defensive and aggressive, if his record was anything to go by.

He had researched Cambourne House before retiring the previous night, having learnt that planning ahead was undoubtably still the way to go, and was pleased to see that it had received exceptional reviews from guests over many years. Many reviews referred to the owners and he quickly realised that Bradley Franklin was not the person running the establishment. He assumed that he was letting the place to the hosts but questioned why he was still registered there on the voters register. He was hoping to find out soon enough.

When he reached the hotel, he saw the car park still had plenty of cars in it, indicating a good rate of occupancy. He walked through the main entrance and was met with a brightly lit hallway, immaculately decorated, with a faint but delicious smell of breakfast coming from the nearby kitchen. There was no reception area, just a small table with a signing in book and a bell, which he rang.

'Can I help you, sir?' asked the man that approached from where Harvey assumed was the dining room.

'Good morning, I hope you can. I'm looking for a Mr Bradley Franklin. I believe he is the owner of this fine establishment?' Harvey queried.

The man regarded Harvey and paused before answering.

'May I ask why, sir?'

'Of course. I am trying to find out where Mr Franklin is currently living, as he is still shown on the voters register as living here. Can you tell me where I can find him? It's in relation to a legal matter going back to the 1950s, I can't really tell you much more than that, sorry,' Harvey replied.

'Are you from the police?' the man probed, peering behind Harvey to see if there was anyone else with him.

'I was with the police, but I'm here in a private capacity,' Harvey replied cryptically. 'I'm not from the tax man or whoever you think I'm with, I just need to speak to Mr Franklin, that's all.'

'Please, let's speak outside, I don't want anyone to over-hear us,' the man returned, walking out and keeping the door open for Harvey.

When they were a few metres away from the front door, the man turned to Harvey.

'I've been telling that man to change it for years, he shouldn't be shown as registered here,' he shook his head as he spoke. 'I'm sorry for any confusion, we run a legitimate business here and I always thought that Mr Franklin was a decent man. As you can see, this is a hotel, and he certainly doesn't live here.'

'Can you tell me where he is?' Harvey asked.

The man nodded.

'He lives in one of the flats on The Esplanade, number 37 Paulian Court. Please don't tell him I sent you there, I don't want any grief; we're good tenants and I want to keep our relationship with him on good terms. I hope you under-stand,' the man replied, his tone sheepish.

'I'm not going to cause any problems, I assure you,' Harvey confirmed, 'and thank you for letting me know, I appreciate it. Just to clarify, he's your landlord?'

'Yes, but weirdly I think a reluctant one. I've offered to buy the place many times but for some reason, he doesn't want to sell.'

Because it isn't his to sell, Harvey thought as he nodded. 'Thanks again, and apologies for the intrusion. It looks like a wonderful place to stay.'

'You're welcome any time, we're famous for our break-fasts, and the location here, as you can see, is pretty spectacu-lar,' he waved towards the sea with his words.

'You'll get no argument from me,' Harvey agreed. 'I'll be

sure to recommend you to my friends. Thanks again,' he added, shaking the man's hand.

On the walk back to the cottage, he looked up the address that he'd been given: a small block of apartments opposite the boating lake near the beach, where the famous old Grand Hotel used to be before it was demolished in 1974 and replaced by the more modern apartments. When he got back, he called Steve McGarry.

'I need another small favour,' he said. 'Can you find out from Land Registry who owns number 37 Paulian Court in Sheringham? It would take me a few days to get a result, and I know you're far more efficient than me,' he continued.

'Plus, it's cheaper for me to do it, isn't it?' Steve snickered.

'Apparently it's where Bradley Franklin is living, not at Cambourne House, which he is renting out to someone. I'm interested to see if he bought the flat or is renting it.'

'Leave it to me, it shouldn't take too long,' Steve replied. 'I'll give you a shout later this afternoon.'

'Thanks, Steve.'

He sat down and gathered his thoughts, absently stroking Max's head as he did so. He glanced down at the terrier with a smile, grateful for his presence these past few weeks.

'I wonder why your mum hasn't called you yet, eh, boy? Her cruise must be almost over by now.'

He decided to pre-empt the call with Becky, hoping that she'd appreciate him reaching out to arrange for Max's return.

> Hope all is well. Are you back yet? When shall I bring Max? H x

Before he had a chance to put the phone down, it pinged. Becky had responded instantly.

> Sorry, Harvey. Been meaning to call. I'm
> going to be away for a bit longer. You okay
> with Max staying another couple of months?
> B x

'Get in!' Harvey exclaimed out loud, as if his favourite team had scored a goal. 'You hear that, Max? You're staying for a while longer!'

He regained his composure and typed out a short reply, not wanting to give his elation away.

> No problem, Max is good company. Have
> fun. H x

Becky replied with two '*x*'s, ending the conversation. He didn't ask why, and he wasn't concerned, realising just how much he enjoyed having Max around. It got him thinking that it was probably because Max was the one he spoke to the most. The last few days had been somewhat different as he tried to get to the bottom of the mystery he was now investigating, and he had enjoyed integrating himself again on such levels, even with complete strangers.

'I need to make more friends,' he proclaimed out loud as he continued to scratch behind Max's ear.

———

'WHAT DID YOU FIND, STEVE?' Harvey asked when McGarry called shortly after.

'That Bradley Franklin does not own 37 Paulian Court, which suggests that he is renting it. I've sent off to see if there are any bank records for him that we can have a look at. If what you've said is true, he'd likely have a pretty penny tucked away for a rainy day,' Steve informed him.

'It'll be interesting to find out, for sure. I appreciate your help with this, by the way. This is getting very interesting indeed,' Harvey replied.

'Well, I'm here if you need more. As long as it isn't too criminal, then I'm happy to assist,' Steve laughed, referring to some privacy laws he had no doubt broken.

'Thanks, Steve. Send my regards to the rest of the team.'

Harvey decided that he should visit Paulian Court sooner rather than later, so he had a quick lunch and left the cottage on foot for the pleasant twenty-odd-minute journey, choosing to take the promenade route that he liked so much. The two-storey block of flats, one of four in the same style and built in a typical 1970's basic design, were just yards from the immaculate beaches close to the lifeboat station to the west of the town, and next to the popular Sheringham Golf Club. Harvey made a mental note to look into joining the club as golf was one of the few hobbies that he'd enjoyed back in London. He entered the block and took the stairs to the top floor, where he had seen a sign for number 37. He could hear that the TV was on when he got to the door and knocked. The TV sound was turned down, and seconds later, the door was opened by a middle-aged woman in a nurse's outfit.

'Can I help you?' she asked.

'Good afternoon. Sorry to disturb you, but I'm looking for a Mr Bradley Franklin,' Harvey replied.

'May I ask who is calling?' .

'My name is Harvey Ross, and I need to ask Mr Franklin a few questions about his father,' he explained.

'You're not a long lost relative, are you? He told us he didn't have anyone,' the nurse continued with her interrogation, scowling suspiciously.

'No, I assure you I'm not a relative or anyone here to cause any trouble at all. I'm hoping Bradley... Mr Franklin... can tell me what happened to an old friend of mine that he knew many years ago,' Harvey stated, not feeling any guilt for the little white lie.

'Well, I'll check and see if he's awake. He sleeps most of the day nowadays... doesn't want to do anything or go anywhere.'

'I'm sorry to hear that, especially living in such a great location,' Harvey apologised.

'It's not much of a flat, but you're right, the location is fab. There's a great view of the sea from the living room. Just give me a sec and I'll see if he's up,' she replied, closing the door.

A minute or two later, the door opened again, the nurse inviting him in in response.

'I'm just about to make him a cup of tea, if you'd like one?' she offered.

'Some water would be lovely, thank you,' he responded gently, following her into what had once been the lounge but had been transformed into what looked like a large hospital room. All the furniture had been removed and replaced by an actual hospital bed, which was now in the upright position with its patient sitting and looking out towards the window and the view beyond.

The elderly patient was a very large, balding man in his eighties, with a large, bulbous nose and dark bags under his eyes. His eyes followed Harvey as he walked towards the end of the bed, blocking the view out of the window.

'This is Mr Ross, Bradley, and he wants to ask a few questions about your dad,' the nurse started. 'I'll go and make you a nice cuppa, okay?'

Harvey regarded the man that stared at him, a strange neutral expression on his face.

'Mr Franklin, thank you for agreeing to speak with me. How are you doing today?' Harvey greeted.

Bradley Franklin started to laugh, which turned into a cough, lasting a few seconds before he calmed.

'As you can see, I've been better,' he replied with a gruff voice. 'Who are you, Mr Ross? What's this that Jamila mentioned, you want to ask about my dad?'

'Yes, I was hoping you could fill in a few blanks about him,' Harvey replied, 'from the late 1950's.'

'That's going back a few years... I was just a kid,' Franklin answered. 'What makes you think I can help you?'

'Well, I'm trying to get some answers for a historical book that I'm writing, and a few things have confused me, some you can probably help with.'

'Confused you? Like what?' Franklin questioned, coughing again.

'Your father was married to Dorothy Flynn, and my understanding is that you both lived with Dorothy and her son, Percy, after the wedding, is that right?'

'Yes, what of it?' his response came suspiciously.

'Well, this is what's confusing me, Bradley. When both Dorothy and Percy passed away, everyone assumed that Cambourne House and the land and other properties were inherited by your father, him being the husband and all. But somehow, that doesn't appear to be the case. What happened? Can you tell me why your dad didn't end up owning anything but you are still earning from it despite that?'

There was a moment of fear in Franklin's eyes before it passed, and defiance took over.

'What business is this of yours, Mr Ross? What has it got

to do with you what I am earning?' Franklin spat defiantly, the cough returning for longer this time.

'Mr Franklin, I'm not here to make any accusations or point any fingers, I'm merely trying to get to the bottom of what is clearly a mystery,' Harvey justified, his arms out wide in a placating manner.

'Still, it's none of your damned business, so I suggest you get out of here,' Franklin dismissed the man, coughing more as Jamila walked back into the room with a tray of drinks.

'Here you are, Mr Ross,' she said, handing him a glass of water. 'And I'll put your tea on the little table there as usual, Bradley,' she added.

'Mr Ross is leaving, please see him out,' Franklin insisted, waving his left arm impatiently.

'I'll go, Mr Franklin, but like I said, I'm not here to cause any problems. If you can't help me, then I'll have to dig deeper, and that may bring up some things you may not want known,' Harvey shrugged, putting down the glass.

'Are you threatening me?' Franklin's voice was gruff as he questioned the man in front of him.

'Not at all. Can you help me? Or shall I ask elsewhere, which may end up uncovering some unpleasantness that you will want to avoid? It's entirely up to you,' Harvey pressed.

'What's this all about then?' Jamila wondered aloud, confused as to what she had walked into.

'It's nothing, Jamila, please leave us,' Franklin replied, his voice lower and less agitated. He stared at Harvey as she left the room, recognising something in the visitor that had led to a change of attitude.

'I appreciate it,' Harvey said, recognising the reversal.

'Tell me what you think you know, Mr Ross, and I'll tell you if it's true or not,' Franklin declared.

'I'm happy with that. Before I do though, you need to know that the police have in their possession some items that put a different take on what happened back in 1957. That includes an empty bottle of arsenic and a letter from the dead, Mr Franklin, that lays the blame squarely on the shoulders of your father, Robert.'

Bradley shook his head slowly, looking away from Harvey as he did so. When he turned back, Harvey could see that his eyes were glistening.

'Arsenic? That's how he did it?' Franklin muttered in disbelief.

'Yes. You didn't know?'

Franklin shook his head slowly.

'I was just a child, so I never thought about how convenient their deaths were until years later. He was a miserable sod, my dad. If you think I'm a grumpy old git, you should have met him. I don't remember him ever being happy, especially in his later years. I had my suspicions, but never knew,' he expressed.

'That your dad murdered two innocent people? What did you think it was, blind luck?' Harvey probed further, trying not to let his emotions get the better of him.

Franklin shook his head again.

'I knew he'd done something, but I would have never guessed it would be arsenic poisoning.'

'Did you never ask him about it?' Harvey interrogated.

Franklin laughed.

'Heck no, not directly, anyway, he would have battered me. You have no idea how twisted he was.'

'Well, I think I do, he killed two people, didn't he?' Harvey shot back.

'What do you want from me, Mr Ross?' Franklin pleaded,

clearly wanting the visit to end soon. 'I suspected he'd done something wrong but was too scared to ask him outright. It was only when he got drunk one night and threatened to kill me that I realised he'd actually killed them.'

'What happened?' Harvey demanded. He could see clearly that Franklin was struggling with his emotions, shifting uncomfortably as he gathered his thoughts.

'That one night, he was in a foul mood. He'd lost a lot of money gambling and couldn't sell anything to ease the debt. I made the mistake of criticising his addition and he punched me full-on in the stomach. While I was on the floor, he stood over me and said, *'You're lucky I don't kill you, boy. I've done it before, and by God, I'd happily do it again. Remember that, and think yourself lucky to be in this house. You can thank me for that, and I still have some poison left,'* Franklin said almost in a whisper, the memory still both powerful and painful.

'He said that?'

'Those very words. I'll take them to my grave,' Franklin uttered.

'I'm confused as to why you're living here in this small flat when you must have a ton of money coming in from the land and property rentals. You must have earned a fortune all these years, where's all the money gone?'

Franklin laughed and then coughed heavily.

'Look at me, Mr Ross. Do I look like a man who's done a day's work in his life? There may have been some money coming in, but my dad spent every penny on gambling and drinking, and what came in after his death went on a lavish lifestyle that I thought I was entitled to. Once I was aware that none of the land or houses could be sold, it was all I could do to keep a low profile and enjoy myself as much as I could. And then it all caught up to me, as you can see, and most of what comes in nowadays pays for Jamila and this flat, along with all the medication and everything else needed to keep me alive. So, I ask you, Mr Ross, do you think it was all worth it?'

'You're asking me? You may be sick now, but you know-ingly and willingly enjoyed the fruits of your dad's murderous deeds, Mr Franklin, so I'm probably not the best person to ask that, and you'll certainly not get any sympathy from me,' Harvey stated.

'What will you do with this information?' Franklin pleaded.

'There's not a lot that I can do,' Harvey shrugged, making his way towards the door. He stopped and turned back to the sick, old man. 'But the police may be able to do something... and if I can help them, I will.'

13

RENTAL UNIT

Harvey returned to the cottage and took Max straight back out, wanting to clear his head with a long walk across the common and then through towards the coastal path and the Beeston Cliffs. The fresh air was invigorating, helping to clear his head as he continued to make sense of what he had found out.

In his mind, Bradley Franklin was an accomplice to his father's crimes, and although he was unaware of what had transpired and subsequently resulted in the murders of Dorothy and Percy Flynn, he was very much aware that his father had something to do with the heinous crimes. Choosing not to do anything about that, thereby taking advantage of the situation for decades and living off the proceeds of the murders, was, in Harvey's opinion, something that he should no longer get away with, despite his age and current health.

Harvey was determined to put that right, but as a civilian, how could he possibly make a difference and have justice dispensed as it should? He had some serious thinking to do about that, but for now, all he could think about were the next steps in his quest for justice.

———

LATER THAT AFTERNOON, as Harvey was feeding Max after their long walk, Steve McGarry kept his promise and called.

'What did you find, Steve?' Harvey greeted.

'Not as much as I thought,' Steve frowned. 'The Franklins kept things to a minimum, I'll give them credit for that. In their attempt to keep a low profile, they clearly disclosed the minimum they could get away with. I found two bank accounts for Bradley Franklin: one personal account which has twelve thousand pounds in it, and one business account that has approximately twenty-five thousand pounds deposited each month from various tenants. Interestingly, the business account name is Flynn Enterprises. That account currently has a balance a little over seventy thousand pounds in it.'

'Wow, if that's not a blatant attempt to keep the wolves at bay then I don't know what is,' Harvey joked with a laugh.

'Franklin has ten thousand pounds a month deposited to his personal account. He pays out almost two and a half thousand on rent and bills, and most of the rest goes on medical services, including a full-time nursing package and the extensive medication that he needs. There is something interesting though that you may want to investigate.'

'What's that?'

'He pays a thousand pounds a month from his personal account to rent a unit on the Weybourne Industrial Estate, unit 57, which is actually on the outskirts of Sheringham. He pays a few bills quarterly there, but it isn't much and it suggests that he doesn't use it for much other than storage.'

'Good to know, thanks. I'll take a wander over and see if I can figure what he's hiding there,' Harvey replied.

'Other than that, there's very little. He has a tiny footprint online, no social media to speak of, and has done a very good job keeping a low profile... just like his dad before him,' Steve added bitterly.

'I'm sure there're more skeletons in their nasty cupboards, but it's time to put a stop to it all, I think. What do you reckon, Steve, are you up for helping your old boss out with this?'

'As long as there's no risk to my job and my pension, then count me in,' Steve jested. 'Just please don't get me into any trouble, not now after all this time,' he quipped after a brief pause.

'Don't worry, old chap, I have a cunning plan that will make this more official and hopefully lead to the Franklins answering for their crimes,' Harvey's response came cryptically.

'Well, I'm here if you need me. Now, if you don't mind, I shall go and enjoy a nice glass of that five-year-old Châteauneuf-du-Pape that you sent me,' Steve proclaimed.

'That's a good one, glad it arrived safely. Thanks again, Steve, and enjoy the wine,' Harvey ended the call after saying their goodbyes.

'More and more unravelling, eh, Max?' he stroked the terrier's head as he spoke his question aloud. 'What do you fancy doing tomorrow, searching a church or sneaking around a storage unit?'

BEFORE RETIRING FOR THE NIGHT, Harvey decided to continue the tradition that his Aunt Agatha had started. He took out the large binder that held all the information and notes she had gathered over decades about all the unsolved mysteries and local legends before making his way to the back, where he added some perforated, clear envelopes that he had found in the loft. On one of them he stuck a label and wrote: *Flynn Murders – 1957.*

He took all the notes he had gathered, including the copies of the newspaper clipping from the museum, and put them in the envelope, effectively continuing on from Agatha's sterling efforts and legacy.

'*Thanks for the motivation, Aunt Agatha, I'll try not to let you down,*' he muttered to himself, closing the binder and patting it affectionately.

14

ALL SAINTS CHURCH

T he following morning couldn't come quickly enough for Harvey, now completely energized and full of enthusiasm for his newfound quest for justice. Figuring that Max wouldn't be allowed to wander around the church, Harvey first fed him and then took him for a brisk walk before setting off in his regular, inconspicuous saloon car, saving *Archie* for sunnier, more relaxing days.

The journey took just five minutes, whereby on arrival, Harvey parked on the grass verge in front of the small, gated entrance to the churchyard. Despite its age, the medieval church was in great condition and still very much in use. It sat proudly, overlooking the nearby holiday park, its neat churchyard home to rows of graves from centuries past. Instead of overcrowding the churchyard they had, they instead added another small yard to its western flank, enclosing it with a neatly trimmed, tall hedge.

Harvey spent a minute taking the sight in before opening the gate and walking towards the south-facing entrance to the church. An open arch to a covered porch led to the

ancient, gothic-style wooden door, with large, wrought iron
hinges, evidence of its timeworn appearance. Harvey turned
the handle, unsurprised to feel it open without any resistance, having read online that the church was open to the
public during the day. Walking inside, he immediately looked
up and noticed the high, vaulted, wooden ceiling, separated
into three sections by vaulted, pillared arches. The wooden
pews were lined up in three sections, separated by the arches,
along with bright red carpet, all facing the altar on the east
side.

Harvey was pleasantly surprised at how much light
flooded into the church, considering its age, and nodded in
appreciation at the large, stained-glass windows responsible.
As he walked slowly along the red-carpeted passages, he
looked carefully for places where Percy was likely to have
concealed any of the family treasures, wondering whether
there was anything actually here, or if it had been found
decades ago. He walked around twice, including the gallery
that overlooked the congregation and several side-chambers
that he was able to take a peek in.

When he checked the time, he realised that he'd been
inside for more than an hour, having lost all sense of time. He
shrugged his shoulders and decided it was time to go, when
something caught his eye that he hadn't seen earlier. To the
left of the ornate, rood screen—the partition between the
chancel and the nave—were some wooden, carved panels,
bearing the names of and dedications to some prominent
members of the parish from the past. He leaned forward to
check one and saw the name of James Flynn, Percy's father,
the war hero. This signified the importance of the man who
had clearly been revered in the community, making it all the
sadder that his family had ended up the way they had. The

moving words were expertly carved into the wooden, panelled screen:

To the glory of god and in loving memory of Captain
James Flynn,
3rd Battalion, Parachute Regiment,
Aged 30 years
Who was killed in action during Operation Market
Garden, the Battle of Arnhem,
This panelling was erected by his devoted wife,
Dorothy, and Son, Percival.

Harvey crossed himself and quietly thanked the man who had saved so many lives during a vicious battle. After a few moments of paying his respects, he decided to check the churchyard and try to locate the graves of the Flynn family, hoping there would be a clue that could help him. Having seen that the new addition was for later graves, he checked the eastern side of the churchyard and found the three graves close together in one of the last rows. James Flynn was five away from his beloved Dorothy, and young Percy was next to his mother. Harvey paid his respects, standing still and crossing himself before bowing his head in acknowledgement of the three lives that were lost under tragic circumstances. The gravestones were very basic, giving the names and dates of birth and death, the only other acknowledgement showing them as parents and son.

Despite not having found any sign of any treasure, Harvey was not disheartened, he was pleased that he had visited and found the dedication and the graves. After making a vow to them all, he then turned and left to head back.

'I'll make sure the world knows what happened,' he promised quietly.

———

UPON HIS RETURN to the cottage, Harvey took Max for a walk, having found that it helped clear his mind and bring clarity to his situation. Max was more than happy to be going on another walk, and the pair found that it was the best way to learn the layout of the town. As they walked through the centre of town, taking roads that they hadn't visited before, Harvey was struck by the peace and quiet, something he hadn't encountered in London, having gotten used to the sirens and traffic noise that went on into the early hours of almost every single morning. All the while, he was planning on the next steps, figuring out his strategy on how best to deal with what he had discovered.

He had planned to visit the storage unit later in the afternoon, in the hope that it could shed some light as to what Bradley Franklin was up to, because Harvey was convinced that there was plenty that he was keeping to himself—a trait going back with his father to the late 1950s, and one they had seemed to excel in.

Another angle Harvey was considering was how to formalise the discovery and thereafter the dispensing of justice, which was something that he couldn't do by himself as a civilian, and something that his ex-team in London couldn't assist with as it wasn't their jurisdiction. That meant just one thing.

He had to speak to the local constabulary.

———

Weybourne Industrial Estate was located on the far western end of Sheringham on Weybourne Road, next to the recently built Reef swimming pool. There were a dozen or so buildings that primarily housed varying types of engineering and motoring businesses amongst them. Unit 57 was one of the smaller units to the south of the estate, separated from the others by trees and bushes that concealed it to almost all, except those who knew it was there. The only sign of anything there was the single concrete track that wound around the foliage to the single-storey building with its up and over steel garage shutter. There was a single wooden access door to the side, with a large padlock supplementing the normal Yale lock.

Strangely, Harvey noticed that there was no evidence of an alarm, which surprised him, but the brick-built building did look relatively secure, and the lack of an alarm suggested there wasn't much of value within. Having checked that he wasn't causing any concern to anyone watching, Harvey strolled around the building, hoping that there was a window or two that he could peek into. There were several large windows up high, maybe seven feet up, that he couldn't see into. He decided to take a chance and climb one of the trees, careful again to look around for any potential witnesses.

He thanked Max for keeping him fit these past few weeks as he pulled himself up to the first main branch of the nearest tree, some five feet up. Standing precariously on the branch as he held the trunk for safety, he could just see through the window. The building was approximately forty feet in length and twenty-five feet wide, with what seemed to be a small office or toilet in the top corner that he could see. He imagined there'd be something similar on the opposite corner where he didn't have the angle to see.

What he could see were eight cars under covers on the one side; maybe something similar on the side he couldn't see. He had no clue what type of cars they were, how old they were, or whether they were valuable or not—just that he was sure they were cars. He took a couple of pictures, unsure whether they'd help, and made his way back safely to the ground. He took a few photos of the exterior before walking back to his parked car and setting off for home.

'Why so many cars, Bradley?' he muttered to himself, shaking his head and his mind raced with possible theories.

———

15

NORFOLK CONSTABULARY

The next morning, Harvey made the decision to contact someone within Norfolk Constabulary to see if they could get them to formalise an investigation. Before doing so, he rang Steve McGarry.

'Do you know anyone in Norfolk?' he asked his former deputy. 'I figured if anyone in the team would have a contact there, it would be you.'

'As a matter of fact, I do,' Steve rejoined, 'but I personally do not want to reach out to her.'

'Uh oh, is this something I should be staying away from?' Harvey teased.

Steve laughed.

'I can literally hear your evil mind ticking over, thinking I've been over the side or something. Yes, it is someone I had a relationship with, but no, not while I've been happily married,' he defended.

'What about when you've been unhappily married?' Harvey joked, making light of it.

'Funny, but wrong again. Emily and I were in the cadets

together. We dated very briefly, it didn't work, and we've stayed in touch. She is also very happily married to Akira, and they have two gorgeous daughters, five and seven. Anything else you need to know?' Steve shot back.

'If you've stayed in touch and are still friends, why don't you want to contact her?' Harvey probed.

'Because I missed their anniversary again and she vowed to kick my arse, so it's not a conversation I'm looking forward to until her infamous anger has passed.'

'Won't she take that anger out on me if I contact her as a result of *your* connections?' Harvey quizzed.

'Yes, most probably, but I don't mind that at all. In fact, you should record it so I can listen to it later,' Steve chuckled.

'You're an arse, McGarry; making a mountain out of a molehill has been your thing, for sure. I'll be sure to take sides with Emily when we speak. Send me her contact details, please,' he requested, his formal tone teasing his friend.

'I'll message her number and email after the call. Let me know how you get on, and don't be too unkind about me, eh, boss?'

'I won't, but remind me to ask you about your time in the cadets. You kept that very quiet indeed,' Harvey bantered in return.

He grinned as the call ended; shaking his head at Steve's antics was something he'd gotten used to for many years now. But one thing was sure, he had never let Harvey down, and despite those antics and frequent humour, he was great at his job. True to his words, the message came through with DS Emily Leclerc's email and phone number.

Before making contact with her, Harvey laid everything out on the table, including his notes, the photos he had printed of the arsenic bottle, and a photocopy of the letter, going through it all to ensure that she would have enough to be enticed by. He purposely withheld the tracing paper and anything he'd found from his searches, wanting to see that through fully before involving the police. When he was ready, he dialled the number Steve had given him.

'This is DS Leclerc,' she answered.

'DS Leclerc, my name is Harvey Ross and I'm Steve McGarry's old boss. I was hoping you could spare a few minutes to discuss something of a delicate nature,' he greeted.

'McGarry sent you?' the icy tone in her voice was evident, along with her initial hesitance.

'Yes, he did, and before you say anything, I will be happy to help you give him a good thrashing. Forgetting your anniversary again is a crime that must be punished.'

There was a pause before the laughter began.

'Honestly, don't tell him this because he'll take even more advantage, but I can't get angry with him for too long, He's been a great friend over the years, despite being an idiot at times,' Emily replied.

'Fair enough, but my offer of helping to beat him stands, whatever you decide,' Harvey quipped.

'It's funny that he didn't make a formal introduction, I'm guessing he's scared of my response, right?' she assumed.

'Spot on; he is staying away until he thinks you've calmed down a little.'

'Dear, oh, dear. Like I said, an idiot. Anyway, what can I do for you, Harvey?' she asked.

'Well, I've moved to Sheringham now that I've retired, after having worked with Steve and my team on cold cases back in the Met. I was kind of resigned to living a boring, retired life when I came across something that you should be aware of. It's a little off the beaten track, but I am convinced that I've stumbled across an unsolved murder from 1957,' he announced.

'Really? How so?' she challenged.

'My dog, Max, found an old satchel after part of Beeston Cliffs collapsed in a storm. Inside was a letter implying that the victim and his mother had been poisoned with arsenic. There was an empty bottle with the letter, amongst other things. I did a bit of investigating and found more information that suggested murder. Is this something you can look at?'

'It certainly sounds interesting enough to look at, for sure. Can you pop in for a chat?'

'Sure, where are you based?' Harvey countered.

'We have an office in Wymondham, can you pop over tomorrow?'

'Sure, what time is best?' he rejoined eagerly.

'Come in the morning, I'll make sure I'm around. Is the number you rang from your main contact number?' she asked.

'Yes.'

'Great, I'll see you in the morning. Bring whatever information you've gathered and we can go through it properly,' she returned.

'Thanks, Emily, see you in the morning.'

He sat back in the chair and gathered his thoughts, wondering whether he'd get into much trouble by not disclosing some of his findings.

'Well, we'll play it by ear and see whether they take us seriously, eh, Max?'

HARVEY ARRIVED the following morning and was asked by the desk officer to sign into the visitors' book whilst waiting for Emily Leclerc to come and escort him inside.

'Harvey? Good morning, it's good to meet you,' she approached him with a smile, extending her hand.

'It's good of you to see me, Detective Sergeant,' Harvey nodded as they shook hands.

'Please, it's Emily. I thought we could have a cuppa in the canteen instead of the stuffy interview rooms, follow me,' she replied, leading the way to the canteen.

They found a table in a quiet corner and sat with their beverages.

'So, I'm intrigued by our phone call yesterday. It isn't what we would typically deal with in the Major Investigations Team, but something different spices things up a little, eh?' she rose an eyebrow as she spoke.

'That's what I loved about my old team; every case was very different from the last, so it was never dull,' Harvey recalled.

'You mentioned the victims and implied they were poisoned?'

'Yes, I have a copy of the letter and photos of everything with me,'

'Where are the originals?' Emily wondered aloud.

'When I found the satchel, I took it home first to see what was inside, hence the photos. I then took it to North Walsham police station where it was logged in,' he replied.

'Ah, okay... I guess we'll have to get that out and sign it in as evidence instead,' she insisted.

'I guess so. I was going to claim it after 28 days and try to locate any descendants, but I guess you can do that, right?'

'Of course. Let me see what you brought with you,' she indicated to what Harvey had with him.

'Here you go,' he replied, handing over a plain folder with copies of everything he'd removed from the satchel, except the tracing paper.

Emily took her time and studied everything carefully, which took several minutes.

'It's a shame there's so much water damage to the paper-work, that would have helped a lot,' she remarked.

'I think there's enough to track down any records that may assist at Land Registry,' Harvey offered.

'So, you think the suspect's son is still benefitting from the alleged murders?' she clarified.

'I do. I had a brief chat with him, and he made it clear that he knew something was not right. He's turned a blind eye to it all his life whilst benefitting from the crimes. He's in a sorry state at the moment, but still benefitting, so that's something you and the courts may have to negotiate when the time comes,' Harvey looked at her as he spoke in an attempt to gauge her reaction.

Emily smiled kindly, nodding before answering. 'I see what you did there, Harvey, and I've been doing this job long enough to figure out whether something is worth pursuing or not. Trust me, if what you say is true and the evidence points to a crime, victims, a suspect, and the proceeds of crime, then we will be able to put this one to bed. I'll need to request the inquest reports, as they may help confirm the possibility of any irregularities.'

'You'll probably want to interview the son, also. He may

know more than he told me, so if you negotiate and he believes that he's safe from prison or losing his carer, then he may cough up and live out the rest of his life without looking over his shoulder each day. Not that he deserves it; although he didn't kill those poor people, he knew there was foul play involved,' Harvey added.

'Don't worry about that; as Steve will tell you, I am a firm but fair negotiator,' she gave a gentle laugh with her words.

'That wasn't the impression he gave, but having met you, I absolutely believe it,' he replied.

'Well, if you think of anything else, please do give me a call. I'll make a start on this later today and will make sure to keep you appraised,' she said, standing. 'I'll walk with you to your car.'

As they exited the police station and walked towards the car park, Emily stopped him.

'Before you go, do me a favour and tell Steve that I'm still fuming, okay? I want to see what he does,' she grinned mischievously.

'Oh, I will, don't worry,' he snickered.

They shook hands, and Harvey was soon back on the road to Sheringham, pleased that he had done the right thing.

'Let's hope they can put this one to bed quickly,' he mumbled to himself.

16

THE ACCIDENT

Harvey was soon home and took Max straight out for a long walk. He varied the routes they took as part of his plan to learn more about the town, and on this occasion, decided to walk along the mile-long promenade, ending at the RNLI lifeboat station before turning back. Instead of walking the same route back along the promenade, they walked up the slope and turned right towards the boating lake, almost directly opposite the block of flats that he had visited Bradley Franklin at. He looked up at the top-floor flat where Franklin was no doubt watching the sea view from, and nodding knowingly as to the repercussions coming his way should the police come to the same conclusions that he had.

'You have some interesting visitors coming your way soon, Franklin,' he muttered.

They sat at one of the benches in the small park area next to the boating lake, watching the world go by for half an hour or so as Harvey pondered on the last few weeks. He glanced down at Max, now lying down after the vigorous walk, and grinned as he realised that he had much to look forward to in his new life by the sea.

'Let's go explore some more, Max, shall we?'

They crossed the road away from the sea and soon found themselves at the roundabout that hosted the Sheringham War Memorial and garden. The impressive twenty-six feet tall cross memorial was unveiled in 1921 to commemorate those who lost their lives during the great wars. After paying their respects, they continued their walk and zig-zagged down several streets before ending up on Church Street, where they took a right onto Station Road, the busy one-way street that housed many of the town's shops. Harvey had walked and driven down the road many times, but hadn't paid as much attention to the shops as he'd wanted to. They slowed their walk and looked in every window, acknowledged many fellow pedestrians, stopped at least half a dozen times for Max to get a familiar pat on the head from strangers that adored dogs. And that was just the first hundred feet.

It was as they were about to cross the road that things took a turn for the worse. Max, still excited from the attention that he'd been receiving, noticed another dog being walked across the road and decided to act before Harvey was able to check if it was clear. The terrier pulled on the lead in his eagerness to cross over, and before Harvey could stop him, was halfway across the road, just as a silver Nissan Leaf was approaching. The electric car wasn't moving very fast, but was silent as it approached, heading right for Max. Harvey's instincts and previous training kicked into action as he sprinted towards Max and scooped him up with his free hand, hurling the surprised dog towards the opposite pavement and diving after him in an effort to avoid the car.

The heroic effort saved Max from being run over, but not

Harvey, whose right leg was clipped by the car, spinning him around before forcing him to land heavily just short of the pavement. He groaned in pain as the car slammed its brakes and several bystanders ran to assist.

'Are you okay?' the elderly male driver rushed over as he led Harvey into a sitting position. 'I'm so sorry, it happened too quickly for me to stop in time.'

'Can you stand?' a younger lady voiced soothingly, holding his other arm.

Harvey shook his head, which he had scraped on the road as he'd landed. His right leg was throbbing, but he was able to move it freely, meaning it wasn't broken.

'I'm okay, just a little groggy. Where's my dog?' he looking around worriedly for Max, smiling as he saw the dog sitting next to him, enjoying the attention of other bystanders who had come to assist.

'He's just fine,' another lady insisted. 'Do you want me to call an ambulance?'

'No, I'm fine, thank you. I just need a minute and I'll be okay,' Harvey reassured.

He grabbed a hand and was helped to his feet. After flexing his leg several times, he became confident that he could walk despite the pain. Lifting his trouser leg, he saw that a nasty bruise had already formed on his right calf.

'You sure you're going to be okay?' the driver's question came hesitantly once more.

'Yes, thank you. You might want to think about moving your car though. Look,' he responded, pointing to the traffic that had backed up almost to the railway station. 'I'll be fine.'

'Don't you want my details?' he came back with.

'No, it was an accident. It wasn't your fault and there isn't any damage to your car, so you don't need mine. Let's leave it at that,' Harvey asserted, shaking the man's hand.

'Fine by me, you take care, young man,' the man nodded with a smile.

Harvey grinned, having not been called that for many years. After thanking those that had helped, he limped away back towards the cottage. The journey took twice as long as a result and Harvey vowed to call the doctor if it wasn't feeling better by the morning.

When they eventually arrived, Harvey quickly fed Max before sitting down in the armchair and resting the leg on a footstool.

'Well, Max, you can't say that nothing happens in this town, that's for sure.'

AS HE HAD FEARED, the pain hadn't subsided by the morning and even taking painkillers didn't ease it. He called the local medical practice where he had registered when moving in. After explaining his predicament, he was told to attend later that morning. When he arrived at the modern practice he was booked into, he sat, waiting for his turn. He didn't have long to wait and went to the room he was assigned to once he got called.

'Good morning, Mr Ross,' the doctor greeted as he made his way in. 'Please come and take a seat.'

Harvey was taken by surprise when he saw the attractive, middle-aged doctor that sat at the desk watching him as he walked in, indicating to the chair next to her desk. The man guessed her to be in her mid to late fifties. Her shoulder-length hair was blonde with occasional white streaks, and her smile was friendly and genuine.

'Good morning, Doctor. Thank you for seeing me so quickly,' he bumped into the chair slightly before awkwardly sitting.

'Are you okay? You seem a little flushed. I thought you had a problem with your leg,' she asked quizzically, tilting her head slightly to one side.

Harvey hadn't blushed for a very long time. It had caused him problems in his youth when dating. He'd completely forgotten about it until now, it had been so long.

'Um, no... I'm fine. Thanks for asking. I suppose I'm a little hot, nothing more,' he stammered. *This could be a problem*, he thought to himself.

The doctor smiled knowingly before looking back at her computer monitor. 'Okay, Mr Ross... tell me what happened,' she urged, her voice gentle as her eyes darted between her monitor and the man in front of her.

'Please, it's Harvey,' he replied. 'I ran into the street to save my dog, getting clipped by a car in the process. I tried taking some painkillers, but it seems to have gotten worse overnight.'

'Did you succeed?' she asked.

'Succeed in what, taking painkillers? I suppose...'

'No, no,' she interrupted, trying to bite back a laugh and failing. 'Did you succeed in saving your dog?'

'Ah, yes, I did. Sorry, I thought you meant... It's quite warm in here, isn't it?' he said, his red cheeks deepening even more.

'I'm glad to hear it. I have a little pooch of my own, she keeps great company, and I don't know what I'd do without her,' the doctor replied, easing his nerves a little.

'That's... that's good.'

'Can you confirm which leg?' she enquired.

'Pardon?'

'Can you confirm which leg you hurt?' she clarified.

'Ah, okay. Sorry. It's my right leg,' he watched her type as he answered her question.

'No need to apologise, Harvey. I can see you're a little nervous, but I can promise you that I don't bite,' she reassured.

'Yeah, it must be the temperature in here, right?' he asked, with little attempt to hide his confusion and embarrassment.

'Can you show me?' she avoided the man's previous question, obviously made in an attempt to save him from his nerves.

'I beg your pardon?'

The doctor laughed, clearly enjoying the exchange more than Harvey, who was getting more miserable with his embarrassment by the second.

'Your leg, Harvey... can you show me your leg?' she repeated.

'Oh, of course,' he replied, standing up. He unbuckled his belt and dropped his trousers.

The doctor looked him in the eyes, trying very hard not to continue laughing.

'Could you not just lift your trouser leg?' she pointed out.

Harvey felt his face burn with embarrassment.

'Oh crap, I'm so sorry, what was I thinking?' he stammered, rushing to pull his trousers up. He was so befuddled that he tripped over and fell backwards against the wall, sliding down comically, as if in slow motion. He ended up on his backside, one leg in the trousers and one without, sitting there with his legs splayed and his eyes wide open in shock.

'Well, Mr Ross, you certainly have a way of introducing yourself, that's for sure,' she laughed, taking a close look at his leg. 'Anyway, I can see from here that you have internal bruising, which could take up to four weeks to heal. Try not to overstretch it otherwise it could take longer. An ice pack will help, and you could also try a compression bandage. Try and elevate it when you can; that will also speed up the healing process,' the doctor gave her guidance, still grinning as he sat there.

'I should get up now, shouldn't I?' he mumbled, finally putting his trousers back on and standing self-consciously. 'What a clumsy idiot I am... I'm so sorry, Doctor. You did not need to see that.'

'I did not, but don't worry, I promise I won't tell anyone,' she laughed softly. 'It's been a while since I've seen boxer shorts, though.'

'Okay, I'll just slip off quietly before I do any more damage,' he began to inch towards the door with each word, eager not to embarrass himself anymore. He turned to leave, grabbing the door handle, before the doctor spoke up again.

'Harvey, come back if it gets any worse,' she requested as he turned. 'And my name is Rose Morgan, by the way,' she smiled warmly as he nodded in acknowledgement.

'I will, thank you, Doctor... I mean Rose... Rose Morgan.'

As he turned to leave, he walked straight into the door that he had partially opened. He stood there for a second, gathering his thoughts and closing his eyes, trying in vain to stop the latest flush. Turning back to the doctor, he saw that she was laughing uncontrollably into her hands. He nodded again, turned, and left the room, shaking his head as if he couldn't believe his behaviour back there.

'What the hell just happened?' he muttered in disbelief,

walking back through reception and outside, ignoring the stares from others waiting to be seen. That just added to the feeling that he did not want to return to the medical practice for a long, long time.

He did, however, hope to see Doctor Rose Morgan again.

———————

17

THE CARS

H arvey slumped into the comfortable armchair upon arriving back at the cottage, still shaking his head in disbelief at his recent antics. After looking up at the ceiling for ten minutes, trying to gain his composure, he peered back down to see Max sitting there, watching him quizzically with his head slightly cocked to one side.

'It's your fault, you know,' Harvey shook his head, reaching out and stroking the terrier's head. 'But it could turn out to be another winner, just like finding the satchel. You are a talented little dog, aren't you, Max?'

Max barked once, almost in agreement, and jumped into Harvey's lap, licking his face enthusiastically now that he knew his owner was okay.

'Alright, alright, let me up and I'll get you a treat,' Harvey chuckled.

After taking care of Max, Harvey looked over the copies of everything that he had collated about the case, the one that was now likely to finally be investigated by Norfolk Constabulary. All other thoughts were banished as he focused, like he had always done in the Met, on the evidence in front of him. He still had questions, but it was mainly two that he could not yet answer that got him thinking of possibilities.

Where is this mysterious family treasure, if it exists? And why does Franklin have a building filled with cars?

He sat with his cup of coffee and pondered for thirty or so minutes. The question about the treasure was one that he could not identify any possible answers to; it was either there somewhere for him to eventually find, or it was not. The cars that Franklin had in storage, however, were another story altogether. If he could find a way to take a look at them, it could potentially reveal the answer, especially if he had registration numbers that he could have Steve check for him.

'I think I'm about to break the law, Max, and not feel guilty about it,' he admitted, making his decision on what was to be the next move. 'It's time to plan for some shenanigans.'

IT WAS early evening when he decided to make his move and investigate the garaged cars, knowing that the neighbouring businesses would all be closed at this time and that it would be highly unlikely to be spotted. Harvey drove to the nearby Reef Leisure Arena and parked in its busy car park. A short walk later, and he was in the industrial estate which was, as he'd expected, quiet and devoid of people. He still looked around him casually, just to make sure, before disappearing behind one of the large bushes that partially hid the Franklin's unit.

He turned on the torch setting on his phone, knowing that it was unlikely to alert anyone like a normal torch would, and used it to help guide him to the tree nearest to the window he had previously investigated. The gap between the tree was too large for him to gain entry, so he looked around and finally found some six-foot scaffolding boards behind the unit, propped up against the wall. He dragged two of them over and leaned them against the tree. Although the window was only seven feet up, he wasn't confident enough to climb and pull himself up to the ledge, so instead elected to walk across on the boards instead. He climbed up to the branch that he had previously stood on and pulled up the first board, laying one end on the branch and the other onto the window ledge of the unit. The six-inch ledge was enough for the board to have decent purchase. Not wanting to take any chances, Harvey pulled up the second board and did the same again, laying the second board on top of the first, giving them the strength to handle his weight comfortably.

Taking a deep breath before making his move, Harvey tentatively stepped onto the boards with one foot, trying it for stability before bringing up the other foot. Happy that it took his weight well and knowing that moving too fast could dislodge the boards, he shuffled across slowly, taking his time until he got to the window. He breathed a sigh of relief when he got there. Removing a small Swiss army knife from his pocket that he'd owned since joining the police some thirty years earlier—which he found useful in many ways—he slid the blade into the tight gap, prising open the handle inside.

Slowly, Harvey pushed the window inwards and was happy that it did so without a sound and without any internal lights coming on from any sensors that he'd failed to antici-pate. Although there was no alarm evident, Harvey didn't want to take any chances, and he'd have a hard time explaining himself if he got caught inside. He turned his body slightly and entered the unit, legs first, slowly descending to the floor, which he was happy to feel under his feet, with no obstructions giving him problems.

Taking his phone out again and using the torch, he made his way towards the far end of the unit, away from the shutters and towards the small rooms that housed a toilet and a tiny office. He found nothing useful in the office, except for a folder that had invoices and receipts from several years earlier. He went back out towards the shutters, where he noticed the letterbox and its mesh cage that looked like it was full. He took a handful of letters out and saw them all addressed to *B. Franklin*. Opening them, he saw that they were more invoices and receipts from the past two years. This suggested that despite continuing to pay his bills, Franklin hadn't visited the unit for a long time. He pocketed some of the letters to look at later.

Moving over to the cars, he lifted the first dust sheet and saw that it covered a red 1975 Triumph Stag. He could see that it was in great condition. Noting the registration number, he moved on to the next car. Another classic British sports car: a 1972 maroon Jensen Interceptor, also in flawless condition. He moved along and noted the registration numbers of all eight cars in the unit. Each was a classic British sports car from the 1960s and the 1970s, except for a 2007 Aston Martin DB9. It was a wonderful collection of cars, and Harvey shook his head at the thought of them being bought by the Franklins off the back of their evil crimes.

He covered each car back up and looked to make sure that he hadn't left any traces of his visit, before heading back to the window. Using a nearby chair, he was able to lift himself up and onto the window ledge, carefully levering himself up and ready to cross the boards to the safety of the tree. He closed the window behind him but left it unlocked, unable to use the knife to lock it. His confidence now high from his discovery, he began to cross back over towards the tree, forgetting to shuffle over slowly as he'd done on the way over.

It wasn't the fall so much that hurt, but the two scaffolding boards hitting him on their way down that did most of the damage. He rubbed his head where one of them had struck a glancing blow, wincing in pain as he did so. Unfortunately, the other board struck his right thigh, and not with a glancing blow, but a full-on blow that made it difficult for him to stand. Taking his phone out again for the torch, he saw that his hand had blood on it from his scalp. Shaking his head, he pulled the wooden boards back to the rear of the unit before limping slowly back towards his car.

'That's going to be sore tomorrow, that's for sure,' he muttered. 'Just with a few more bruises than I'd have liked,' he added ruefully.

———

WHEN HE ARRIVED BACK HOME, Harvey called McGarry.

'Isn't it past your bedtime?' Steve teased.

'It isn't that late, smartarse,' Harvey rolled his eyes, even though the other man couldn't see.

'Yeah, I know that, but you retired folk go to bed before it gets dark, don't you?' More laughter persists from the two of them.

'Funny man, you are,' Harvey quipped. 'When you eventually decide that we're worthy of a visit, I'll show you exactly what we retired folk can do.'

'This is fun, making fun of you. It wasn't so easy when you

were my boss, but now it sems to flow naturally,' Steve teased again with a grin.

'When you decide to grow up a little, I'll tell you why I'm calling, shall I?'

'Fine, what can I do for you, boss?' Steve sighed in mock defeat.

'I've got a bunch of car numbers I was hoping you could check for me. I just want to know whether they've been reported stolen, the owner details, that sort of thing...' Harvey explained.

'Sure, go for it.'

Harvey read out the make, model, colour, and registration number of each car.

'Blimey, that's a decent collection of vintage cars there,' Steve remarked. 'Got to be a quarter of a million pounds worth, at least.'

'Maybe more, they're all in amazing condition. I don't think they've been driven in years,' Harvey informed the other man.

'Are they part of this ongoing private investigation of yours?' Steve wondered.

'Yes, and before I do anything about it, I want to know what their statuses are, before I take it further with the local police. If they're stolen, it will be a little extra insurance for a conviction if they don't find the evidence that I gave them compelling enough.'

'Give me until tomorrow afternoon and I'll let you know,' Steve announced. 'Do you need anything else?'

'No, that's it for now, Steve, thanks. Seriously, though, try and get yourself down here for a few days. I'm sure your lovely wife would appreciate you taking some time away with her.'

'I'll see what I can get away with; as you can imagine, it's been a lot busier for me since you decided to abandon us,' Steve acknowledged.

'That's exactly why I retired, Detective Sergeant, so you could benefit from my workload,' Harvey teased. 'I'll speak with you soon.'

He grinned after ending the call and sat thinking of that workload that he realised he wasn't missing at all, stroking Max's head as he pondered the past.

'I much prefer what I'm doing now, eh, Max? Much more fun and without any of the stress.'

18

THE DOCTOR

Harvey was surprised to feel so much more pain when he woke earlier than usual the following morning. His right thigh was throbbing, even more than his calf had been after being hit by a car, and his head was very tender from the glancing blow, coupled with a nice, fresh scab from the shallow cut it had caused. Despite the pain, it was only when he got up to go to the bathroom that he realised it was worse than he thought, his leg almost buckling under him.

Oh no, he thought ruefully, *I have to go back.*

DOCTOR ROSE MORGAN stifled a laugh when he limped into her consultation room two hours later. She watched as he sat, clearly uncomfortable in her presence again, and waited for him to settle down in his seat before speaking.

'It's been such a long time, Harvey, we missed you here,' she teased, grinning broadly.

Harvey sighed deeply, shaking his head as he looked down at the floor before looking back up at the happy doctor.

'Before you say anything else, I didn't purposely hurt myself just so that I could come and see you again,' he insisted firmly. 'I hope that's clear.'

Rose nodded exaggeratedly, her eyebrows furrowed as if to lightly mock his presumption.

'Why would you say that, Harvey? Is there something you haven't told me?' she asked innocently.

'It's... well... I didn't want you to think... for goodness' sake... it doesn't matter. My leg hurts, please fix it,' he gave up, his voice showcasing his defeat.

Rose stifled another laugh as she pointed to his leg.

'You mean it got worse? Can you lift your trouser leg please?'

'Yes... no... well, it's the same leg but in a different place,' he spluttered.

'I'm confused, Harvey, what exactly has happened here?' she probed.

'Don't be alarmed again, but I need to drop my trousers to show you... Please try not to laugh this time,' he pleaded.

The doctor laughed out loudly.

'You should never tell anyone not to laugh when something is funny, Harvey, because it just makes it funnier. Go ahead and drop your trousers, I can promise you that I won't be alarmed,' she insisted. 'Something I haven't said so cheerfully in a long time.'

Harvey did as he was told, trying to cover his modesty as best he could as the doctor examined the fresh bruising on his thigh.

'Was it another car?' she queried, having finished her brief examination.

'No, it was a scaffolding board,' he shook his head.

'You got attacked by a scaffolding board?'

'No... well, I suppose so, yes. Actually, it was two. One fell on my leg and the other on my head,' he replied, showing her the top of his head and pointing to the scab.

'Well, you're on a hat-trick now, Harvey. Two visits in as many days, what do you think you'll be in for tomorrow?' she bantered.

'I'm glad you find it funny, Doctor, but you know it isn't very professional of you to mock the wounded,' he shot back.

'It absolutely is, especially when the wounded need to be mocked. Now, why don't you go home and put some ice on that, take some painkillers, and take it easy for a few days. That way, you will avoid being hit by something else. Unless you absolutely want to come and visit again?' she asked with a raised eyebrow, trying to stifle a laugh once more.

'I will do that, thank you. Wait... what do you mean visit...'

'It's been a while since someone made me laugh this much, and so innocently too. I'm somewhat intrigued by you, Harvey Ross. Is there a Mrs Ross here in Sheringham with you?'

'There is not. There is an ex-Mrs Ross out at sea somewhere on an extended cruise, though,' he replied, unsure of where this conversation was leading.

'So, there isn't anyone out there who would object to you going out for a coffee and a chat?'

'A coffee and a chat? Wait... are you... as in a date?' he stuttered. 'I'm pretty sure that's not allowed, is it? You know, ethically and all that.'

'You are quite correct, it is most definitely not allowed,'

she grinned. 'I can tell you, however, that an accidental encounter *is* allowed,' she added.

'An accidental encounter, eh? So, let's say that did happen, would that then be considered a date?'

'Call it what you want, Harvey, just remember that as a doctor it would be considered unethical for me to get involved with a patient at work. Maybe I'll see you tomorrow when you come in with another injury,' she jested.

'Do you have a thing for men who make a fool of themselves?' he asked, 'or is this some sort of prank that you're looking to pull off?' he continued.

'I suppose I like men who make fools of themselves,' she laughed again. 'Just stick some ice on that and rest, okay?' she offered. 'Now leave me to my work, there's lots of people who need my attention.'

He waved and left the room without saying a word. Standing in the corridor, he tried to make sense of the last five minutes, frowning as if he'd forgotten something or couldn't work anything out.

'Sometimes you have to just stop overthinking and crack on,' he muttered lowly, trying to piece together the last few minutes.

The grin on his face stayed the entire trip home.

'IT DIDN'T TAKE AS LONG as I thought,' Steve started when he called early that afternoon.

'What did you find?' Harvey demanded excitedly.

'Unfortunately, none of the cars are stolen. They're all registered to Robert Franklin at the Cambourne House address, with one exception, the Aston Martin, which is registered to Bradley Franklin at that same address. All cars were bought after 1957, if that helps.'

'I didn't see that coming, if I'm honest. I guess they were bought from the proceeds of their crimes though, if all were bought after the death of Dorothy Flynn, right?' Harvey asked.

'Most definitely, as long as Robert Franklin was found to have killed Dorothy and Percy, yes.'

'I guess that the police should be made aware of them, then. My concern is that there's now a trace of the checks on the Police National Computer, which may attract some attention,' Harvey mused.

'I took care of that. I logged an anonymous call about some abandoned cars that a local suspected were stolen, so if anyone comes asking about the PNC checks, they'll see it was anonymous,' Steve shot back proudly.

'You think of everything, don't you? They should promote you,' Harvey beamed with a laugh.

'Well, I'd have to meet them halfway and take the inspector's exam, but I'm working on that. And to be honest, I learnt most of the devious tricks from you, so if it all kicks off, I'll just blame my ex-boss for leading me down the wrong path,' Steve quipped.

'Of course you will, as all good turncoats should do,' Harvey responded.

Steve laughed out loudly.

'Will you please come back already? You've had months off now... surely it's time that you realise that there's no place like home?'

'Steve, I'm just fine and dandy here, thank you. And I am home.'

19

JRR TOLKIEN

Before the end of the business day, Harvey decided to call Emily Leclerc to see if any decisions had been made on pursuing the case for murder.

'It's good of you to call, Harvey. How's that scoundrel friend of yours doing, did you tell him what we discussed?' Emily greeted in response.

'I did, and he told me he's staying away until things calm down a little... I guess he knows what you'll do to him,' he joked.

'Good, he needs a lesson taught. I guess you're calling to hear if we're doing anything with the investigation?' she assumed.

'I am, and I apologise if this isn't a good time, I can call back if you wish.'

'No, no, it's fine. We had a meeting about it yesterday and decided that our team was best placed to investigate it. You'll be happy to know that we are now officially on the case,' Emily confirmed. 'Weirdly, we must log it as a new crime, as it was never reported as such in the past. It isn't so much a cold case, but a new case that's come to light. The downside is that our murder stats will take a hit, but the head honchos will just have to take it on the chin.'

'That's great news, Emily, I am very pleased to hear that. There should be no escape from justice, right?' Harvey enthused.

'Absolutely. We've transferred the items from the lost and found report and are working on making a list of the people we'd like to speak to, so hopefully there should be some news next week or so when we start interviewing.'

'Marvellous. If there's anything at all I can assist with, please do let me know,' Harvey offered.

'I will do, and thanks again for bringing this to our attention, Harvey.'

'The pleasure is mine, Emily, I appreciate you listening to me in the first place, although I suppose I owe that buffoon a thank you also,' he jested again.

'Yes, well, you can tell him that things have calmed down and to reach out to us again, unless he wants to feel our wrath once more,' Emily chuckled.

Harvey was elated at the news and tried to anticipate the next moves that Emily's *Major Investigations Team* would take. It was likely that they'd research Franklin and find out about the unit and the cars at some point, so that part was taken care of. Percy's letter, the empty arsenic bottle, the inquest open verdict all pointed to the murder, but was it *actually* enough? Harvey suspected that Bradley Franklin would have a big part to play in the outcome. His age and health suggested that even with a conviction for the crimes he had committed, a custodial sentence was very unlikely, but maybe there could be negotiations for him to tell the investigators everything that he knew to assist in confirming the murders, in exchange for leniency in his sentence. A confession of sorts.

If that was how to best get justice for Dorothy and Percy, then Harvey was fine with that.

HARVEY DECIDED to listen to the doctor's advice and rest his leg. After taking care of Max's feeding, he made himself a coffee and limped over to the armchair, pulling a footstool close for him to raise and rest his leg. Before sitting down, he wandered over to the bookcase and looked through the wonderful array of first edition books that his aunt had so thoughtfully left him. He was slightly reluctant to touch some of the rarer volumes, but then thought that Agatha would scold him.

'I left them so that you could read them, young man!' he imagined her saying.

He laughed at the thought and nodded, his mind made up. He reached in and gently took out a first edition of *The Fellowship of the Ring* by J. R. R. Tolkien, the first book in the epic *Lord of the Rings* trilogy, from 1954. He cradled it carefully as he sat down, marvelling at the condition of this rare and wonderful book.

'Thank you, Aunt Agatha. I shall endeavour to take care of this amazing gift as best as I can,' he said.

Turning to the first page, Harvey almost choked when he saw that the book had been inscribed and signed by the famous author with an impressive penmanship rarely seen nowadays.

To my dearest friend Agatha,

It was wonderful working with you on such an intriguingly stimulating 'project'.

Please accept a gift of this first edition from my own personal collection in gratitude.

I hope that you enjoy reading it as much as I enjoyed writing it so long ago.

I look forward to our next equally stimulating 'project'!

Your faithful friend and sometimes collaborator,

J. R. R. Tolkien

February 1st, 1969.

'Aunt Agatha, you surely are full of surprises, aren't you? More and more each day!' Harvey exclaimed, wondering what it was that the pair had worked on together. He worked out in his head that Tolkien would have been seventy-eight years of age and his aunt in her early thirties, so discounted a romantic project.

Something to do with her spying, no doubt, he thought to himself.

He was too excited to start reading such a significant book, not just as a book, but more so the personal nature of how his aunt had come into its possession. It was a rare and wonderful gift, indeed. He decided instead to take another look through her journals in the loft, forgetting the condition of his leg and immediately regretting the way he stood so quickly. He collected himself and slowly limped towards the stairs, hoping that the pain wouldn't impede his progress too much. It took twice as long to reach the top of the stairs than normal, but he managed to do so without too much of an issue, releasing the ladder and slowly scaling it into the loft.

Sitting down by the dresser, having selected and then retrieved two of the clothbound notebooks, Harvey marvelled at the detail that his aunt had written. One of the journals was dated **1969 #1**, which he opened first, intrigued by Tolkien's inscription in the book, wondering if there were any clues to the 'project' mentioned.

'Here we go,' he muttered, turning the page to January 4th, 1969.

Followed Agent 223 to vicinity of RAF Hurn, Dorset.

Agent 223 took discrete photos of base but no aircraft or personnel in view.

Reported to main office.

He turned the page and saw another entry made on January 7th, 1969.

Met with JRR and Edith at their bungalow in Woodridings, Lakeside Road.

Explained my predicament regarding foreign agents watching RAF Hurn.

JRR excited to assist and set me up in a room overlooking the road.

Good view opposite to Agent 223's current residence.

On the opposite page was an entry made on January 9th, 1969.

Agent 223 returns to Lakeside Road with unknown male after meet near perimeter of air base.

Main office informed immediately of collaborator involvement.

Advised I continue surveillance until they can respond.

7.16pm - Arrest team enter residence by force and make two arrests.

Equipment seized and taken away.

JRR and Edith overjoyed to witness the forced entry and removal of foreign agent and collaborator.

Edith and JRR insisted we celebrate with a glass or two of sherry.

Stayed the night and left midday the following day with a headache!

Harvey grinned and imagined the elderly author's excitement watching the events unfurl before him. Knowing his history in the military, Harvey believed that Tolkien would have thought that as an adventure and a half, and had no doubt continued the friendship with his aunt as a result. He took out his phone and searched for Tolkien's home at that time. It didn't take long; Woodridings was a lovely bungalow at 19 Lakeside Road in Poole, Dorset, and the final home of the Tolkien's before Edith's death in 1971 and his in 1973. Having retired some years earlier, such an event taking place on their doorstep and helping considerably in the end result must have been a hugely symbolic and entertaining to the elderly couple. Harvey nodded and smiled at the positive impact his aunt would have made.

One more gem to hold on to, Auntie, he thought, placing the journal down.

He sat for a while, thinking about his own life and the impact he had made on others so far, hoping that he had been a force for good and positive, at least to some. Not wanting to rest on any laurels, Harvey realised that he still had much to offer to many people; it was never too late to do more in life. Granted, some of the people that he was likely to be able to help in the future were no longer alive, thanks to his cold case investigator speciality, but there were still living relatives that would benefit from his discoveries, and he was now even more determined to find the truth and ensure that justice was served.

His aunt had shown him the way, and he was determined to follow that path.

'That's my life now,' he said, nodding happily to himself with his words.

20

COFFEE

The following day, buoyed by the revelation that helping people find closure and peace—having been wronged in the past—was the way forward for him now, Harvey decided that being bold and adventurous was most certainly one way to continue living his new life. After a bracing walk with Max and a breakfast of porridge and tea, he decided to use his rediscovered bravery and message Rose Morgan.

> Good morning, Doctor. I forgot to ask you if you know of anywhere that makes a decent coffee? I'm new here and I don't know anyone else to ask.

He crossed his fingers briefly before realising his mistake and typed again.

> This is Harvey Ross, by the way.

Grinning and very pleased with himself to have messaged

instead of calling in the hope of an answer, he put the phone down and picked up his aunt's notebook, flicking through to see if there were any more Tolkien references. He found another in the second of the journals, marked **1969 #2**, dated September 19th, 1969.

Received call from JRR.
House previously used by Agent 223 now occupied again.
JRR watched for several weeks, making notes.
Identifies new agent, now known as Agent 277.
Main office informed with all information from JRR.

Flicking forward a few pages, another entry came to his attention, dated September 24th, 1969.

Main office confirm that Agent 277 now identified as a friendly visiting agent from America, who is assisting main office with ongoing Top-Secret operation.
Confirm that residence now owned and operated by MI6.
JRR informed that agent is friendly. Apologises profusely, insists I visit.
Next holiday booked, Poole here I come!

Harvey grinned at the thought of the famous J.R.R

Tolkien being mortified at his error, but delighted that
Agatha was visiting again.

'We all make mistakes, old chap, and that wasn't actually
a bad one to make,' Harvey mumbled, imagining the laughter
at their reunion.

His phone pinged, making him jump out of his reverie.

> Good morning to you, Harvey Ross. I like
> Gangway, their coffee is very nice, especially
> around 7 when they change baristas.

Harvey grinned knowingly.

> This is Rose Morgan, by the way, lol x

Harvey pumped his fist and shouted, 'Yes!'
He sent another message.

> That's very kind, thank you.

He looked down at Max whose tail was wagging excitedly,
recognising that something was afoot.

'That's right boy, things are looking up, eh? How about a
treat?'

THE NEXT FEW hours dragged on interminably as Harvey
deliberated on what to wear, whether to drive or walk, how
early to be there, and a dozen more questions that he hadn't
asked since his days as a single young man. Momentarily, he
also questioned his decision to be going on a date, before

recovering quickly and remembering his new mantra... bold and adventurous.

'Life is too short, Harvey. Grab what you can by the scruff and enjoy it,' he mumbled several times, convincing himself to relax a bit as he changed his shirt for the third time.

Eventually, it was time to leave. The butterflies in his stomach got progressively worse as he had neared the time, the frequent deep breaths doing nothing to allay them. He'd made his mind up on one thing, and that was that he'd take Archie. Although it was a cool evening and the roof would remain up, it gave him a boost to get in and listen to the lively engine purr the way it did. It was a short drive to the car park opposite The Gangway and he parked in a spot where he could see the car from inside.

He got out and locked the little roadster, the butterflies in his stomach as bad as they had been all day. He checked his shirt and jacket, happy that there were no stains or tears to embarrass him, when he heard the familiar voice.

'You should zip that up, you know,' Rose Morgan said from ten feet away where she'd gotten out of her car.

Harvey had been so focused on parking and then his jacket that he hadn't noticed her sitting in her car, waiting for the right time to head towards the coffee shop. Her voice startled him.

'Zip what up?' he asked, confused.

'You're flying low, Mr Ross,' she laughed, pointing to his trousers.

'Oh, dear God!' he exclaimed, turning and zipping up his trousers. 'I can't believe I did that.'

He turned back to see tears rolling down Rose's cheeks as she failed in her attempt to stifle the laugh.

'I didn't do it on purpose, honestly,' he defended, joining in with the laughter.

'I think that's one of the best icebreakers I've come across,' she teased, walking up to him. 'Thank you, it helped ease the nerves somewhat. Fancy bumping into you here... accidentally,' she added.

'Yes, what a... coincidence,' he replied. 'Wait, you were nervous?' he asked, pausing before continuing once more. 'Because I can tell you that I'd be a gold medal contender if there was a sport on dating nerves.'

'Yes, I was a little nervous. I think you should be on an... accidental first date, shouldn't you? Otherwise, there isn't much point, is there?' she replied.

'So, it is a date!' he exclaimed, as if catching her out.

'Come on, Harvey, it's a figure of speech. Let's just go and have a coffee, shall we? We can discuss your nerves inside,' she grabbed his arm to loop hers through it as she spoke, guiding him towards the coffee shop.

There was a constant murmur of voices and passing cars as they sat outside with their coffees a few minutes later.

'So, here we are,' Harvey started, the nerves still very much there.

'Yes, here we are. It seems like only yesterday you were falling over yourself to take your trousers down,' Rose grinned. 'And look at us now, drinking coffee in a very civilised setting.'

'You certainly have a way with words, Doctor Rose Morgan,' Harvey replied. 'And I should add that it is partly your fault. Actually, it is entirely your fault that we are here.'

'And why is that, Harvey? I don't recall twisting your arm in any way,' she shrugged.

'It wasn't so much that, more so the fact that you turned

me into a blubbering fool, something I assure you that I am not. Not normally, anyway. I can only deduce, using my extensive detective abilities, that you are to blame, as you are the only variable that could have affected me in that way.'

'That's a lot of complex words to use to say that you were attracted to me, Harvey. Do I make you shy, detective?' Rose replied.

'Yes. Yes, you do. And it's infuriating. I'm very much used to being in control at all times, and for some peculiar reason, that all goes out of the window when you are in close proximity,' he huffed.

Rose laughed.

'I'll take that as a compliment, and a nice one it is to hear too. I didn't think I could have such an effect anymore, who would have thought it, eh?' Rose winked.

'Me, for one. Anyway, enough about my embarrassment... tell me about yourself, Rose. How long have you lived in Sheringham?'

'Straight to the point, I like that. I moved here about four years ago after I sold my share in a private practice in London. I accepted the post here on condition that I only work three days a week, which is as much as I want to do nowadays. It's worked out well, if I may say so.'

'Interesting, a privateer giving something, that's very honourable of you. Where in London was your practice?' Harvey asked.

'Harley Street, where the wealthy were drawn to when they had their health problems. I was one of four partners, so when I had enough, they bought me out. I always wanted to come back here after my holidays here as a child, it seemed fitting.'

'That's an odd coincidence, I ended up here for the same

reason, although it was given a healthy nudge by my aunt leaving me her cottage here when she passed away,' he replied.

'Oh, I'm sorry to hear that. That is a special gift that she left you, indeed.'

'As well as Archie, there,' he said, pointing to the red sports car she'd seen him in.

'Wow, she must have loved you a lot!' Rose exclaimed.

'I suppose she did. I was her only living relative, so that played a part, but I'm very happy to be here regardless. It's turning out to be an entertaining retirement,' Harvey reasoned.

'That's good to hear. I'm wondering about what to do with myself when it's my turn, so tell me more.'

'Oh, I haven't joined any clubs or anything, I found myself something to keep me busy and to put right a few wrongs at the same time,' he replied.

'That's cryptic of you, Harvey, I'm guessing you don't want to say much more.'

'It wouldn't be fair, to be honest, not while it's ongoing. You'll just have to be patient with me... and no, I didn't mean that as a pun!'

'I should hope not, it was dreadful,' she chuckled.

'So, Rose Morgan, what do you like to do in your spare time?' Harvey probed.

'Before I answer, I think it's time we stopped being so formal, so I promise I won't call you detective anymore if you promise not to call me Doctor... unless you are in my surgery as a patient, of course. Harvey and Rose it is from now on. Deal?'

'Deal,' Harvey agreed with a cheerful laugh.

'Good. Well, now, what do I do in my spare time? I read a

lot, I potter around in my garden, and I have a secret passion that I'm not sure I should disclose on a first date,' Rose teased.

'Okay, I'll make it easy for you. If it is something personal that is of an embarrassing nature, then I demand that you say nothing... yet. If it's anything else, then I demand that you do,' he joked.

'That's fair. Okay, brace yourself. I'm a science fiction geek,' she admitted, watching closely for Harvey's reaction.

'As in, you love Star Trek and Star Wars, or you like watching the stars through a telescope?'

'A bit of everything, I suppose. I love speculating what the future holds for us all... I dream of going to space and floating in zero gravity... I imagine what extra-terrestrial life is like... that sort of thing,' she replied sheepishly.

'Okay, that's not overly embarrassing. I mean, it would be if you were in church and started talking about Captain Spock or Yoda, but in the privacy of your own home, that's a pretty cool hobby.'

'The fact that you know Spock and Yoda is a big positive, I can tell you,' she smiled gently.

'I like to think of myself as a well-rounded, well-educated man, who often forgets to pull his zip up,' Harvey made a humble joke of his prior embarrassment.

'That's very good,' she said, joining in the laughter.

'Going back to my question, what do you like to do in your spare time if you were going out with someone on, say, a second or third date?'

'Look at you, one minute you're falling over yourself, and the next, you're planning our next two dates. Have the nerves completely left you, because that may not be a good sign,' she replied.

'The nerves are still there, I assure you. I'm doing a good job of masking them, which is a better sign because it means I can be less of a buffoon around you.'

'That's good. Well, I do like a long walk in the park or along the seashore, in all weathers, but preferably when the sun is out. I also like the cinema and eating out at restaurants. Later, when I no longer think you are a danger to me, and we've been out enough times, I also like to snuggle up with a hot chocolate and watch television, but only at the end of the day when I'm too exhausted to do much more.'

'That's a decent start, I suppose, nothing too controversial. I was half expecting a helicopter ride or skydiving, something like that. I can handle a nice meal and a movie, for sure,' he grinned.

'I'm glad to hear that. That's quite a significant minute or two, don't you think?'

'Why's that?' he asked, knowing full well what she meant.

'In the space of two minutes, we basically agreed to go on at least two more dates, with a potential snuggle on the couch thereafter,' she laughed.

'Which means, of course, that this first date, despite the horrific start, turned out to be a spectacular success, wouldn't you think?' he offered with a cheesy grin.

'Absolutely. Now, how about a glass of wine now that we won't be storming off in a hurry?'

HARVEY WAS STILL GRINNING BROADLY when he arrived back at the garage to park Archie. As he locked the door and started walking towards the cottage, he heard the sound of an engine starting. Thinking nothing of it, he continued to walk normally. It was only when he heard the engine noise increase to a roar that he turned to see what it was. The vehicle came at him at high speed: a dark Transit van with a solitary driver, a man that Harvey locked eyes with momentarily, long enough for Harvey to realise he was in trouble. He instantly recognised the determined, fanatical look in the man's eyes enough to know that. Just before the van struck him, he dived sideways into the front garden of another cottage. The landing was rough, and he felt a searing pain in his elbow, just as the van struck a glancing blow to the flint wall protecting him. Harvey got up in time to see the van speed off. He noticed that one rear light wasn't working and that the first two letters of the registration number were 'BN'.

'That's an interesting turn of events,' he muttered as he dusted himself down.

He limped back to the cottage and examined his elbow, which he was able to move freely but was still painful.

I daren't go back to the doctor for this, he thought.

He picked up the phone and called the police.

'I'd like to report an attempt on my life,' he told the operator.

21

LEMON JUICE

Harvey woke with a smile the following morning, despite the incident with the van. It was a smile that continued throughout his morning walk with Max, and for most of the morning, until his face started to ache a little. He had enjoyed spending time with Rose immensely, something that he hadn't experienced with Becky for many years, and something that he hadn't expected to experience again. In fact, it was almost alien to him—the first date nerves, chatting about things that he hadn't with anyone for many years, that sort of thing.

'I'm not a fan of teenagers at the best of times, but if this is what it's like dating again then I may have to overlook some of their behaviour and give them the benefit of the doubt... at least some of the time, eh, Max?'

Shortly after lunch, as he looked through the evidence and information he had gathered again—a task he'd employed many times as a detective to refresh his memory in the hope that something missed earlier would reveal itself—his phone rang.

'Mr Ross? This is Millie Parry from Holts Road. I hope this isn't a bad time?'

'Not at all, Millie, it's good to hear from you,' Harvey replied. 'What can I do for you?'

'I just wanted to see if you'd had a chance to check out the locations from the tracing paper, that's all,' Millie replied.

'Yes, I did, but unfortunately, I couldn't find anything that looked like it had been buried or hidden. I think it's a bit of a dead end at the moment,' Harvey frowned slightly.

'That's very unlike Percy...' Millie trailed off.

'What do you mean?'

'He was so meticulous with everything that he did. He was studying to be an engineer, you know. Whenever we used code to communicate, it was always correct and clearly understandable... I can't think why, on the most important occasion, he would get it wrong,' she huffed.

'I don't know what else to do or say, Millie, I spent hours looking and found nothing.'

'Mr Ross, do you have the tracing paper with you?' she implored.

'Yes, why?'

'Can you smell it for me?'

'Excuse me?'

'Please humour me, just try smelling the tracing paper and let me know if there is a scent of any kind,' Millie pleaded.

Harvey took the tracing paper out of an envelope and tentatively smelt it.

'Well?' Millie's question came eagerly.

'I'm not sure what to say... it smells like old tracing paper. There's a very faint hint of lemon, but no fancy scent or anything like that. What were you expecting?' Harvey's confusion was evident in his tone.

'I wasn't expecting a perfume or anything like that, silly. I wanted to know if there was a lemony smell, which it sounds like there is. Can you bring it round to my house? I think there's a secret message hidden on the paper, and I know how to retrieve it,' Millie announced.

HARVEY ARRIVED at Millie's house less than thirty minutes later, both intrigued and impressed; it seemed as if Percy was still leaving clues from beyond the grave.

'Hello, Harvey, please come in,' Evelyn greeted when she answered the door. 'Millie is waiting for you in the dining room. Would you like a tea or coffee?'

'Nothing for me, Evelyn, thank you.'

Millie was sitting in her favoured chair when he entered the room and started to rise.

'Please, don't,' Harvey insisted. 'Don't do that on my account.'

'That's very kind of you, Mr Ross,' Millie gave him a kind smile.

'Please, it's Harvey.'

'Harvey it is. Did you bring the tracing paper?' she cut to the chase almost immediately.

'I did, and I'm very intrigued by your request, Millie. What do you have in mind?'

'It's all in the book, Harvey. It was right there in front of you,' she smiled.

'Which book?'

'*Fun with Science*, of course. Don't you remember? We

used to send each other secret hidden messages using lemon juice. Nobody ever figured it out, but it's all there in the book as to how it's done,' she informed the man.

'I didn't bring the book, so please enlighten me,' Harvey solicited.

'Of course. Bring me that lamp please,' she instructed, pointing to an ornate lamp on a nearby table. 'Lemon juice has carbon compounds in it that are colourless at room temperature, but when exposed to heat, the compounds break down and release the carbon. That then oxidises and turns brown when it comes into contact with air, making the invisible message visible. Shall we try it?'

'How on earth did you know all that?' Harvey was astonished.

'I never told you, but I was a chemistry teacher at the high school in Cromer for many years, and you never forget that stuff,' she grinned proudly. 'Please, take the lampshade off and switch the light on.'

Harvey did as he was instructed after handing the tracing paper to Millie. She held it against the warming light bulb for few seconds before a hint of smoke started emanating from the tracing paper due to the heat.

'And voila!' she exclaimed triumphantly, showing Harvey the result.

Harvey was stunned when he saw that there was a message next to the dot indicating the position of the pillbox that had fallen with the cliff collapse.

Outer north wall
Middle
12 inches
12 inches

'What do you think that means?' Millie speculated.

'I imagine it means that whatever Percy hid there was outside, twelve inches from the wall and twelve inches deep,' Harvey surmised.

'I'm very confused, Harvey,' she countered.

'About what?'

'Percy was supposedly found dead outside after a bad storm. How was it he managed to bury everything *and* write this note? It doesn't make sense to me,' she shook her head in awe.

'I have a theory that he was just very unlucky, Millie. The poison had started to take its toll, and when Percy realised that he and his mother were being poisoned, he put a plan together to hide everything from his stepfather before it was too late. He was on his way back home and likely to have posted the letter to you when he realised that he may not make it in the storm, and just left it in the satchel hidden, in the hope that he would survive and get back to it the next day.'

'So, if it wasn't for your dog finding the satchel, nobody would ever have known about this all,' Millie whispered. 'Poor Percy.'

'He was just very unlucky... I'm so sorry, Millie.'

Harvey could sense that even after all these years, Percy's demise still affected Millie.

'He was a good man,' her eyes watered slightly at the memories of her love rushing through her.

'He was, and a very clever one to use this method, that's for sure. What do you say we solve this crime and get some justice for Percy, eh?' Harvey encouraged.

'Yes, absolutely,' she responded, her determination shining through.

'Let's see what other clues Percy left us,' Harvey brought the tracing paper close to the bulb once again as he spoke. He moved the paper around slowly so the heat would reach it all, when he noticed several more messages appearing.

'Will you look at that...' he said, nodding respectfully.

'There's more?' Millie asked.

'And then some,' Harvey replied. 'Look at this, Millie.'

Harvey showed her the tracing paper which now had three additional messages on it. Two were next to the dots marking the Beeston Regis Priory and the All Saints Church, and the other was in the top left-hand corner, away from the markings, a personal message to Millie.

I love you, Millie x

When she saw the words, Millie let the tears flow freely, smiling at Harvey, proud of the young man that she had loved so long ago.

Harvey kneeled beside the woman and hugged her gently.

'Let's make him proud,' he whispered.

'Yes, let's.'

Harvey looked at the other messages. The one to the left of the dot marking the location of the ruins at Beeston Regis Priory had a rudimentary sketch of a square with the east side missing, with a dot in the middle and a few words.

Chapel
Chancel
12 inches

'This one is a little trickier. I'll need to check it against the plan I have of the Priory and see if it matches to anything. I assume that the dot mark is where something is buried twelve inches down,' he said.

'What about the other one?' Millie asked, pointing to the All Saints Church message.

There was another rudimentary sketch of what looked like the letter Z but with a straight vertical line instead of a diagonal one. There was a dot marked on the upper end of the vertical line.

Father
North aisle

Latch

'Whatever does that mean?' Millie wondered.

'I have an inkling, Millie. When I went to the church, I noticed there was a wooden panel with a dedication to Percy's father, on the north side of the church. I think this message is a clue as to something hidden there, where the dot is,' he answered.

'I remember when they added that; we were children and the church was filled to the brim with people, Percy's father was a much-loved man,' Millie nodded.

'It certainly seems that way. The more I learn about the man, the more respect I have for him,'

'Percy lost him when he was very young, but frequently spoke of him proudly, so to leave this clue at his dedication is typical of him,' Millie added.

'Well, now, thanks to Percy, it seems I can revisit the Priory and All Saints and see what I can find. The search is back on!' Harvey exclaimed happily.

'Harvey, can I ask you something?' Millie diverted the subject with her question.

'Of course, what is it?'

'If you do find anything, what do you intend to do with it?' she replied, her tone gentle as always.

'I hadn't thought about that, to be honest. It's unlikely Franklin will have a claim to it, now that it is very possible that his father will be revealed as the murderer and he as a knowing accomplice. I imagine there will be a hunt for existing relatives or something like that. Why do you ask?'

'No reason,' Millie responded, suddenly quiet and distant with her thoughts.

'Millie, if there's any consolation, I will do anything I can to make sure that the right person or persons take possession of anything I find, I promise you that,' Harvey reassured.

'Thank you, Harvey, that means a great deal to me,' she replied, smiling as she turned back to face him.

'On that happy note, I shall leave you to it. I'll be in touch if I find anything or if I hear anything else,' he said, standing.

'Thank you, Harvey, it's been delightful getting to know you. I hope you will keep in touch after this is all over,' Millie wished with a smile.

'You won't be getting rid of me that easily, Millie. You're my friend now and it shall remain that way until you get fed up with me,' he grinned.

Millie laughed.

'Well, let's not let that happen, eh? Evelyn, would you mind seeing Harvey out, please?'

'Bye, Millie, see you soon,' Harvey said his goodbye, giving her a peck on the cheek before he left.

Upon arriving back at the cottage, Harvey made sure to take photos of the tracing paper, just in case, before making a few notes and then sitting down to plan the next days ahead.

He found a plan of the Beeston Regis Priory and compared the sketch that had revealed itself on the tracing paper. It didn't take long to match the shape to a spot on the plan in the northeast corner. The dot marked a spot outside, halfway between the walls of the chapel and the chancel.

He did the same with a plan of All Saints church and saw that the shape matched the location along the east wall at the north end of the church—exactly where James Flynn's dedication panel was located. Now that both locations had been pinpointed to him, he knew exactly what to do the next day.

'It seems we'll be looking for treasure again, Max. Never a dull moment, eh?'

22

TREASURE

The following morning, Harvey awoke at dawn, having set an early alarm to act while most of the town was still fast asleep. Armed with the precise locations of the two venues, he equipped himself with a backpack that had the tools he'd likely need for the day, including a trowel for digging, a small knife, and various hand tools such as screwdrivers for whatever was required at the All Saints church. He also added several large bin bags for any findings he discovered until he could get them home safely.

He decided the first stop would be the Priory, where he didn't expect anyone to be passing by so early in the morning. He parked nearby and walked the short distance, aiming for the exact spot that Percy had marked on his rudimentary sketch. He made sure to take a good look around for any early morning walkers before starting to dig in the centre of the area between the walls, as marked by the dot. The ground was harder than he thought, so digging with the trowel took some time, but eventually, and about a foot or so down, he struck something hard.

'Here we go,' he muttered as he cleared the soil from around what looked like a rotting cloth bag containing the object.

As he lifted the sack out carefully, he realised there were, in fact, two objects inside. He placed the bag on the ground and carefully cut away the string tying it together, revealing two small, ornate wooden boxes within. There was some obvious damage to them from being underground for so long, but they were still in reasonably good shape. Both were made of mahogany with gold inlay and the initials *'DF'* engraved into small, circular-shaped, golden buttons about an inch and a half across.

'Dorothy Flynn, maybe?' Harvey mumbled lowly as he cleared remnants of soil away.

Gently placing them next to each other on the grass, Harvey released the small clasp on the first and opened it slowly.

'Wow!' he gasped in awe. 'Dorothy Flynn indeed...'

The box was divided into six compartments, each with four or five gold rings in them of all shapes, sizes, and designs, and many set with vibrant, coloured gems as well as clear, sparkling diamonds. They had been well-protected in the box and looked like they were freshly bought from a jeweller. He closed the box and repeated the same with the second one, nodding appreciatively at the contents. The second box was also divided into six compartments. These were filled with gold and silver brooches inlaid with precious stones of all colours, along with gold crosses and chains, with one compartment filled with a dozen gold sovereigns. It was a precious haul indeed—a real treasure that had become part of local folklore for decades; a treasure that had never been found.

And Harvey had found it... or part of it.

He took a minute to think about the circumstances leading to the hoard being buried here by a young man who knew he was dying and who tried desperately to protect the family legacy form the murderer.

Well done, Percy, well done indeed, he thought, patting the ground respectfully.

He put both jewellery boxes into his backpack and quickly filled the hole, leaving minimal trace of his being there. Before too long, he was in his car on the way to All Saints Church, buoyed by his discovery and excited about what he would find there.

It was still before eight in the morning when Harvey arrived at the church. There were no cars parked anywhere, so Harvey felt reasonably comfortable that it was unlikely that there would be anyone present. He entered via the porch entrance way, as before, and walked in, as before, knowing that the door was always open to the public. He was always surprised at how at peace he felt when entering churches, and this morning was no exception, despite the reason for him being there. He looked around, seeing nobody present, as expected, and walked down the central nave towards the chancel. There was a wooden table with two candlestick holders and a plain wooden cross in front of the decorative panel that he was aiming for, but there was enough room to the left of the panel for him to get close. The dot that Percy had marked was in line with the edge of the panel, so he slowly ran his fingers along the side of the panel, looking for a latch that the young man had mentioned.

There was no evident latch of any kind, so he repeated the action, but slower, until he felt a slight depression in the wood. He turned his fingers inwards and used the nail on his forefinger to trace the outline of a very well-constructed switch that was level with the rest of the frame. He tentatively pressed against it, feeling for any resistance, which there was. He pressed again more firmly, and there was a faint click as the switch did its job and released the panel from the wall.

Harvey felt and saw the panel move very slightly away from the wall, maybe half a centimetre, but enough for him to use his fingers to pull it slowly downwards. He saw that the panel was hinged at the same level as the top of the table, so he gently moved the table away from the wall before pulling the panel as far as it would go. He pulled it back about twelve inches from the wall before it stopped and would not move any further. Peering behind the panel, he could see that there was a void behind, something that Percy would have likely known about. Inside the void was something wrapped in a sackcloth, about eighteen inches long and five inches deep, fitting snugly within the narrow void. Next to it was a small, blue, glass vase with a beautiful silver rose in it, and next to that a small, brown teddy bear with the words '*I love you, Daddy*' embroidered on its white belly in red cotton.

Poor boy, Harvey thought. He couldn't imagine what Percy had endured, losing his father at such a young age, and then realising that he wasn't long for the world. The young man's bravery was beyond measure.

Reaching carefully into the void, Harvey pulled out the item that was wrapped in the sackcloth. It was dusty, with a strong musky smell, typically of something that was old and hadn't been moved in decades. He was about to open the sack when he heard a car arriving outside. He quickly closed the panel, hearing the faint click when it did so before he pushed the table back against it. The item retrieved from the void went into his backpack quickly before Harvey then sat at a nearby pew, head bowed, as if deep in prayer.

His timing was good, as the door to the church opened seconds later. He turned and looked to see who had arrived, the natural thing to do, and saw that it was two elderly women carrying brooms, along with a bucket and mop.

'Morning, young man, you're here bright and early,' one of the ladies greeted.

'Good morning to you. I was just passing by and thought it would be a good time to reflect. I was just about to leave and get out of your way,' Harvey replied.

'We wouldn't want you to leave on our account, but it is mop-the-aisle day so at some point, you'd likely have wet shoes,' the other lady laughed.

'Well, we can't have that now, can we?' he replied, standing. 'I shall return when it is safer to do so.'

'Thank you, young man, will we see you at services on Sunday?'

'I shall try my best, yes,' Harvey nodded softly. 'It will be my first, is it busy here on Sundays?"

'Not as busy as it used to be, but we have a coffee morning on Saturdays that are busier, if you prefer that. There are a couple of clubs that meet here some evenings... book clubs and that sort of thing; there's a leaflet by the door on the way out if you want to know more.'

'I knew it was a good day to pop in, thank you kindly,' Harvey waved his goodbye before leaving them to their cleaning.

'You're welcome, love. We look forward to seeing you

again soon. We could do with some new blood here, so do try, okay?'

Harvey laughed.

'I haven't been called *new blood* before, so thank you for that also. I will do my best but make no promises. You have a wonderful church here and I already enjoy living in Shering-ham, so it is a no-brainer for me,'

'Good, then we'll see you soon.'

Harvey left, pleased with himself for achieving his aims at the church. He had not lied, intending at some point to come to the church. Having not been to services for many years now, and having seen the lovely, well-kept ancient interior of All Saints, there was an incentive to meet more people and learn about the community here... past and present.

In the meantime, he was champing at the bit to find out what was in the sackcloth that he'd retrieved.

BACK AT THE COTTAGE, he removed the contents of the backpack and placed them on the table. The two jewellery boxes were placed to one side and he laid the larger item wrapped in the sackcloth front and centre with careful move-ments. The sackcloth was tied with string at one end and had been folded behind for many years. Harvey slowly unfolded it to minimise the dust coming from it before cutting the string. He looked inside, nodding before reaching in and pulling out two small paintings facing each other, both sixteen inches long and ten inches wide. He gently separated them, keen to avoid any damage and assuming they would be fragile. He placed them both, face up, on the table, whistling in disbelief as his eyes settled on the artwork before him.

'Oh my, they are incredible!' he exclaimed.

One of the paintings was signed on the back, where Harvey could see the faint signature of *J. M. Turner* and *1840*. The painting itself was a beautiful landscape typical of Turner's style, with the green and brown hues of trees and foliage in the foreground and a farmhouse in the distance. The second painting had a more vibrant colour palette and was a study of fruit in a bowl. It was signed *John Constable*, also on the rear, and dated *1832*. Both were remarkably well preserved thanks to the way they had been stored behind the panel in the church.

Harvey knew enough to know that although small and not the size associated with both artists, they were still likely to be valuable. It wasn't every day that a new Turner *and* Constable were rediscovered. He looked back and forth between the paintings and the jewellery boxes and, along with the priceless medals and pocket watch he'd handed in, figured the haul to be worth many hundreds of thousands of pounds. He recalled Millie Parry's question about what he would do with anything he found, which made him contemplate what he would do next.

I have no idea, none at all, he thought.

23

INTERVIEW

Harvey decided that the best way forward would be to keep his findings quiet for now, with the exception of Millie, until he could figure out what to do with them. After taking photos of everything, he wrapped the paintings in bubble wrap and placed them in the briefcase that he'd used in the Met. The two jewellery boxes went into the backpack, also carefully wrapped, and all items went into the loft in one of Aunt Agatha's ottomans.

As he was closing the loft hatch, his phone rang.

'Detective Sergeant Leclerc, it's good to hear from you. To what do I owe the pleasure of the call?'

'Hello, Harvey. Please, call me Emily, unless you want to feel the wrath that I am so famous for,' she bantered.

'Emily it is,' his response came sharply, with no hesitation at all.

'I thought I'd bring you up to speed with the investigation. Do you have a few minutes?'

'Yes, please go ahead,' he welcomed the update.

'Well, as you know, when an allegation of murder by

poisoning is made, we'd typically exhume the body and conduct the usual checks, yada yada. In this case, there is no point, because we know that it was arsenic and there would be no trace, but especially since it has been over sixty years since the murder. What I'm getting at is that what we have is not concrete evidence, just circumstantial, and you know that after such a long time, it would be a tough one to prove,' Emily explained.

'I appreciate that, Emily, that's why it's critical that you speak to Bradley Franklin as soon as possible. He's ripe for a confession and willing to make a deal if it means he doesn't get thrown out of his flat and can keep his nurse. I think that's a good offer, don't you?'

'That's exactly what I thought, and my next point. You beat me to it, so typical of an inspector, I can't tell you,' she teased.

'What are you saying, that you've spoken to him?'

'Well, I was trying to say it until you beat me to it. Yes, Harvey, I spoke to Mr Franklin earlier this morning and we conducted an interview in his flat with his solicitor present. Weirdly, his nurse answered the door in a bright red silk dressing gown. That took us by surprise, I can tell you,' she informed, her attempt to hold back her laughter failing.

'That is weird... I suppose she must be a live-in nurse,' Harvey replied.

'Anyway, Franklin told us that he believed his father had killed Dorothy and Percy Flynn by poisoning them. Didn't actually witness anything, but knew he'd done it from conversations they'd had. It's not a confession because he wasn't involved in the actual murders, best we could do is charge him with perverting the course of justice by not coming forward with his suspicions. He's a good witness though, and a strong one that confirms your theory about the murders,' Emily continued.

'How did you leave it?' he probed.

'We agreed that we wouldn't press charges if he came forward with the information that essentially solves two murders we didn't know about. We also told him we wouldn't make any attempts to recover any funds spent and that he could keep what he had to continue paying for his flat and nurse.'

'What about the outstanding property and future revenue from rents that he would have received, what happens to that?' Harvey challenged.

'Well, it is recoverable property that was obtained through unlawful conduct, so we'll seize it until we can find a Flynn descendant that has a claim.'

'And if there isn't?' Harvey probed, hoping that Emily would help him figure out what to do with the treasure he'd found.

'It goes to the Government, what do you think?' she laughed.

'Ah, okay, fair enough...'

'You look disappointed,' Emily pointed out. 'What's up?'

'I just think it's sad, that's all. Two good people were killed and the murderer, and later his son, have lived pretty good lives off the back of those murders. And now that we know, it seems like justice hasn't really been done, does it?' Harvey challenged.

'Better this than leaving things as they were, Harvey, don't forget that. Anyway, I thought I'd let you know that we're working on the paperwork and hope to have it wrapped up in a few weeks.'

'There is something else you should know, which may be

connected to my prying, Emily. Someone tried to run me over the other night, a dark van driven by a man aged around thirty. I only managed to get a partial number plate, BN, and I reported it the same night. I can't think who would want me out of the way, though, but thought you should know,' he added.

'Interesting. I'll check on the crime report and let you know if anything comes from it, okay?' Emily replied.

'Thanks, Emily, I appreciate the call. Keep in touch, or even better pop over for a coffee any time, okay?'

'Will do, bye Harvey.'

Harvey was slightly deflated by the news. He was delighted that the murders were now officially declared and solved, but felt that the Franklins, both of them, were too lucky. That didn't sit right with him, and it made the decision about what to do with the treasure even harder.

'What do you reckon, Max? Shall I just give it to the police?'

Max barked, happy to be involved in whatever Harvey was doing, cheering his companion up to no end.

'Good boy, Max, good boy,' he stroked Max's coat, his mind made up.

He picked up his phone and called Millie.

'Hello, this is the Parry household,' Evelyn answered.

'Hi Evelyn, this is Harvey Ross. May I please speak with Millie?'

'Of course, I'll just pass you over.'

'Hello, Harvey, how did you get on?' Millie asked.

'If it's alright with you, can I pop over and I can tell you over a cup of tea?' he asked.

'It'll be on the table waiting for you,' the woman insisted, the smile on her face evident through her tone.

EVELYN LET Harvey into the house less than ten minutes later. As promised, there was a steaming cup of tea waiting for him when he entered the room, and he saw Millie, her hands together, eager to hear the news.

'Evelyn, be a dear and go to the shops for me, will you? Harvey will keep me company, don't worry,' she requested.

'Of course, I'll be back in about twenty minutes. Harvey, if you can sit with her?' Evelyn asked.

'Absolutely, I'll be here, don't worry,' Harvey assured.

Millie waited until the front door had closed before she asked.

'Don't keep me in suspense, Harvey. What did you find?'

'Percy was a genius, Millie. His markings were spot on. I found these at the Priory,' he showed her photos of the jewellery boxes as he spoke.

'They're beautiful,' she whispered, looking through the photos slowly.

'There's more, Millie. At All Saints church, I found these two paintings,' he added, showing her the Turner and Constable.

'Fabulous, aren't they?' she said.

'They were hidden behind the dedication panel, along with a small vase with a silver rose in it, and a teddy bear with a message from Percy to his father,' Harvey continued.

'Bless him, what an amazing thing he did,' Millie said.

'I know it's sad remembering these things, Millie, but have in mind that we now know that he was a very brave, young man who did something very special. That's how we should remember him, don't you think?'

'I do, yes. I never forgot about him, you know, I still think of him almost every day. I had a wonderful marriage, and I loved my husband, but Percy was the true love of my life, and he was taken away from me,' Millie replied. 'But you're absolutely correct, I shall remember the positives, and nothing will change that now.'

'That's good, I'm happy to hear that. I have more news, by the way.'

'What is it?' she asked.

'The detective leading the investigation into Percy and Dorothy's deaths interviewed Bradley Franklin, and he basically told them that he knew his father had poisoned them.'

'Really? That's great news. Did they arrest him?' she quizzed.

'No, sadly the only way to get that information was to make a deal with him to avoid any charges,' Harvey declared, his tone slightly defeated.

'So, they got away with it then?'

'It seems that way, but actually, they'll be taking all the properties and land from him, and he's only allowed to keep what little money he has left... there will be no more coming.'

'Lucky him,' Millie spat. 'That family deserves to rot in Hell forever for what they did.'

'It was a compromise, Millie. Would you rather not know the truth?'

'What do you think will happen to everything they're seizing from him?' she challenged.

'They said they'd be searching for any Flynn descendants, but if they don't find any, then unfortunately, it all goes into the Government coffers.'

Millie sat in silence, looking towards the door with a frown.

'Are you okay, Millie?'

'It doesn't seem like a happy ending, or that justice was really done, does it?' she whispered, suddenly frail again.

'You know, I don't think they'll find anyone from the Flynn family. You were the closest thing to a next of kin, and you certainly deserve it as opposed to the Government,' Harvey disclosed.

'That would be nice. I don't really need anything, Harvey but...'

'What?'

'It's nothing. Oh, look, it's Evelyn back early,' Millie announced, pointing towards the front door.

'Okay, well, I'll leave you to it for now. I'll be in touch when I know more, is that okay?' .

'Yes, please do, Harvey,' Millie expressed her gratitude with a smile. 'Evelyn will see you out.'

Harvey gave her a peck on the cheek and left the room.

'She seems a little upset, Evelyn, I hope it isn't anything I've done,' he mentioned as they made their way out.

'Don't worry, Harvey, I'm sure it's nothing, she's just tired, that's all,' Evelyn expressed kindly.

'I'll be in touch soon, call me if you need anything, okay?'

'I will, bye now.'

Harvey left and drove home, unsettled by Millie's reaction towards the end of their conversation.

I wonder what that was about?

Upon returning to the cottage, Harvey took Max for a long walk while he deliberated his next steps. He had a mental checklist of everything he'd done and the things that needed doing. The most prominent were the actions he'd need to take when he decided whether to approach the police or not with his findings. It was the list he made when he returned from the walk.

Cars in garage
Tracing paper
Jewellery boxes / paintings

He considered informing Emily Leclerc and letting her deal with it, but then realised that the only beneficiaries to everything found would be the Government, which he considered wholly unfair. He was pleased to have withheld the tracing paper that would have potentially allowed them to find the items, or worse, to miss the markings and archive the evidence, meaning the treasure would never be found, forever remaining a local legend.

Harvey decided not to make any rash decisions and simply put a question mark alongside each, leaving it for another day. He suddenly realised that the issue had consumed more of his time than he thought possible, almost from one extreme to the other, when he'd initially had concerns about being bored. He turned to Max and grinned.

'We saw what happened the last time I let work take over, didn't we, boy? Not this time, I promise,' he reassured the terrier, and himself, before picking up his phone.

'Hi, Rose, it's Harvey. I thought I'd check in and see whether you fancied another coffee, or maybe even step it up a little and have dinner? What do you think? Let me know when you hear this message.'

24

DATE NIGHT

'Well, this is much nicer than I thought it would be, thank you for the recommendation,' Harvey thanked Rose as they sat down at the table.

'This is one of Sheringham's greatest secrets, Harvey; it's time you learnt some of them,' she grinned.

Rose had recommended *North at Burlington*, a restaurant that was part of *Burlington Berties Boutique Hotel*, considered to be the best in Sheringham by many.

'The food here is fab, and the atmosphere is friendly and cozy,' she explained.

Harvey noticed the impressive range of artwork that hung on the walls and saw the kitchen staff hard at work in the open kitchen, from which there was a delicious aroma. A lot of care had gone into the design and layout of the hotel and restaurant, which he found impressive. They soon placed their orders and sipped on the cocktails they'd ordered upon their arrival.

'So, is this your go-to place for second dates?' he asked, trying not to sound too mischievous.

'It is not, cheeky. I usually wait until at least the fourth date, so think of yourself as being very fortunate, Harvey Ross,' she retorted. 'If you must know, I've been here a few times with my family, that's how I know this place; it's my favourite,' Rose added.

'That's good to know, and lucky me, eh? All joking aside, tell me about your family, we never really spoke about things like that last time, did we?'

'No, I guess we didn't. I suppose that's a good sign, that we had plenty of other things to talk about. It's a positive sign that we're not bored of each other... yet,' she teased. 'My family are all living in London. I divorced my husband, Keith, many years ago, and my two daughters are both in their late twenties and married with a child each, also in London. My parents are still both alive, thankfully, and live in Southwold in Suffolk, which isn't too far, so I get to see them quite often,' she explained.

'That's great. Do you get to visit your daughters in London, or do they come here?'

'A little of both. I see them maybe three or four times a year, which isn't a lot, but they both have busy lives, so I can't complain too much. I speak to them a couple of times a week and FaceTime my grandchildren, so I do keep in touch fairly often,' she answered with a smile.

'Thank God for modern technology, eh? I see my daughters even less, unfortunately; I think they're still a little sore at us over the divorce. I haven't seen them since I moved here, but I try and call once a week. My parents have both passed away, unfortunately,' Harvey disclosed.

'Oh, I'm sorry to hear that. So, you have no family close by anymore?' Rose asked.

'Sadly, no. My aunt was the only one that lived here and everyone else is in London,' he shrugged.

'I imagine it's been somewhat lonely for you here, then?'

'A little, especially the first few weeks... until Max changed everything,' Harvey chortled.

'The satchel? How is that going? Last we spoke, you were tight-lipped about it,' she wondered.

'I must be, really, there are people still alive involved so it's quite personal and very confidential. I learnt not to mess with either of those things nowadays,' he replied. 'When it's all done and dusted, I'll tell you everything you need to know, don't you worry.'

'I'm not interested in their identities, silly. I just want to know the fun stuff. You know, if there's any scandal, if anyone is likely to be jailed or anything like that.'

'No, there's no risk of that, but there's a lot of property and valuables at stake, so finding the rightful owners is going to be a little tricky. I'm hoping someone is found otherwise the government will grab it, which will be sad,' he revealed.

'That doesn't sound like fun at all, is there much still to do? And what will you do next?' Rose pressed.

'I think it should be all resolved within weeks, I imagine. After that, I hope to move onto something else, maybe take on one of my aunt's projects, I'm not sure yet,' he disclosed.

'Your aunt's projects?'

'Yes, the binder I told you about.'

'Oh, the myths and local legends? What will you do?'

'It's mainly unsolved crimes that I'm interested in, and there's a couple that may still be viable for me to solve,' he told the woman in front of him. 'I just need to go through it again and figure out which ones.'

'I guess as long as you keep busy doing something you enjoy, then good for you,' Rose expressed with a gracious smile.

'What about you, have you decided what you want to do when you retire?' he enquired.

'Well, for one, I want to travel a bit. I have a bucket list of countries I'd like to visit. After that, or even during, I want to try my hand at writing a science fiction novel,' she revealed.

'Bucket list, eh? What are your top three countries?'

'Australia, Canada, and Peru,' her voice came almost instantly, no hesitation in her answers.

'Wow, no need to think on it, eh?'

'Nope, I know exactly where I want to go, and I can't wait.'

'How long before you think you'll retire?'

'If all goes well and they are able to recruit a new doctor, then as early as next year,' she said, crossing her fingers.

'I shall keep my fingers crossed for you too. The sci-fi book sounds great also, it sounds like you know exactly what you want to do... I like that,' Harvey encouraged.

'Life is too short for indecision, Harvey. Just go for it, and even if it doesn't work out, at least you tried, eh?' she voiced with a grin.

'Exactly right,' he agreed. 'Cheers to that.'

They toasted, just as their food order arrived. The food exceeded Harvey's expectations, enjoying every morsel. They ordered another round of drinks, having decided that walking home was best. It was several drinks and several hours later when they finally left, both grinning from ear to ear after another very enjoyable evening.

'Before you get too nervous, or anything like that, I insist on walking you home,' Harvey asserted as they walked arm in arm.

'I wouldn't have it any other way, Harvey. Nothing wrong with being a gentleman,' she nodded appreciatively.

'Where do you live?'

'Cromer, it's only five miles,' she giggled.

'Really? I thought... oh, I see, you're being funny again, that's very good,' he nodded with a humorous grin. 'You have a vicious sense of humour, Rose Morgan.'

'Sorry, it's been such a long time since I've been able to act a little mischievously, you seem the perfect person to do that to. You know, with dropping your trousers, falling over, that sort of thing,' she jested with a cheeky grin.

'That's very good. I see that you're unlikely to forget those little episodes, eh?' he rolled his eyes playfully.

'Absolutely not. They give me far too much enjoyment to simply forget them,' she shook her head as if the idea of forgetting what had happened was offensive.

'Well, I suppose if it makes you laugh, that's a good thing, and maybe that means you'll want to go out with me again. If so, then I'd consider that a fair price to pay,' he smirked.

'How very gallant of you, Harvey, and a little cheeky too, sneaking another date in like that. Impressive indeed.'

'I try; you know, all that training does come in useful occasionally. Anyway, now that we've established that you don't live five miles away, how about you point me in the right direction?' he asked.

'I live in West Cliff, opposite the Shell Gallery,' she replied. 'It isn't far.'

'I know where that is, nice and close to the promenade,' he replied. 'A very nice location.'

'It is indeed. Now, about this third date that you

mentioned, what did you have in mind?' she rose an eyebrow as she awaited the man's answer.

'Well, you've introduced me to that fabulous restaurant, so I figure I need to step up a little and do something just as nice. How about fish and chips?' he grinned. 'The location isn't as fancy, but the fish is as good as you'll ever find.'

'That's stepping things up a bit, is it?' she laughed. 'Well, I'm game for a laugh, so let's go for it. Any time after six works for me during the week.'

'I shall endeavour to book early and let you know when and where,' he said, bowing playfully.

They arrived at her flat a few minutes later.

'Thank you for another wonderful evening, Harvey,' she smiled happily.

'I think it's me that should be thanking you, Rose. I had no idea about that restaurant, it was incredible. I hope you feel that way about the fish and chip shop I'll be taking you to,' he delivered a playful grin with his words.

Rose laughed and then leaned up and kissed Harvey gently on the lips, taking him by surprise.

'Goodnight, Harvey,' she said, walking into her block.

Harvey stood there, motionless, for several minutes.

'Harvey Ross, you are an imbecile,' he finally said out loud before walking away.

It was a good, long walk to the cottage, so he had many opportunities to think of the date and, in particular, of that kiss and how he could have handled it so much better. He was grateful to have another chance.

Roll on the third date! he thought.

'ARE YOU DRUNK?' Steve asked when he called, shortly after Harvey had arrived home.

'What makes you think that?' Harvey feigned his offense in the tone of his voice.

'Well, you're in a good mood, for one, you haven't made a snide remark yet, and you've slurred at least two words,' Steve replied.

'That's very forensic of you, Steve. I'll have you know that I'm not drunk, just a little bit merry, that's all. I haven't had a good drink for a long time.'

'Ah, that's so sad, getting merry all by your lonesome. I told you, get yourself back to London where you have at least one friend you can call upon,' Steve bantered.

'That's very good, as usual. I'll have you know that I was not drinking alone, I had a very pleasant companion. And I have no intention of moving back to London, even if I do have a single friend there. Who is that, by the way?'

'That's so typical. Wait... a pleasant companion? That's your code for a lady, isn't it? You sly shrew, boss, you've been out with a lady!' Steve exclaimed.

'There's no fooling you, is there? No wonder you made sergeant,' Harvey chuckled.

'Don't you change the subject. I need more information, so crack on, tell me all about it... and her,' Steve demanded.

'No and no.'

'Wow, it must be serious if you won't disclose. That didn't take anywhere near as long as I thought. I had you down for five years before you had the courage to ask someone out,' Steve uttered playfully in disbelief.

'Seriously, how did we work together when you have so little faith in my abilities?' Harvey questioned in mock disappointment.

'It's all about the salary, boss... I played the game to get the money, it's that simple.'

'You're a buffoon. Why are you calling me so late, anyway?'

'I had a call from Emily earlier. After she tore into me for my poor friendship skills, we had a nice long chat about everything, and she insisted I visit soon. I'm thinking of coming down on the weekend and thought I'd save on hotels by staying at your place, if that's okay?'

'Of course, you have an open invite, remember? Is it just you or the family?' Harvey asked.

'Just me. The missus insisted so I can have a catch up with you. I couldn't say no, could I?'

'Such a gentleman. Just get yourself down here before I change my mind,' Harvey remarked.

'Great, see you on Friday night,' Steve replied before hanging up.

Harvey sat with a coffee, grinning at the thought of Steve coming up to see him.

'Do you reckon I can train you to bite him by then, Max?' he asked his little companion.

————

25

THE VISIT

The next few days went by far too slowly for Harvey, which he quite accurately recognised as impatience... he was impatiently waiting for the third date with Rose and impatiently waiting for his friend and ex-colleague to visit for a catch-up weekend. During that time, he made sure to have the guest room ready for Steve, but more importantly, a table reserved at Dave's Fish and Chip Restaurant for the all-important third date. He'd ordered takeaway fish and chips from there before that he'd enjoyed and saw they had an adjoining restaurant, allowing him to keep his promise for such a venue.

Rose agreed to see Harvey the following Monday, after Steve's visit, as she'd be visiting her parents in Southwold over the weekend, leaving late on Thursday after work.

'It's far too early for you to meet my parents, Harvey, so you'll just have to be patient,' Rose had teased.

'Gulp,' was his reply, before adding, 'that is a good decision. Thank you for saving my blushes.'

He'd spent an hour at the supermarket getting in the supplies for the weekend, knowing which beer Steve was a fan of and that he had always enjoyed an unhealthily large, cooked breakfast. The rest they would play by ear, which would give Harvey a chance to introduce Steve to several quality venues that he was sure he'd enjoy. He made sure that Max had a good supply of extra treats so that he didn't feel too neglected. Everything was ready when Steve eventually arrived.

'And about time too,' Harvey exclaimed, hugging his friend, 'I thought you'd got lost again.'

'I blame the directions. If I'd have known you lived in a park, I would have hired a Jeep,' Steve stated with a comical glare.

'Steve, you've been in London far too long if you think Beeston Common is a park,' Harvey laughed. 'Come on in, you old goat.'

Steve was met by an excited Max who yelped and jumped up excitedly, welcoming him to their home.

'Hello, boy, are you being kept prisoner here?' Steve taunted with a laugh.

'He loves it here, I'll have you know. He trots around with a permanent grin, loving life,' Harvey countered with a roll of his eyes.

Steve nodded appreciatively as he looked around.

'Well, now, this is a surprise. When you said you lived in a cottage, I had visions of having to duck down to get through the front door. This is actually very nice and spacious, and really well appointed. Kudos to your aunt, bless her,' Steve walked around the ground floor as he spoke, taking in his surroundings.

'She was special, that's for sure. How about you grab a

seat, and I get you a beer?' Harvey asked, indicating towards the lounge.

'I thought you'd never ask.'

Harvey quickly returned with two beers for them and a chew for Max.

'Cheers, boss. It's been too long,' Steve acknowledged.

'Entirely your fault. I've been telling you to come since day one. Are you that busy?'

'Yep. You made it look so easy, but all that time, you were hiding the fact that there was a lot of work in the background that none of us were aware of,' Steve grinned.

'You should know by now that is how you build an empire, Steve. Never give all your tricks or secrets away... it will make it too easy to replace you,' Harvey shot back.

'That is true, which is why I shall be picking your brains for years to come; you know all the dirty tricks to succeeding in life.'

'Well, you know where I am now, and I'll always be happy to help,'

'I'll probably go and visit Emily and Akira tomorrow, if you fancy coming along?' Steve offered.

'No, I think you need to go alone to that one, you have a lot of catching up to do. Just make sure you take lots of presents for their kids as well as for them, it'll give you a chance of escaping with minimal damage.'

'Yeah, I will. I feel dreadful but I always make it up to them, they understand,' Steve spoke convincingly.

'What do you fancy to eat? I'm guessing you're starving, right?'

'You know me too well. I'll let you decide, you know what's best around here,' Steve shrugged.

'I'll take you to The Bank,' Harvey declared.

'Eh?'

Harvey laughed, expecting that response from any Sheringham newcomer.

'It's a restaurant called The Bank, because it used to be... you guessed it, a bank. It's a Nepalese restaurant that also serves Asian food, you'll love it,' Harvey insisted.

'Sounds good to me.'

They drove down and parked across the road from the restaurant.

'Interesting place,' Steve nodded, looking around the décor, which included a bank safe on the opposite wall.

'Trust me, the food is great,' Harvey told him.

Before too long, they had ordered a curry each, along with a Tiger beer.

'It's like old times, this, only much more civilised than the Edgware Road,' Steve reminisced.

'So, tell me what's happening with the team, Steve. How is everyone?'

'I hate saying this, but the team miss you a lot. The new boss is okay, but she's a little cold and doesn't really mix as well with us. She keeps her distance and that takes away that incentive you always gave us through loyalty, to do that little bit more, you know?'

'Just give her time, Steve. It isn't easy taking over a successful team, there's a lot of pressure from those above, so you, especially, should step in and help her when you think she needs it,' Harvey suggested.

'I do that anyway, Harvey. And I get it, don't worry, the team will give her all the time she needs.'

'That's good. By the way, thanks for helping me out with those checks, it has helped me a lot,' Harvey acknowledged and expressed his gratitude.

'I told you, as long as it isn't massively illegal then I'm happy to help,' Steve bantered, firm in his belief that massively illegal was crossing the line, but slightly illegal wasn't.

'Thanks, and I know you could get into a spot of bother if anyone found out. I wouldn't ask for anything controversial; these are the checks that will help with the investigations that Emily is undertaking, so she will be conducting them anyway.'

'So, you've decided to tell her everything?' Steve quizzed.

'Not everything, I feel there's a moral issue that I need to get my head around. I'll let her know about the cars soon, so she can connect them with the murderer's surviving son. That way, she can issue a confiscation order that will hopefully result in the proceeds going to a descendant of the victim,' Harvey explained.

'That's the boss I remember—never giving up on justice, no matter how long ago the crime. You would have been perfect for the war crimes reparations unit, I don't know why you didn't go for it,' Steve disclosed.

'Honestly, up until a few weeks ago, I had no idea what I was doing or even where I'd end up. If it wasn't for Max finding that satchel, I don't know what I would've done. I was getting pretty bored up until then, with no friends and not a lot to do except explore the town. The investigation I've conducted so far—if I'm allowed to call it that—has made me realise that I have plenty left to offer this town, which incidentally does have a lot to offer, and the lovely people that live here. I'm good with that,' Harvey voiced contentedly.

'I can't argue with that, so good for you.'

Their curries arrived and they were soon tucking in.

'You weren't wrong, boss, this is a fabulous curry,' Steve announced between mouthfuls.

'Glad you like it, because tomorrow you're making breakfast.'

'Fair enough,' the other man shrugged in understanding.

'So, are you ever going to tell me the real reason you're visiting?' Harvey broke the brief pause in conversation suddenly.

'What? How the hell—'

'I know you better than you think. Spit it out, Steve,' Harvey insisted.

'I came to ask for advice,' Steve admitted sheepishly.

'About what?'

'Things aren't going well at home and we're discussing divorce. I know it's a delicate matter for you, but I thought it would help me... learning from the way you dealt with it,' the friend's confession came.

'You think I dealt with mine well?'

'Yes... well, no... look, it doesn't matter, you went through it so you know far more than I ever will,' Steve continued.

'It all depends on what you want, Steve. Do you want to stay, or do you want to go?'

'I want to stay, but I don't know what to do to make that happen,' his voice was defeated, and slightly deflated as he trailed off.

'I'm going to take a wild guess here. Your wife thinks you spend too much time at work and not enough time at home, correct?'

'Bang on the money,' Steve nodded.

'Then there's only one thing for it, Steve. If you want to stay and give your marriage, and your family, a chance of surviving, then you need to work less or change your working hours to something more... normal. Ask for a transfer or refuse overtime. If I were you, I'd speak to your new boss and ask her if you can work nine to five or eight to four.'

'You think they'd go for that?'

'If they want you to stay, then they'll make it work. To be honest, it's probably the ideal time to ask, while the new boss is still getting to grips with the new job,' Harvey suggested.

'That's not a bad shout. I love my job so would rather stay, even if it meant changing to more regular hours. That could work,' Steve nodded. 'I appreciate you suggesting that, Harvey. I didn't think it would be a realistic option, but if my ex-boss would consider it, then maybe she would also.'

'If you don't ask, you don't get. Now, get that beer down your throat, it's a decent walk home from here.'

THE ROADS WERE quiet at that time of the night as they turned into Station Road from the restaurant on the walk home. The pair planned to cut down Co-Operative Street and go along Beeston Road before cutting across again to Curtis Lane for the final stretch. As they turned into Beeston Road, and before they had a chance to turn off into Avenue Road, Harvey heard a vehicle approaching them from behind. He turned to see two blinding beams coming towards them at great speed and instantly knew that the dark van that had tried to run him down previously was back.

'Look out!' he hollered, shoving Steve into the forecourt of a bicycle repair shop, diving quickly behind him just as the dark van reached them.

Harvey peered up to see the van continuing at speed, still

without one of the rear lights, confirming it to be the same as before.

'What the hell was that all about?' Steve sputtered in astoundment, standing and dusting himself down.

'Someone doesn't like me, Steve. It seems I'm getting too close for comfort. Come on, I'll tell you all about it when we get back,' Harvey replied.

———

'WHY DIDN'T you tell me about this happening before?' Steve demanded once Harvey had explained.

'I reported it, Steve, and Emily is aware, but there wasn't a lot more I could do. I thought... hoped... it would be a one-off, but it seems someone is on a mission to shut me up.'

'So, what are you going to do about it?' Steve urged.

'I'm reporting this attempt also, and will keep Emily in the loop. There's not a lot else I can do, is there?'

'You can keep me in the loop too, for starters,' Steve demanded.

Harvey laughed. 'Yes, mate, of course I will.'

'Good, now I think I deserve another beer. My shirt is ruined thanks to you.'

———

STEVE WAS true to his word the following morning and was up bright and early cooking a full English breakfast for them both.

'Blimey, I haven't had one of these since I left the Met,' Harvey gave a cheesy grin as he sat down to eat.

'I made Max an extra Norfolk sausage, I'm sure you don't mind,' Steve announced.

'Not at all, he's going for a walk after this, so it'll be out of his system soon enough,' Harvey shrugged.

'Lovely, thanks for that,' the man's reply came sarcastically, making a face as he took another mouthful of bacon.

'Where are you meeting Emily and her family?' Harvey diverted the conversation with his question.

'At their house in Holt. Nice part of the world; have you been there since moving in?'

'I have, a couple of times. Lots of great shops there and some interesting art galleries. It's a nice town for sure,'

'They have an old Georgian house with a weird layout. One of the upstairs bedrooms has two doors, one regular one, and another to a different hallway where you can access the loft. Whoever designed it must've been a heavy drinker or wanted to keep that part of the house as a secret.'

'Give them all my regards. Don't mention to Emily about the cars or anything yet, I'd rather tell her myself,' Harvey pleaded.

'Don't worry, your secret is safe with me.'

Steve left shortly after breakfast at the same time as Harvey took Max out for his morning walk. It gave him time to think more about the moral obligation he felt for returning the treasure to the rightful owner, but had no clue as to who that would be. His attempts at tracing descendants from Percy's mother, Dorothy, had also been unsuccessful. Using the limited resources he currently had, Harvey could see very few options other than to let the police locate them using far more effective technologies than he would ever have.

'Just doesn't seem right,' he murmured, his tone disappointed, as he continued walking.

It was some twenty minutes into the walk when he realised that he was in Holts Road, very close to Millie's house.

'There's a message there, somewhere,' he said to Max as he walked to the front door and knocked. Evelyn answered the door.

'Hello, Harvey, it's nice to see you again. And who is this gorgeous fellow?' she questioned with an instant smile, leaning down to pat a delighted Max on the head.

'This is Max and, as you can see, he loves being pampered. Is it possible to have a chat with Millie?' he wondered.

'I'm sure that will be fine, let me just check,' Evelyn confirmed. 'Come inside and wait in the hall.'

She returned a few seconds later, ushering him into the lounge.

'Come through, Harvey. I can take Max to the park, if that's okay with you. It'll be more exciting for him than sitting around here,' Evelyn offered.

'Are you sure? He'll love you forever if you do, you know,' Harvey replied, handing her the lead.

'That's the plan, Harvey. I just love dogs. My daughter has two and they spend more time with me than with her, I adore them,' she replied.

'A woman after my own heart,' Harvey grinned. 'Does your daughter live locally?'

'Not too far, she lives in West Runton with her husband and my three grandchildren, just a few miles away. She has a studio at the back of the house; she's an artist if you ever need a painting for a special occasion,' Evelyn informed him.

'I'll keep that firmly in mind, Evelyn, and thank you for looking after Max.'

He walked into the lounge where Millie was waiting for him, leaning over and giving her a peck on the cheek.

'It's lovely to see you again, Harvey. How are you?' the woman's face instantly lit up as she greeted Harvey, their friendship something the pair were both very grateful for.

'I'm fine, Millie, thank you for asking. I wanted to pop in and see how you were. I think I may have said something to upset you the other day.'

Millie glanced down with a frown, considering her words carefully before speaking.

'You didn't say anything wrong, Harvey. I was just a little unnerved by what you said. It hit a raw nerve that put me out a little, that's all. Please don't feel guilty on my being a silly old fool,' she asserted.

'There's nothing silly about you, Millie. You're clearly upset that the man who murdered Dorothy and Percy—the man you wanted to spend your life with—has clearly gotten away with it, as has his son, who has profited from the crimes.'

'It's not just that, Harvey. This whole episode has hurt a lot, like having a plaster ripped off a fresh wound. I can't stop thinking about it,' she conceded, the pain in her voice palpable.

'Is there anything I can do to help, in any way at all?'

'Not really. You've already made sure that some semblance of justice will be served, and that people will know that Percy and Dorothy were poisoned, not that anyone else will care much. It sets the record straight, I suppose.'

'I haven't quite finished with my sniffing around, Millie, not until I'm happy there's absolutely nothing else that I can do. I fear that I don't have the means to find any living descendants of the Flynn family, or even Dorothy's. It may have to be passed on to the police to deal with. We can only trust that they find someone to give everything to,' Harvey's voice was hopeful, trying to find the light in the situation that had become a dark cloud looming over them.

They sat in silence for a few minutes while Millie digested the information. Harvey could see that she was still on edge, as if she wanted to say something but couldn't bring herself to do it.

'If it helps put your mind at ease, I won't do anything until you are comfortable with me doing so. Does that sound like a plan?' the man suggested.

'I feel terrible, Harvey, putting you in such an awkward position. Nothing about this feels right. I'm so sorry,' the woman's voice was almost tearful as she spoke, the current state of everything not what either of them had hoped for.

'Let me make us some tea and we can talk about something else, how does that sound?'

'That would be lovely. Let me get up and show—'

'No, no, you stay put. I know how to make a pot of tea, Millie. I'll be back in a few minutes,' he insisted.

It took a little longer than at home, looking for cups and a pot, but he got there in the end. They sat and sipped their tea, chatting about life in general. Millie asked about his police career, and Harvey asked about Millie's marriage. As planned, her mood improved, and the anger and frustration she had felt were replaced by a beaming smile as she spoke about holidays in Wells-Next-The-Sea and Holkham and the long walks along the coastal path.

'They were lovely times, peaceful and free from the dark times we seem to be living in nowadays,' she reminisced. 'My daughter loved those beaches, she'd always build the largest sandcastles with moats; they were wonderful memories.'

It was at that time that Evelyn returned with Max. He was panting, his tail wagging at superspeed when he walked in and lay down next to Harvey, clearly exhausted.

'Oh dear, he isn't going to like walking back home in a minute, he's properly knackered,' Harvey laughed, smiling down at the terrier.

'He'll be fine, he's like a little whippet, aren't you Max?' Evelyn grinned down at the dog. 'Can I get you anything, Harvey, another tea maybe?'

'Not for me, thanks.'

'How about you, Mum?' Evelyn asked.

Harvey was startled by the revelation and turned to Millie, who was now looking at him knowingly.

'You're Evelyn's mum? I thought she was your carer?' he asked.

'I wouldn't trust anyone else to care for me in my old age, Harvey. Evelyn has been wonderful,' Millie said gratefully.

'Sorry, Harvey, I thought you knew. Don't you think we look alike?' Evelyn asked, grinning as she posed next to her mother.

'It didn't cross my mind at all, I'm so sorry,' Harvey apologised.

'I'm a little tired now, Evelyn, can you help me to my other chair?' Millie requested suddenly.

'I'll get out of your way. Thank you for the company, as ever, Millie, and thank you for looking after Max, Evelyn,' he thanked.

'Why don't you pop over tomorrow morning for another cup of tea, Harvey? Evelyn has an appointment so I could do with some company, just for an hour or so,' Millie offered as she was helped to her feet.

Harvey could sense that Millie wanted to talk to him more, just in private.

'Of course, Millie. I'll be here at nine, as I need to be back at ten for my guest, if that's okay?'

'I'll see you then,' Millie replied.

Harvey left with Max in tow, who was slower than usual but still happy to walk.

I think I know what you want to talk to me about, Millie, he thought.

————

26

BLAKENEY

H arvey was deep in thought and on his second coffee when Steve returned from his visit with Emily and her family later that afternoon.

'How did it go?' he wondered.

'It was great to see them again, I won't leave it so long next time. We had lunch in town and walked around all the shops with them. I can't believe how well behaved their kids were; they were more than happy to shop and made no fuss at all. They're certainly doing a grand job with them.'

'Good to hear. Did Emily bring up the case at all?' Harvey quizzed.

'Very briefly. Apparently, her boss wasn't excited about creating two new murders from sixty-odd years ago, but she persuaded him that it would be a good career move for him to show people that the police never give up on justice. She's learnt the politics of the job good and proper, I tell you,' Steve chortled.

'Good for her. Hopefully she'll get the credit she deserves, also.'

'So, what's the plan today?' Steve rubbed his hands in anticipation, awaiting the answer from his friend.

'I thought we'd take a drive over to Blakeney and have dinner at the Blakeney Hotel, if you fancy that? I've been there once before and their menu is excellent,' Harvey suggested.

'Works for me; as long as it hits the spot, I won't feel so hangry,' Steve laughed.

'There's some savoury snacks in the cupboard if you can't wait,' Harvey offered. 'They don't open until six for dinner.'

'Snacks it is then. What have you been up to today?'

'I went and saw Millie; do you remember I told you about her, she was the murder victim's girlfriend at the time.'

'Oh, okay... yes you did. Are there any new developments?'.

'I think there are, but I won't know until I have another chat with her tomorrow morning. Will you be okay if I slip out for an hour?'

'Yeah, sure. I can go for a wander if you leave me a key,' Steve shrugged.

'There's a spare one hanging up on the hook by the door. I should be back around ten,' Harvey replied.

'Great. In the meantime, how about a game of backgammon until we go and eat?' Steve suggested.

'Blimey, we haven't played that for a while. What made you remember that?' Harvey immediately thought back to the good old days, when they used to play religiously together.

'I figured that old age would have affected your game, so now's the best chance I have of beating you,' Steve bantered with a cocky grin.

'Fine, but it will be a serious dent to your confidence

when you find out that old age actually improves my game,' Harvey retorted.

'So, while you're getting everything ready, you can tell me more.'

'More about what?' Harvey asked.

'You don't think I'd stay a weekend and not ask any questions about your new girlfriend, do you?' Steve's voice was playfully astonished.

'She's not my girlfriend, Steve. I've only met her a couple of times, that hardly qualifies,' Harvey defended.

'So, why is it that you're blushing a tad, is it an embarrassing subject for you? Is there something odd about her? Is there something wrong with her? Does she know what you're like?' Steve shot back with a laugh.

'Yes, and she's lovely, okay? I'm looking forward to seeing her again, and that's about all you need to know.'

'Oh, come on, Harvey, what do you think I'm going to do, take the mickey on social media or something?' Steve pleaded.

'Fine, but there's nothing juicy to tell you, so don't get your hopes too high. Her name is Rose, and she's a doctor. We met at her clinic when I had my accident, and then the following day after my second accident, and she found that amusing. I then... bumped into her... accidentally. It sort of started from there, really,' Harvey thought back to their meetings, hesitant to disclose the *slightly* embarrassing encounters that occurred.

'Two accidents, eh? My, my, how the mighty have fallen.'

'She thought I was a bit of a buffoon, especially when I dropped my trousers when I didn't need to. I suppose she thought I was funny and took pity on me,' Harvey bantered along.

Steve laughed and then shook his head exaggeratingly, mocking his former superior.

'You are so lucky that didn't happen in London while you were still in the job... you would have been slaughtered.'

'I know that much, thanks. Anyway, it turned out great and I'm seeing her again on Monday. I'm looking forward to it,' Harvey grinned.

'Good for you. Does Becky know?'

'No, why would she?'

'No reason, I thought it might pre-empt any bad feelings, but what do I know?'

'It won't be like that, Steve. Becky is off travelling the world and has probably met someone herself by now,' Harvey spoke contentedly.

'Maybe, maybe not. It hasn't been that long since you divorced, has it? She may take it badly.'

'Then there is no reason to say anything until she gets back, right? I can tell her then, if I am still seeing Rose, which may not be the case,' he replied.

'Okay, well I'm sure you know what you're doing,' Steve smiled.

Harvey thought it over as they played their game, and it clearly affected his concentration.

'Ha! See? I told you that you're not quite with it, old man,' Steve teased.

'Well, it's your fault, bringing up that business with Becky. Was that a ploy? A nice bit of sportsmanship?' Harvey suspected.

'Maybe it was, but it proved my point. The Harvey I remember would never have fallen for that, so I guess I was right,' he continued to boast.

Harvey won the next four games straight... with ease.

'I guess you were wrong, eh, Steve? Now, if you have had enough, let's make a move.'

'There's nothing worse than a smug winner,' Steve sulked as they left for Blakeney.

27

EVELYN

Harvey knocked on Millie's door at exactly nine the following morning. He was keen to speak with her and confirm his suspicions. It took a little longer than normal, but she was soon opening the front door for him.

'Come in, Harvey. I have a nice pot of tea waiting for you,' she invited, grabbing his arm for support.

'How are you doing, Millie? I imagine the last week or so has been somewhat exhausting for you,' Harvey sympathised as they entered and took their seats in the lounge.

'They have indeed. Initially I was worried; I didn't enjoy digging up the past, but you have a way of getting your point across, young man. Your quest for justice—for doing the right thing—has been inspiring, to say the least.'

'Thank you, Millie. Sometimes it takes over and I forget about everything else. It's why I ended up divorced, unfortunately, and there is nobody to blame but myself,' he admitted to himself.

'Don't be too hard on yourself, Harvey. There are many

honourable professions that separate a husband and wife for longer than normal, and sometimes, like in your case, it takes its toll.'

Harvey stopped and turned to face her, clearly hesitating for a moment before he finally spoke again

'Millie, I have to ask... and please don't be upset... Evelyn is Percy's daughter, isn't she?'

Millie paused and looked at Harvey, her face neutral as she weighed her response.

'She doesn't know, Harvey. I was four months pregnant when Percy was killed. That's why we'd plan to marry and elope. I met Reg, my husband, at the hospital when I was there for my six-month check-up, alone and scared for the future. Reg was wonderful and supported me almost instantly; we ended up getting married four weeks before Evelyn was born. It all happened very quickly. Things were different back then, having a child out of wedlock was very much frowned upon,' she confessed sombrely.

'I understand. I suppose you kept it from her to shield her from the heartbreak,' Harvey reasoned.

'That and more. I went to the police to tell them of my suspicions that Percy had been murdered, but the police officer I spoke to was a cousin of the Franklins, and they both warned me off saying anything. I didn't want that to follow me around, so I just kept quiet. I've felt guilty about that ever since... please believe me,' she sobbed.

Harvey made his way to her and kneeled beside her as she wept, giving her a gentle hug.

'Millie, you did the right thing, never feel guilty about that. You protected your daughter from harm and raised her to be a wonderful person, a mother to your grandchildren.

You did that, and Percy would have been so proud,' Harvey explained.

'They both threatened me, Harvey—first the stepfather, and then a few years later, the son, who knows that I suspected foul play. That's why I got upset the other day, because I know more than anyone what they did and how they changed everything. I hate that family,' she continued tearfully.

'The police will take care of that now, but I think you should consider telling Evelyn, as soon as possible. Also, you should tell the police your side of the story. Do you see how significant that is now?'

'How?'

'Because Evelyn is Percy's legitimate heir, Millie. That means if the police can prove that, then all the land, the property, and those valuables—the legendary Flynn treasure that I found—rightfully belong to her.'

'Really? I hadn't thought of that. How could they possibly prove that, Harvey?' the woman's voice came doubtfully, wanting to believe the best, but struggling to.

'I know exactly how, but I will need you to speak to the police and also tell Evelyn what is going on, today if you can. She'll understand, trust me, and she won't hold it against you for keeping it from her all this time. You did it for the right and honourable reasons. Reg will always be her dad—he raised her, and she knows that. But she should also know that Percy was her father and what happened to him. Explain it all to her, and she will understand and love you for it,' Harvey said.

'Are you sure about this, Harvey?' Millie's voice was fearful and gentle as she pondered the possible outcomes of the truth coming out.

'Absolutely. Tell Evelyn and then let me know. I'll speak to the police on your behalf and arrange for them to meet with you here. Once they get your story, it will most certainly help with their investigation. They'll take a DNA sample from Evelyn, and once it comes back as a match, then all the land and houses can be legally transferred to Evelyn. She'll also be entitled to her grandfather James's medals, which I can tell you are worth a small fortune on their own. And there's a garage full of vintage cars that she can also lay claim to,' Harvey clarified.

'That's a lot to take in, Harvey,' the woman spoke, analysing the new turn of events in her head, her face clearly flustered

'Millie, I will be here the entire time for you, okay? You won't be alone—either of you—I promise.'

'I knew the first time I saw you that you were a good man, Harvey. I am grateful to have you in our lives,' Millie praised, squeezing his hand.

'Thank you, Millie. Now, how about you pour me a cuppa, eh? I think I've earned it, don't you?'

It was a little later than he'd promised when Harvey returned to the cottage, having gone through the plan again with Millie to ensure she understood what needed to be done.

'There you are,' Steve said, sipping his tea. 'What's the plan today?'

'I think we should go and see Emily,' Harvey grinned.

'What? I saw them yesterday and you turned the invite down, remember? Are you going senile or something?'

'I have exciting news for her investigation, Steve, and it's important I tell her in person,' Harvey explained. 'It won't take too long, and I'll treat you to a beer later.'

'Fine... but it'll be more than one beer, that's for sure.'

THEY WERE JUST PULLING up at Emily and Akira's house when Harvey's phone pinged, indicating a message. After parking, he saw that it was from Millie.

> Evelyn knows everything. Thank you x

'Perfect timing,' he murmured.

'What's that? Steve asked.

'Never mind, you'll hear everything I have to tell Emily soon enough,' Harvey beamed proudly.

'I've seen that look before,' Steve trailed off. 'Just before we made an arrest. That excitement and confidence, I'd recognise it anywhere.'

'Honestly, Steve, how much do you think a person changes just because they retire?'

'In this instance, not at all,' Steve joked with a chuckle.

'Let's go and break the news... did you message her we were popping in?'

'I did, and she's waiting.'

The door was answered by Emily who grinned spectacularly when she saw them both.

'Two days in a row is a record, McGarry, what is the world coming to?' she exclaimed in mock disbelief. 'Hi again, Harvey, I have a feeling I know what this is all about. Come in, both of you.'

'Harvey, this is my wife Akira, she's just on her way out to pick the kids up from my mother,' she introduced her wife to the pair with a loving smile.

'Lovely to meet you, Akira, I've heard nice things about you from this reprobate,' he replied, pointing to Steve.

'He's alright when he gets his act together, eh? You know what'll happen if you leave it too long next time, don't you?' Akira pointed to Steve jokingly.

'Yes, ma'am, I do. But surely two days on the trot counts for something?' he replied innocently.

'No, it doesn't!' Akira laughed loudly, waving a quick goodbye before leaving.

'You don't know when to stop, do you?' Harvey admonished.

'He doesn't, Harvey, he's way too gone. Please, come through and I'll make us a brew,' Emily invited.

They followed her through to a large, open-plan kitchen diner with a sizeable island where they sat on stools, waiting for their tea.

'Like I said, I think I know what this is about, Harvey. Something to do with our friend Franklin, right?' Emily looked up to gauge the man's response as she poured.

'Sort of. I've made a discovery—or two—that you need to know of and act upon. Don't get angry, but I found a storage unit that has eight valuable vintage cars in it, all belonging to Franklin. You need to seize them and ensure that Franklin doesn't benefit from them in any way.'

'Okay, I won't ask how you found out about what was inside... why are you telling me this now?' Emily enquired.

'Percy Flynn has a daughter, born five months after his death. She is the legitimate heir to the Flynn estate, all of it. Most of it is still in the Flynn name; Franklin couldn't change it over because of the bestowal by the Crown that meant its return when the Flynn lineage comes to an end. Now that we know there is a surviving descendant, all of that can continue under her proprietorship,' Harvey continued.

'I'm slightly confused, Harvey. Why didn't this daughter come forward years ago to claim her inheritance?'

'Because she was only made aware of the fact that Percy Flynn was her father within the last hour. It's why I'm here now, because you'll need to act quickly to ensure that all the right procedures are conducted.'

'Wow, you don't miss a beat, do you?' Emily acknowledged.

'I think we're both on the same page, Emily. We want justice for Percy and his mother, and one surefire way of that is to make sure his daughter inherits everything she deserves, not just morally, but also in law.'

'How on earth can we prove that she's Percy's daughter? I'm not asking for an exhumation, that's for sure; I doubt it would be given for something like this. We have the confession from Franklin so there's no need to dig poor Percy up... the crime has been effectively solved,' she replied.

'That's the thing, Emily. You don't have to!' Harvey exclaimed.

'Then how on earth will we be able to compare DNA?' she questioned back.

'You already have a sample... a few dozen, actually,' Harvey explained.

'Where?'

'The pendant that I handed in to lost and found, which is now in your possession, has a lock of Percy's hair in it.'

'Well, I'll be damned if I would have remembered that,' Emily nodded respectfully.

'All you need to do is get a sample from Evelyn, Percy's daughter, and match it with the DNA in Percy's hair, and you can legally announce them to be a match, right?'

'That's a simplified way of doing it, ignoring all the complex legal channels, but in a way, you're right as there is unlikely to be any opposition, now that Franklin has cooperated,' she shrugged.

'Great, so will you do it? Will you make sure Evelyn is looked after?' he pleaded.

'Don't worry, Harvey, I'll make sure that she is dealt with exactly as she should be.'

'Marvellous, I can sleep better for it,' Harvey slapped Steve on the back in content, pleased with himself.

'I had no idea you were that involved, boss. You're just as big a nightmare here, retired, than you ever were back in London,' Steve laughed.

'And don't you forget it,' Harvey replied. 'Now, about that beer I owe you, we should go and celebrate. Fancy tagging along, Emily? Bring Akira with you.'

'Sorry, no can do, we have dinner plans tonight, maybe next time,' the woman apologised.

'Let's make that happen soon, you know where I am now, so no excuses,' Harvey rose an eyebrow and pointed a finger.

'Good to know, Harvey, good to know.'

28

DNA

The celebration beers went on into the early hours of the morning, with Harvey and Steve catching up on life in general, as well as the Specialist Casework Team.

'Make sure you tell them... actually, you should order them to come and visit,' Harvey insisted. 'I miss them all, it would be nice not to lose touch.'

'They will, don't you worry, and they always ask about you, so you know,' Steve assured.

'Getting back to our earlier conversation... have you decided what you're going to do when you get back?' Harvey pushed.

'I have. In fact, I already spoke to the new DI about changing my hours. We're due to discuss when I get back so, all being well, she'll accept it, and I can fix things at home.'

'Here's a tip for you. Before you go into that meeting, do a bit of research into it. I know for a fact that it's a statutory request—you have a legal right to ask for changes. I think there's a new law that will help you. If you go armed with that knowledge, then she'll find it difficult to deny your request,' Harvey suggested.

'You are a fount of all knowledge, boss. I'm glad I popped over, it's been good to catch up properly,' Steve nodded gratefully.

'Don't leave it too long next time, otherwise I'll set Emily and Akira onto you,' Harvey threatened with a laugh and a playful, pointed glare.

'Yep, a lesson learnt, that one.'

'ONE FINAL FULL English breakfast from me,' Steve introduced, placing a plate in front of Harvey the following morning.

'It'll take me days to walk this off. Porridge it is, from tomorrow,' Harvey replied. 'What time are you heading off?'

'I was going to leave after breakfast, if that's alright. It's a fair drive and I want to catch up with my family before going back to work tomorrow,' Steve replied.

'Good idea, I'll keep my fingers crossed for you.'

'What's your plan for the rest of today?'

'I'm going to go and see Millie again, and hopefully Evelyn, to make sure they're okay with everything. I promised I'd be there with them throughout the process, which could take months, and I know that Millie in particular is a little nervous about it.'

'She's made a good friend in you, boss, a knight in shining armour... if they had sixty-year-old knights back then,' Steve teased.

'Steady on... I may be close, but it's not quite sixty, okay?'

'Ooh, so touchy, old man,'

They finished breakfast and had a final coffee before Steve brought his holdall downstairs, ready to leave.

'Drive carefully, Steve, and thanks again for popping in. I hope it was worth the drive,' Harvey hugging his friend goodbye.

'It was, and thanks again for your advice; you don't know how much I appreciate it,' Steve thanked.

'Well, if you have any more kids, you can name one of them Harvey,' he replied, laughing.

'Only if I want them to be bullied senseless at school. Mind you, it would probably toughen them up a little nowadays, the young generation could do with it, eh?'

They shook hands before Steve got into his car and drove off.

'Take care mate, see you soon,' Harvey waved his friend off before turning to go back inside.

———

HARVEY HAD CALLED and planned to visit with Millie after Steve's departure. He decided to walk there with Max, hoping to walk off the extra-large breakfast as well as think over the events of the past few days. Things had gone surprisingly well despite the hurdles that came with solving historic crimes. When they arrived at the house, Harvey saw that Evelyn's car was in the driveway, which he was glad to see.

It was Evelyn who answered the door, with a kind smile, as always.

'Hi, Harvey, and hello lovely Max,' she instantly kneeled down to pat Max, who revelled in the attention.

'Morning, Evelyn. How are you doing?' Harvey greeted.

'You mean apart from finding out that my dad wasn't

actually my dad, and that I may be inheriting a fortune? All is dandy, thank you for asking,' she replied, attempting to make a light joke out of a situation that was sure to be overwhelming.

'It's a lot to take in, I know,' Harvey nodded, noticing her tension. 'I'm glad that you're here, so that I can assure you that I'll be with you both all the way until the end.'

'Sorry for being so rude, Harvey, it's come as a massive shock. Mum was in tears when she explained it all, mainly because she thought I'd be angry and ashamed of her. She couldn't be further from the truth, bless her.'

'That's good to hear. How about we go and see how she's doing?' Harvey suggested.

They went into the lounge where Millie was sitting. She instantly smiled as she saw Harvey come in.

'Hello, Harvey. I'm glad to see you again. Please, sit down and Evelyn will make us both a nice cup of tea,' she indicated to an armchair.

'How are you doing today, Millie? I imagine yesterday was very trying for you.'

'You can say that again. Luckily, Evelyn understood my reasons and I think she's forgiven me, so I can't ask for more than that, can I?' she questioned.

'I think you'll both be fine, Millie. It's been a painful few weeks, but when the dust settles, your lives will be better for it and your spirit will be free from the guilt that you've carried for so long.'

Evelyn came in with a tray and served them both a cup of tea, before sitting down with one herself.

'I wanted to make sure you both know what's coming next, and also, that I'll be with you for all of it... if you want me along, that is,' Harvey offered.

'Don't be silly, Harvey, we wouldn't be in this position without you; I'd be upset if you didn't stay with us,' Millie responded.

'Ditto,' Evelyn piped in.

'Okay, that's good. I spoke to the Major Investigations Team from the local police who are dealing with Franklin, and they now know of your existence, Evelyn. They also know about some very valuable cars he's kept secretly stored, so hopefully they'll be able to confiscate those, meaning he won't benefit any further from the crimes of his father that he's lived off for so long,' Harvey informed.

'What'll happen next, Harvey?' Evelyn wondered.

'They'll be getting in touch with you both to take DNA samples. One of the things I found in the satchel was a locket with a photo of Percy as a toddler and his parents. There was a lock of hair in it, which forensics can use to take a good sample from. Once they match it to yours, then the police and lawyers can announce officially that you are Percy Flynn's daughter and the legitimate heir to the land and properties thereon,' he replied.

'Wow, I still can't believe it,' Evelyn shook her head in awe.

'It's a good thing, Evelyn. It's rightfully yours, don't ever doubt that. Robert Franklin took your father from you, and the life you would have had would have been very different. Luckily, Reg was a great dad to you, but don't feel like you don't deserve it, because you do,' Harvey clarified.

'Thank you so much, Harvey,' Millie spoke up. 'It makes me so happy to know that Evelyn and her family will be so well looked after.'

'Millie, the same goes for you; never feel bad about what is happening here. Franklin took so much away from you.

There's one other thing that I want to tell you, but it's important that you keep it to yourselves,' he continued.

'What's that?' Evelyn asked.

'Your mum knows, but I found the famed Flynn family treasure, the one that everyone thinks is a myth around here. There's a couple of valuable paintings and your grandmother's jewellery. You'll also be returned the items I found on the beach: your grandfather's Victoria Cross, a gold watch, and the pendant. Again, they are absolutely yours by birth, but if people find out about them now, they may challenge that and give you problems, so keep it quiet for a while, and then in years to come, your mum can say that she held them safely until the time was right. Does that work for you?'

'It does, thank you, Harvey,' Evelyn expressed her gratitude, a gentle but sad smile gracing her lips.

'Now, the next step is the DNA tests, like I said... are you both still okay with that? Do you want me to be here with you when they're taken? They'll also ask you questions about the past, to confirm you are who you are... that sort of thing. Millie, you have enough keepsakes, I'm sure, to confirm everything. That'll all be clarified after the DNA results come back.'

'When do you think that will be?' Millie asked.

'I've asked them to do it quickly, to get everything confirmed as soon as possible,' Harvey answered.

'If you could be here, that would be wonderful, Harvey,' Millie replied.

'Of course,' he stated without hesitation. 'In the meantime, are you clear about everything? Do you have any questions?'

'You mentioned vintage cars, Harvey. If Franklin bought

them, how is it that they can seize them from him?' Evelyn asked.

'Because they were likely bought from the proceeds of Franklin's crimes. Namely, the money he earned as a land-lord. Everything he earned because of Dorothy and Percy's deaths can be seized as a result. The Financial Investigations Team will then, hopefully, confiscate it all and make the simple decision to pass it on to the legitimate heir: you, Evelyn.'

'I understand. Mum told me about his son's current arrangement with the police... what do you think about that?' Evelyn asked.

'I think the compromise was necessary to confirm that his father had, indeed, murdered Percy and Dorothy. If we didn't have that, then it would have been difficult, sixty-odd years later, to do that with just what I found in the satchel. He's an unhappy old man, Evelyn, who understands that it was wrong. He did what he needed to do to stay where he is until he passes away. Think about it, if he had been evicted from the flat, then the council would have housed him somewhere else, and the taxpayer would have paid for his accommoda-tion and care. It's better this way, I think,' he replied.

'That sounds fair to me. Mum isn't happy though, are you, mum?'

Millie shook her head slowly, still clearly upset that Bradley Franklin isn't to be punished.

'He may be old and unhappy, but he lived a great life for decades off the back of my Percy's murder, so you'll get no sympathy or understanding from me,' she mumbled, feeling disheartened about the lack of punishment.

'Yes, but he's been found out, Millie, and something is being done about it. The alternative would have been unthinkable, don't you think?' Harvey tried to spin the situation, making light out of the current outcome.

'I'm sorry, Harvey, of course it's better this way. I won't complain any more. I'm pleased the truth is out finally.'

'Good. Now, you both have my number, so call whenever you want, for whatever reason, and I'll be here to help, okay?' he told them both.

'Thank you, Harvey, so much,' Evelyn stood to give him a long hug.

'Yes, thank you, Harvey,' Millie also preparing to stand, but was swiftly cut off by the man in front of her.

'Don't get up, I'll come to you,' he insisted with a laugh, leaning down and receiving a warm hug from Millie.

'Right then, I'll be off on my way. I shall hopefully see you both soon,' he waved, picking up Max's lead and walking off.

'Bye, Harvey,' Millie waved back at the man.

As they walked back to the cottage, Harvey felt good at what he'd done for them both, knowing that Evelyn and her family—Millie's grandchildren—would lead a better life for it.

'How about we celebrate, Max? I fancy a steak tonight, and I'm sure you'd like one too, eh?'

Max barked, knowing that he'd be going to sleep with a full belly that night.

29

FISH AND CHIPS

'Yep, this is an absolute first... a third date at a chip shop,' Rose announced as they tucked into their fish and chips.

'I promised you, didn't I?' Harvey grinned. They sat at a corner table in Dave's Fish and Chip Restaurant, away from others, which Harvey had requested, so they could talk without being overheard by other diners.

'I have to say, I can't fault the food, it's delicious. The setting isn't the most romantic, but I guess it's early days, eh?' Rose winked.

'Are you teasing me again?' Harvey asked. 'Because last time, you mentioned your parents, and now, you're talking about romance. You're trying to freak me out, aren't you?'

He wasn't sure if she was doing it on purpose and felt silly as a result.

'Of course, I am, silly. Keeping you a little nervous makes me laugh, it's when you tend to react in a way that's usually... unpredictable and funny.'

'So, you are happy to watch me embarrass myself because it amuses you?' the man raised his eyebrows as he awaited the woman's response.

'Absolutely, is that wrong?'

'Who knows how the dating game works nowadays? I think that's where I embarrass myself—my lack of experience in how to woo someone nowadays—I'm not very clued up, I'm afraid,' he replied.

'Woo? I haven't heard that term for a while... woo,' she laughed. 'You're doing just fine; I'm having a nice time and that's what matters, right? Anyway, how was your weekend with your guest?'

'It was great catching up, I hadn't seen him for many months. We did have an incident that almost resulted in another visit to your clinic,' he admitted.

'Oh, what happened?'

Harvey told her of the attempt to run them both down, and of the previous one on him a few days earlier.

'Oh no, you're both lucky to have avoided injury... or worse,' she shook her head. 'Do you know who it could be?'

'I have no idea at all. I've spoken to several people about the investigation since I started, so who knows what they could have passed on. It's a mystery,' he frowned.

'Well, you'd better be careful until it's all resolved. I was joking about you being on a hat-trick of visits, I'd rather not see you at work again,' she warned. She leaned over and placed her hand on top of his. 'I mean that.'

'Doctor Morgan, you really do care,' he grinned. 'So romance is possible, after all.'

'Not if you keep calling me Doctor Morgan it won't,' she swiftly removed her hand to make her point.

'Sorry, I shouldn't make light of it, those nerves are kicking in again. I'd like to see more of you, Rose, if you can forgive an old fool for his clumsiness.'

Rose took her time before replying with a grin.

'I can be forgiving, but it'll cost you,' she finally responded.

'Fair enough, what's the price?'

'A romantic dinner at a suitable location, that you have to find and arrange,' she insisted, her grin still very much in place.

Harvey nodded respectfully, realising that she had manoeuvred him expertly into position.

'Well played, Rose, well played. It won't be easy, as you well know, but it's a deal,' he extended his hand to make the deal.

'Good, that's settled then,' she shook on it firmly, her grin not wavering.

'I know exactly where to take you, but you'll have to wait and see, it'll be a nice surprise,' he teased.

'I look forward to it, Harvey,' Rose replied. 'Now, tell me more about this van that tried to run you out of Sheringham.'

———

EVELYN ANSWERED the door with her usual smile when he turned up to offer them both support during the upcoming DNA test.

'Come in, Harvey, we're expecting them in thirty minutes,' she welcomed.

'Did they tell you who'll be coming?' he asked.

'Yes, I believe you know Detective Sergeant Emily Leclerc,

and someone from the forensic department, I don't recall his name,' she replied.

They walked into the lounge where Millie was sat waiting, smiling directly as she saw Harvey.

'Hello again, Harvey. Thank you so much for coming,' she greeted as he leaned down to kiss her on the cheek.

'I told you I wouldn't have missed it, Millie. Just so both of you know, Emily is a friend, and the forensic person attending is simply coming to take mouth swabs from you both for the DNA testing, okay? It's nothing more complicated or sinister than that,' he notified them, hoping to ease their nerves slightly.

'That's good to know, thank you, Harvey,' Evelyn poured them a tea as she responded.

'I've asked Emily if it's possible to rush the results through the system, as they can sometimes take weeks,' he added.

They sat and drank their tea, making casual conversation until Emily turned up.

'This is Dan Viera, one of our forensic scientists, who will administer the DNA swab for you both,' she advised after introducing herself. 'As I explained over the phone, we'll take the two samples and compare them with the one that has been taken from the lock of hair that Harvey found. If there is a DNA match, we'll let you know and issue a formal letter for you to use with any legal action that may be required. Do you have any questions?'

'Sergeant, I did some research and found that it isn't likely that you can extract a viable DNA sample from cut hair, has that changed?' Evelyn asked.

'Dan, can you answer that one?' Emily directed the question to her colleague.

'Of course, happy to. That was the case until recently, but technology has advanced enough for a sample to be viable from cut hair. What I can tell you, though, is that the lock of hair in the pendant isn't just cut hair, and some of the strands we tested had their roots intact. I believe it was infant hair collected from a bathtub or something similar, which was common practice back in those days, maybe after the child's first haircut. We have a viable sample from that, so we'll be able to give a definitive result,' Dan explained.

'That's good to know, thank you,' Evelyn nodded in gratitude.

'If you're ready, I'll start with you, Evelyn,' he instructed, taking out a five-to-six-inch plastic tube from an evidence bag and extracting the cotton-tipped swab from within. 'Please open wide, I'm just going to take a sample from the inside of your cheek, okay?'

Evelyn did as she was told, and Dan was soon gently taking the sample. He placed the swab back into the tube and sealed it, writing Evelyn's name, date of birth, and the date and time of the test. He repeated the process with Millie, and the whole thing took less than five minutes.

'That's great, I'm done,' he told Emily.

'Wonderful. I've asked Dan to expedite the tests, so hopefully we should have something back to you in a few days, okay?' Emily offered.

'Thank you, Emily,' Millie smiled gently.

'Do you have any other questions for me while I'm here?' Emily asked.

'Emily, if the tests come back as a match, will Evelyn be able to claim the items I found on the beach?' Harvey asked.

'As it stands, they're evidence that are part of the investigation into the alleged murder, but based on the discussions we've had with Bradley Franklin, and what we have surmised from the items and all your statements, I think that the case will be closed soon. Once I can confirm that, I will personally return all the items found, if that's what you'd like, Evelyn?' Emily informed.

'Thank you, yes. Harvey mentioned them, it will be nice for Mum to have something of Percy... my father, also,' Evelyn looked back at her mother, whose eyes were glistening.

'Of course. There are some very important documents in there that you'll need for the future, although some of it was damaged, but there's enough for you to be able to use and legally request copies if required,' Emily added.

'I'll help you with that, Evelyn, I have a solicitor who can guide you through all of the complex issues that will most likely come up,' Harvey piped in.

'Thanks, I'll definitely take you up on that,' she replied.

'You will own a lot of property and land, you know, including a lovely hotel, farmland, and cottages. You'll be surprised as to how much it's worth. Some of it you can't sell, as it was bestowed by the Crown, and will be returned once the Flynn lineage ends, but you can still rent it and generate good revenue from it. Much of it *is* Flynn property, so that can be sold, such as the hotel. You and your family will be comfortable for many generations, I'm sure,' he communicated.

'Quite right too,' Millie added. 'I'm just happy the Franklin family won't earn another penny.'

'Hear, hear,' Harvey cheered.

'I'll keep in touch, and I'm sure we'll speak soon, both of you,' Leclerc said her goodbyes after answering any concerns they had.

Once Emily and Dan had left, the trio sat with their

drinks in silence for a few minutes as the reality started to sink in.

'Not once have I ever thought this would ever come to pass,' Millie mumbled, holding back the tears. 'I'm ever so grateful, Harvey. It isn't about money, you know that, don't you?'

'Yes, of course I do,' Harvey replied. 'I'm happy for you both, I really am.'

'You're a good man, Harvey. Most people would have kept those things you found. Like you said, the medal alone is worth a lot of money,' Evelyn praised.

'It was the right thing to do, Evelyn, it never once crossed my mind to do anything else.'

'Thank you so much,' she repeated. 'It's incredible to know that my daughter, and my grandchildren, will be looked after now. They've been struggling for years, so this will be wonderful for them.'

'I look forward to meeting them all, but in the meantime, I will leave you both, as I must get back and walk Max. I've neglected him a little recently, and considering all of this has been possible because of his nose, I think I should be looking after him better, don't you?' Harvey stood to leave, shooting them a content smile.

'I'll see you out,' Evelyn insisted.

Harvey gave Millie a now customary departing kiss and left.

At the front door, Evelyn pulled Harvey back and gave him a long hug.

'Thank you, Harvey. For Mum, mainly, she needed this for her peace of mind, so thank you.'

'I'm honoured to have helped, she is a wonderful woman, your mum. See you soon, Evelyn.'

Harvey felt a great sense of pride as he made his way back to the cottage. It was a good feeling, one that he enjoyed a great deal, and it inspired him to want to do more for people like Millie and Evelyn.

'That's exactly what I shall be doing,' he declared out loud.

30

THE ATTACK

The DNA results took just two days, which was when Emily Leclerc contacted Harvey.

'I shouldn't really be doing this, it's somewhat unethical, but I'm sure that Evelyn and Millie won't mind me giving you a heads-up. Dan has confirmed that Evelyn is, indeed, Percy's daughter, and I've already let her know. Additionally, Millie is confirmed as Evelyn's mother, which sounds strange, but is also a legal matter that would have needed clarifying. He's sending the documents to me shortly and I'll arrange for the ladies to have their own copies, as well as a report from us,' she updated him.

'That's wonderful news, Emily, thank you. In fact, Evelyn is trying to call me right now. Can we catch up later?'

'Of course, speak later.'

'Hi Evelyn, how are you?' he answered as soon as he got off the call with Leclerc.

'In case you don't already know, the results came back and confirmed that I am Percy's daughter. I'm shaking a little,

Harvey, if I'm being honest. I'm in my mid-sixties and have just found out I have a different father than I thought and I'm about to inherit a fortune. I'm just elated for my daughter; my life is just fine and dandy, but she will never have to struggle again.'

'As it should be, Evelyn. I'm very happy for you all. How's your mum?' he asked.

'She hasn't stopped grinning since the call, bless her. You're her favourite person at the moment; I hope you don't go off and disappear on us,' she warned, the smile evident in her tone.

Harvey laughed.

'You'll have to go a long way to get rid of me now,' he replied. 'I know exactly where to go for a nice cuppa.'

'Good. Anyway, I'd best get back to her. Will we see you soon?'

'Absolutely,' he reassured. 'I'll try and pop over in a day or two, okay?'

'Great, see you then.'

He was soon out on the road with Max, choosing the trail that took them over Beeston Bump, a challenging hike along the coastal path with stunning views to the sea. Max enjoyed being off the lead and explored everywhere his nose took him. Apart for any close proximity to the cliff edge, Harvey let him roam freely, and whenever there was an opportunity for the terrier to get too close to the edge, he would coax him back with a treat. They exited the walk close to Cambourne House, making Harvey smile at the thought that the original Flynn family home would be back in the hands of a descendant.

A few minutes later, as they were approaching the cottage, Harvey's phone rang. It was Evelyn.

'Harvey, please help us, someone's tried to kill us!' she yelled frantically.

'Are you okay? Your mum?'

'We're fine, but they almost set the house on fire, Harvey,' she bawled.

'Call the police, I'll be there in ten minutes,' he demanded, rushing towards the cottage.

As soon as he'd returned Max, he ran out and into his car, making his way to Millie's house as promised. As he ran towards the front door, he could see the damage that had been caused by the attack. The front window had been smashed, and he could see one of the curtains smouldering. As he reached the front door, it was pulled open by Evelyn, who looked pale and wide-eyed.

'Come in,' she rushed, looking over his shoulder for a potential threat.

'Did you call the police?' he probed.

'Yes, they're on the way, as are the fire brigade,' she nodded.

'Is there another fire?'

'No, but they want to be sure and confirm it was an attack,' Evelyn explained.

'Where's your mum?"

'She's in the lounge. Please, go and see her and reassure her, she's in a real state.'

Harvey found Millie in the kitchen, staring out of the window. She turned as he entered the room.

'There you are. You've missed all the excitement, Harvey,' her voice was eerily calm as she spoke.

Harvey turned to Evelyn, narrowing his eyes quizzically.

'She must be in shock, don't you think?' Evelyn assumed, shrugging her shoulders. 'She can't be this calm, surely.'

'And why is that, Evelyn? You think I'm easily scared? Remember what I've had to put up with all those years ago. This is just another Franklin attempt to scare us off, that's all,' Millie spat, defiant and confident with her response. 'He can go to Hell and meet up with his cowardly father, as far as I'm concerned.'

'Why do you think it's Franklin, Millie?' Harvey queried.

'Well, who else would do this? Can you think of anyone else? It must be him,' she replied, as if stating the obvious.

'I'm just going to check the damage, I'll be back in a minute,' Harvey informed the pair.

He went into the lounge and saw that the damage was limited to the broken window, a burnt curtain, and a section of burnt carpet, which was wet from the liquid that had seemingly put it out. There was a broken wine bottle near the scorched carpet, and a half-brick a little further away. A petrol bomb attack on an elderly woman was as cowardly and evil as they came.

'They smashed the window with the brick first and then threw the bottle in, which caught fire. Luckily, we weren't close enough to be hurt by it, and I'd just brought a pitcher of lemonade for us to drink,' Evelyn explained. 'I threw it onto the fire and then stopped it spreading onto the curtain with a cushion. We were lucky.'

'I think they were trying to scare you, it's a classic attempt,' Harvey analysed, taken aback by yet another awful attempt. 'But yes, you were lucky not to have been close.'

'Do you think it was Franklin?' she implored.

'I'm not sure, it certainly points to him, doesn't it?' he returned.

'What should I tell the police?' she urged.

'Everything you know, Evelyn. Don't leave anything out or

lie, and let your mum tell them her suspicions... that won't hurt,' he advised.

'Thank you. Will you stay until they arrive?' she pleaded.

'Yes. In fact, here they come now,' he indicated to the blue lights coming down the road.

It took an hour for the police and fire brigade to leave, having exhausted their questions for Millie and her daughter. The fire brigade confirmed it as deliberate attack and arson, and the police confirmed that they would escalate the investigation as a result. They called for an emergency boarding service to secure the window until a glazer could replace it in the morning.

'They won't find them, will they?' Millie doubted, after they had left.

'Maybe, maybe not. They'll ask around the neighbourhood to see if anyone saw anything suspicious, a vehicle they hadn't seen before, that sort of thing,' Harvey replied, wondering whether his friend, the van driver, was involved.

'I'm still confused, Harvey. Shouldn't there have been a message tied to the brick or something telling us why they've done this?' Evelyn appealed.

'You'd think that, wouldn't you? The reality is that most criminals are stupid and don't think further than their noses. It doesn't surprise me at all,' he elucidated.

'Like I told you, we don't scare easy,' Millie remarked.

'Good for you. In the meantime, I think it's worth getting some cameras fitted until we know for sure that the threat is over. I'll arrange for someone to come and install them tomorrow, okay?' Harvey added.

'Thank you, Harvey. Is there anything else we can do in the meantime?' Evelyn pondered what might help the pair feel a bit more at ease.

'It may be worth you staying here for a while, until it blows over. Can you do that?' he recommended.

'Yes, of course.'

'I'll be at the end of the phone and just a few minutes away if you need anything, okay?' he soothed, reassuring her as much as possible.

'Yes, thanks again.'

As Harvey drove away, he couldn't help but think it was linked to the two attempts to run him down. Someone was desperate to frighten him and Millie away. The only possible connection was Franklin.

Could the sick, frail, old man be responsible?

31

THE HOTEL

Harvey dialled Emily Leclerc as soon as he got home.

'I just heard from one of the officers attending,' she opened with immediately. 'Are the ladies both okay?'

'Yes, a little shaken but they'll be fine. I'm getting some cameras installed tomorrow,' he notified. 'Emily, I think this is linked to the two attacks on me, I think they're trying to scare Millie off. She's having none of it, by the way, she's a tough old bird.'

'I'm glad to hear that,' Emily expressed with a content nod.

'She's adamant that Franklin is involved, somehow. I can't imagine that he would be, after negotiating a deal to keep him out of prison and keep his flat. I'm stumped, to be honest,' he stated in defeat.

'Why don't you pop over tomorrow? We can go over all the paperwork together, and maybe we can spot something that will help. It's just a case of tidying it all up—a formality —and we can get everything to Evelyn as soon as possible. If it is a threat, then maybe one way to stop it is to formalise everything legally,' Emily encouraged.

'Great, I'll be there first thing tomorrow.'

'I'll have the kettle ready for you, Inspector,' she laughed.

HARVEY WAS true to his word and arrived at the station at nine o'clock on the dot. He was shown into a conference room, where Emily was laying out the paperwork on the large table.

'Good morning to you,' she welcomed. 'Your drink awaits,' she added, nodding towards the steaming cup of coffee at the end of the table.

'Wow, you're good,' he furrowed his eyebrows at the coincidental timing.

'Not really, I saw you parking out of the window there, so I thought I'd be clever,' she quipped.

'Well, you wouldn't be a detective if you weren't clever, Emily,' he replied. 'How can I help?'

'This is all the paperwork relating to the entire case, from the lost and found report you submitted, to the first crime report alleging the murder that I submitted. The next row is all the statements we've taken, including Franklin's, Evelyn's, and Millie's, amongst a few others. I was going to start with those, if you can start on the expenses on the next row.'

'Yes, I can do that,' he agreed.

They spent the next hour in silence as they both read through their allocated documents, until Harvey spotted something that he queried.

'Emily, isn't Jamila Roberts a live-in nurse?' he quizzed.

'Yes, why do you ask?'

'There's a bunch of other expenses for another carer that

I just noticed,' he pointed out. 'Look, a monthly payment is made to Jay Roberts. Is that her husband or her son?'

'I've no idea, to be honest, and it's strange that nobody has queried that before. I guess if she wasn't live-in, nobody would have thought it unusual to have two carers,' she replied.

'Is there any chance you can get some checks done on him? And if you haven't already, I'd check Jamila's background also,' he suggested.

'Absolutely. What are you thinking?'

'When I was on the Specialist Casework Team, one of the things we found consistently was that it was always someone you least expected that was responsible. I'm thinking that in this case, everything points to Franklin, and who else could possibly have a vested interest in the money and position he held before we found him out?'

'I suppose that's why you were on the big money back in London, eh?' she laughed, standing. 'I'll get those checks done now.'

Harvey continued to work on the documents, making notes where he found discrepancies worth checking. When Emily returned with some printouts, he had more questions for her.

'There's a bunch of petrol receipts here, submitted by Jamila. Why does she need petrol if she's live-in? Even if she did the odd shopping trip, we're talking two lots of petrol a week, which doesn't fit,' he suspected.

'Well, this may explain why,' she said, handing him one of the printouts.

'Yep, that answers everything, doesn't it?' he grinned.

'I've informed the duty officer downstairs, and he's dispatched a unit to make the arrest,' she confirmed.

'And that's why you get the big bucks here in Norfolk, Detective Sergeant,' he laughed.

———

'WELL, if it isn't our shy detective,' Rose opened with when she answered her phone.

'We spoke about this, Doctor, didn't we?' he laughed.

'Yes, Harvey, we did. It's not fun at all when you aren't awkward and shy,' she teased.

'I thought I'd let you know that I've made a reservation for two and can pick you up at seven thirty on the dot,' he offered.

'That's impressive, Harvey. I thought it would take you at least a week,' she poked. 'Seven thirty it is, I look forward to it.'

'Me too, see you then.'

Harvey grinned like a teenager and rubbed his hands excitedly.

'It's going to be a lot of fun, this dating lark, Max,' he nodded to his little sidekick laid next to him.

Max barked, his tail wagging frantically.

'No, I won't forget you, boy, don't you worry,' he conversed, laughing.

———

HARVEY PULLED up outside the apartment block at exactly seven thirty, just as Rose walked out. He quickly got out and opened the passenger door of the MG.

'Why, thank you, sir. And seven thirty on the dot too, I am impressed,' she nodded slowly.

'Thanks. I waited around the corner for six minutes,' he pointed out. 'I wanted to make sure I was true to my word.'

Rose laughed.

'I like this confident version of you, Harvey Ross, long may it continue.'

'Glad to hear it, Rose. I thought I'd keep the roof up so as not to mess up your hair,' he added.

'But that's why I brought this along,' she huffed playfully, whipping out a red, nylon headscarf. 'It goes with the car!'

It was Harvey's turn to laugh as he quickly undid the clasps holding the roof in place and pulled it back, revealing the clear starry night above.

'Wonderful... now, where are you taking me?' she asked.

'You'll just have to wait and see, won't you?'

Harvey took the coast road towards Weybourne and continued along the winding, tree-lined road, perfect for open-topped driving, until he turned into the drive towards The Pheasant Hotel.

'Harvey, that is very presumptuous of you, isn't it?' she gasped in mock surprise.

'I thought you would say those exact words,' he shook his head playfully. 'But if you must know, one of Norfolk's best restaurants lies in wait for us inside,' he replied.

'Interesting choice, if I may say so,' she hummed.

After parking the car, they walked in via the main entrance and through the bar to the impressive orangery, where they were met by the waiter. He led them to the table that Harvey had asked for especially, by the window over-looking the gardens.

'This is very nice indeed, Harvey, I am impressed,' Rose admired her surroundings with a grin.

'I aim to impress. I still maintain my belief that Dave's was a great choice though, but now you can see that I can introduce variety if required.'

'Well done you. Now, how about some champagne, eh? This is an auspicious date, after all,' she winked.

'THEY MUST LOVE US HERE,' Harvey joked. 'Three bottles of champagne for two people must be good for business, eh?'

'It's been wonderful, Harvey. Usually, I'm struggling to stand up after a bottle and a half, but we seem to have spread it over three hours,' she bantered, the smile never leaving her face. 'How time flies when you're having fun, eh?'

'It has been a great evening, Rose. I'm enjoying this dating lark much more than I ever thought.'

'It's a shame we have to get a taxi home, Harvey, I hear the rooms here are lovely,' Rose smiled playfully.

Harvey put his hand in his pocket and retrieved a wooden fob with a key on it.

'Great minds think alike,' he winked back.

32

GIN RUMMY

'That's never happened to me before,' Harvey murmured, almost in a whisper.

'It's fine, don't worry about it, it happens to every man,' Rose shrugged.

'It's not fine, it's something I have never experienced before, that means something to me,' he replied.

'Well, I wouldn't worry about it, Harvey. To be honest, you may as well get used to it, if truth be told,' Rose insisted.

Harvey sat up straight, a horrified look on his face.

'Seriously?'

Before he could say anything else, Rose interjected.

'I told you I was a geek of sorts. Geeks are good at games, Harvey, as I have now clearly established. That is now four games in a row.'

'I have never lost four games of Gin Rummy in a row. I'm either dreadfully unlucky or you are a world-class hustler,' he huffed, laughing.

'That will teach you to be so presumptuous, won't it?' she boasted in return.

'Well, I thought it was funny. Bringing out the key like that was a stroke of genius, don't you think?'

'It was funny, I'll concede. You timed it very well, bringing out the second key just as I was about to ready a slap to your rugged face,' she rolled her eyes jokingly.

'It's police humour, sorry. It'll take a few years to get it out of my system. As much as I'm attracted to you, I had absolutely no intention of taking advantage of you so soon. I think I should leave it another couple of dates, at least, don't you think?'

Rose laughed again.

'Let's just see how it goes. I'm having a good time so far; you make me laugh, and that is very important, but it's not everything. I want to learn more about what makes you tick, Harvey Ross. You have a very interesting energy, and I like that, so let's go out a few more times and see where that takes us,' she suggested.

'I'm fine with that. Now, how about one more game?'

THEY HAD a leisurely breakfast together early the following morning before Harvey took Rose back to her apartment.

'I had a wonderful evening, thank you, Harvey,' she mused, kissing him on the cheek. 'I must say, the rooms in the hotel were lovely, and good to know for the future,' she added, winking.

'It's part of my cunning plan, show you all the best places in town and beyond, and hope that you no longer think that I'm a buffoon.'

'Well, it seems to be working, so good job,' she raised an eyebrow with her cheeky reply. 'Speak to you soon.'

Harvey waited until she was safely indoors before getting back into the car and driving off. When he arrived back at the cottage, Max was sitting, waiting for him as he walked in. He stared at Harvey disapprovingly, before walking to the kitchen, turning back every few paces to see that he was following.

'Good morning to you too, Max. Don't you look at me like that, I left you with more than enough food and water to last you until I returned,' he admonished out loud.

Sure enough, Max led him to his bowl, which was now empty. Harvey filled it for him and went upstairs to change into more suitable dog-walking clothes. By the time he got back downstairs, the terrier was eagerly waiting for him by the front door.

'Come on then,' Harvey huffed with a laugh, attaching the lead and opening the front door.

Wanting to make it up to Max, Harvey took him for a longer-than-usual walk, around the Nelson Road and Cromer Road loop via the Beeston Regis Priory that he was now so familiar with. Max ran and explored every patch of ground that he hadn't encountered before as they navigated between fields and across the railway line. They were almost home when his phone rang.

'Emily, how's it going?' he greeted.

'Great, to be honest. Can I come over for a chat?'

'Sure, I'll get the kettle on,' he agreed.

It was just a few minutes later that he was back at the cottage and ready for Emily when she knocked on the door.

'In the neighbourhood, were you?' he asked.

'As it happens, yes. The uniforms found Jay Roberts and made the arrest late last night. I popped over this morning to check on his vehicle, just to be sure,' she briefed the man.

'Was it the van?' he probed.

'Maybe, I just wanted to clarify something... was there anything distinctive about it?' Emily urged.

Harvey thought before replying.

'Sorry, Emily, only what I told you before. It was a dark Transit van with a part index of 'BN' and a thirty-or-so-year-old driver. Oh, and the broken taillight,' he reiterated.

'Great, thanks, I just wanted to confirm,' she nodded.

Harvey waited, sensing that Emily was teasing him but not saying more.

'Is this what you do with Steve?' he passed her a cup of tea after shooting his playful accusation.

'It is a ritual that I enjoy very much,' she confirmed with a proud nod. 'I thought I'd continue it with you seeing as I'm likely to see more of you than him. No sense in wasting a good thing, is there?'

'Okay, I get it. Just remember though, I am nothing like Steve. I won't forget to keep in touch, okay?' he laughed.

'Fine, spoil the ritual, why don't you?' she huffed, spreading her arms exaggeratingly.

'Is the van driver Jamila's son?' he urged.

'Yes, it is, but you didn't hear it from me, okay?' she replied.

Harvey grinned. When he had met with Emily to go over the paperwork, she had shown him a printout of the vehicle that was registered to Jay Roberts: a grey Ford Transit with a registration number of BN05 YTS, which matched the van that had tried to run him down twice.

'Did you get a chance to interview him?' Harvey pushed for an update.

'I had to get a little creative first, which meant also arresting his mother. He wasn't happy when I informed him that she could be charged with conspiracy to commit grievous bodily harm alongside him,' she started, 'so he confessed.'

'He confessed? To what, trying to kill me?'

'That and the rest,' Emily gestured with her hands.

'Why did he do it?'

'Because he and his mother were buttering Franklin up to take over when he passed away. What we didn't know is that Jamila Roberts is more than just a carer to him, she's a... somewhat reluctant, occasional lover, hoping that he leaves her his fortune,' she replied.

'With the help of her son, right?' he added.

'That's correct. He got upset about pandering to Franklin's needs and that he and his mum deserved more, and he wanted to leave Sheringham for the bright lights of Norwich, blah, blah... honestly, he was an idiot,' Emily shook her head in disgust.

'Until I came along and exposed Franklin's history, forcing him to confess to his father's crimes and ill-gotten gains in exchange for his freedom, right? Jamila probably heard everything and realised that she'd not only end up with nothing, but she would have been the... reluctant, occasional lover for nothing,' he put the pieces together, finally making sense of the mystery.

'That must have upset her greatly,' Emily laughed, 'And she probably encouraged her son to do something.'

'That's what I find hard to understand. What did they think would happen now that the police were involved, that hurting me would stop their investigation? It doesn't make sense,' Harvey muttered. 'If anything, it involves the police much more.'

'I think it's because of this,' Emily pulled out an evidence bag with an A4 envelope inside it. The word '*Logbooks*' was crudely written in felt-tip pen on one side.

'The cars? Ah, they're still registered in Franklin's father's name and his own, so Jamila and Jay thought they could salvage something by selling the cars... I get it now.'

'Yes, and thanks for letting us know so bright and early about it, Mr Private Detective,' Emily jested.

'I just want Evelyn to get what she deserves and for that horrible man to stop benefitting, that's all,' Harvey admitted.

'I get it, and we're good, don't worry,' she reassured.

'Did they confess to that also?'

'Yes, the son coughed up to everything, though, says he acted alone, so I guess there's no evidence against Jamila. What I will do, though, is inform Franklin, who will probably fire her and get someone new in,' she acknowledged.

'She's lucky to get away with just being sacked,' Harvey spoke distastefully. 'Because that conspiracy charge is pretty much spot on.'

'Yep. Still, the main thing is that we have the confession for the attempts on you and Steve, along with the criminal damage and arson to Millie Parry's house,' Emily informed.

'That should put him away for a few years, for sure.'

'Good riddance to bad rubbish, I'd say,' Emily added.

'Where are you with the paperwork for Millie and Evelyn?' Harvey asked.

'It's all done now; I think we have everything that they need. They just need a good solicitor who can make the arrangements for the transfer of ownership, etcetera.'

'So, a happy ending it is, then,' Harvey smiled, raising his cup to toast with Emily.

'Yes it is, thanks to you and Max, of course,' Emily ruffled Max's head after toasting to the good news.

'You know, Max is responsible for almost all of the good things that have happened since I got to this town,' Harvey scoffed playfully, reminiscing on everything. 'If he hadn't found that satchel, I wouldn't have met the people that I have, and may have even left by now.'

'He is a lucky charm, Harvey, keep hold of him and look after him,' Emily asserted.

'Oh, don't worry, he isn't going anywhere.'

———

33

THE ARREST

H arvey was surprised when Rose called him that evening.

'Is everything okay?' he asked in a hurry. 'I don't actually remember you ever calling me before.'

'I'm just full of surprises, aren't I?' she joked with a soft chuckle.

'You are. How's it going?'

'I thought I'd invite you out this time, if you're free this Saturday?'

'I am, what did you have in mind?' he posed the question.

'A day at the beach. You can bring Max, and we can just chill out for the day. How about it?'

'I'm up for that, and Max will love a day by the sea. Which beach did you want to go to?' he wondered, ready to make the plan.

'Have you ever been to Wells? The beach there is lovely and goes on for miles,' she recommended.

'Nope, never been there, but it sounds great. Should I bring anything?'

'You can bring the drinks, and I'll bring the food,' she started. 'I have one of those antique basket hampers that you can tie to the back of your little sports car,' she added.

'That settles it then,' he beamed. 'What time shall I pick you up?'

'How does ten o'clock sound? It won't take long to get there, maybe half an hour, and there's a huge car park so it doesn't matter how busy it is,' she suggested.

'I look forward to it, Rose, see you then,' he replied.

Harvey looked down at Max and smiled at the happy terrier.

'You're going to have a lot of fun on Saturday, boy, and you get to meet Rose,' he spoke excitedly, hyping the little terrier up.

As he said those words, he sat down and thought about their previous conversation. This seemed like a positive step —Rose asking him out and including Max—and Harvey nodded appreciatively at the way Rose was guiding what Harvey could now consider to be a relationship, albeit a fledgling one.

'Yep, you're going to like Rose, Max... a lot.'

'So, THEY GOT HIM?' Steve questioned when he called later that day.

'They did. He's bang to rights, registered owner of the van matching the description we both gave, and confessed to the attempts. He and his mother were hoping to benefit from Franklin's now-defunct empire, which is why they came after me in the vain hope it would put off any further investigation and they could end up with something,' Harvey replied.

'Let me get this straight: in the few months that you've been retired, you moved to a town on the coast, found clues that led to a double murder, got involved in investigating it before the police did, was almost killed... twice—as a result— and ended up helping to solve those murders as well as the attempts on your... our... lives. Is that about right?' Steve demanded in awe.

'It's a decent summary,' Harvey trailed off.

'You sure know how to make friends, don't you?'

'Well, there is that too. I now have several friends here, including Emily, I might add. In fact, I may be a better friend than you ever were to them,' Harvey gloated.

'And let's not not forget Rose, the sexy doctor, eh?' Steve teased. 'You didn't mess about, did you?

'That's going to be an awkward conversation, that,' Harvey replied, biting the inside of his cheek as he thought of it, 'with Becky, I mean.'

'Why do you need to tell her? You're divorced, aren't you? It's all finalised. You're not waiting on anything, are you?'

'No, I just feel that I should tell her, that's all,' he responded awkwardly.

'Harvey, you have barely started seeing Rose; don't tell Becky until you know that it is a relationship. You're just courting at the moment, trying to figure each other out, whether you want to continue seeing each other, that sort of thing.'

'That may be the case, but I'm still on good terms with Becky and it feels like the right thing to do,' Harvey argued his point.

'Well, if you want to risk that friendship then go ahead and tell her, but I'm telling you that she'll ask one question and one question alone.'

'What's that?' Harvey asked.

'Don't you think it's a bit soon?'

'Maybe, but I know Becky well and she's a very pragmatic woman who wanted a divorce for the right reasons. She'll approve, I'm sure,' Harvey replied.

'On your head be it,' Steve insisted, pulling back from the debate. 'Anyway, what are you going to do now that everything seems to be resolved?'

'I told you before, I may look into some of my aunt's research and see if I can solve a few of those old mysteries she recorded. It should be a lot of fun,' Harvey grinned to himself.

'Well, if I can help in any way, you know where to call. Also, thank you for the advice, I spoke to my boss and my hours are being reviewed with a view to working regular hours Monday to Friday. Carla is very happy,' Steve updated him, his tone grateful.

'Good, I'm happy for you, Steve. You should bring her to the coast for a visit, I'll leave you a key so you can come and go whenever you want.'

'That's very kind of you, thanks. Anyway, I'm pretty busy at the moment so I'll leave you to it, let's catch up next week,' Steve replied.

After ending the call, Harvey thought about the life he'd left behind in London and realised something. Max popped onto his lap and made himself comfortable, which Harvey nodded at approvingly.

'I know what you mean, boy, life is nice and comfortable here, isn't it? I can still talk to my friends and family regularly; I have plenty I can do here, and I've made new friends... one of them particularly lovely. What's not to like?'

34

WELLS

Harvey and Max visited Millie and Evelyn the next day.

'How are you both doing?' he asked the pair as they sat with their tea in the lounge.

'I'm fine, but my daughter here is fretting about everything,' Millie shook her head playfully, grinning as she nodded towards Evelyn.

'I'm not fretting, Mum, I'm a little nervous, that's all,' Evelyn countered.

'What are you nervous about?' Harvey asked.

'It's just a little overwhelming, Harvey. In the space of a few weeks, I found out that my dad wasn't my dad, that my real dad and my grandmother were both murdered before I was even born, and that I am about to inherit a fortune that I haven't a clue how to manage. That's a lot to process.'

'I can see how that is overwhelming, but surely you can see that it has turned out very nicely, can't you?' he soothed.

'That's what I've been telling her, Harvey,' Millie interjected. 'We now know for sure what happened back then, and that Evelyn's inheritance is rightfully restored.'

'You can't argue with that, can you?' Harvey shrugged, turning back to Evelyn. 'And you said it yourself, your family won't have to worry about anything anymore—their struggles are over.'

'Yes, that is wonderful, but it has come at a cost, Harvey. I've caught Mum crying a couple of times now; she didn't think I could see her, but I know the memories that she tried so hard to bury have resurfaced. And who's to say that we won't get another brick through the window?' Evelyn opposed.

'That's something I was meaning to tell you: they caught the man responsible, and he won't be bothering anyone for many years,' Harvey reassured.

'Oh, that's very good news. Who was it?'

'I'm not really supposed to tell as I shouldn't know myself... actually, sod that... it was the carer's son who thought he would take Franklin's fortune when he passes away. Just don't tell anyone I told you, but you can rest assured that he won't be bothering you again,' Harvey insisted.

Millie turned to Evelyn with a gentle smile.

'Sweetheart, they weren't tears of sadness you saw, they were tears of joy and love. Percy and I weren't together very long but we were very much in love, and we also made you. I cried because I know he's looking down at us and approving of everything that has happened these past few weeks.' Anybody could hear the love and adoration that Millie had, and will always have, for Percy in her voice.

Evelyn walked to her mother and held her tightly. Both cried silently at the realisation of the events that had transpired over recent time, and the fact that it was now over, and they could get on with their lives. Millie, in particular, was finally free from the burden of guilt and remorse.

'I can't tell you how happy I am for you both,' Harvey nodded appreciatively.

'You can start by joining us for lunch on Sunday, seeing as your schedule is now free,' Evelyn insisted, with no room for arguments. 'Say, one o'clock?'

'Sounds like a plan to me, can I bring my trusted side-kick?' he replied, indicating to Max, who was gnawing at a rope toy that Evelyn had given him.

'If you don't bring him then you'd best not come at all,' Evelyn gasped in pretend shock at the idea of Max not being at lunch.

'Then I shall see you both on Sunday,' he said, waving as he left.

As he walked back to the cottage with Max, Harvey smiled at the thought of what his actions had resulted in.

'Long may it continue,' he spoke into the universe.

THE WEATHER on Saturday morning was sunny but a little windy, something that Harvey was now getting accustomed to in Norfolk, especially by the sea. Taking no chances, he'd purchased a bottle of 2006 Châteauneuf-du-Pape, a six-pack of Brewdog alcohol-free beer, six tins of Sanpellegrino Aranciata, and two large bottles of still water.

'Can't drink too much wine, boy, otherwise I won't be able to drive Archie back home.'

As he had done previously, he waited around the corner for a few minutes so as not to be too early. When he drove up to the apartment block, he saw Rose waiting for him, a small vintage willow hamper on the pavement next to her.

'You waited round the corner again, didn't you?' she shook her head, smiling, as he opened the door for her.

'Well, you know how much I hate being early... or late,' he grinned.

'Me neither, which means we both need to stop doing this, I've been waiting here for ten minutes,' she beamed with a teasing roll of her eyes.

'This is Max, by the way,' he said, introducing him to Rose. 'The best detective dog you can ever hope to meet.'

The terrier greeted the newcomer enthusiastically, and it was a few minutes before they were able to get a move on.

They drove for forty minutes along the coast road to Wells-Next-the-Sea, passing Weybourne, Cley, and Blakeney Point along the way to the impressive, wide beaches that it was famous for. Frequently described as the perfect English beach, with its colourful and unique beach huts, it was an ideal place for a quiet picnic amongst the miles of sandy dunes. Harvey parked the car and together, with the provisions, they walked along the path to the stairs that led up and then down to the beach.

'Hell of a view,' Harvey admired as they reached the top of the stairs.

'It's one of my favourite places to be; you can escape the frenetic world here and walk for miles without anyone bothering you,' Rose took a deep breath of fresh, sea air and nodded in appreciation.

They walked along the beach for a few hundred meters until they passed the row of impressive beach huts, before stopping close to the trees and laying out a tartan blanket. Rose had brought cheese and cucumber sandwiches, crab rolls, a selection of cheeses and pickles, and an array of fruit that a restaurant would have been proud of.

'This is going to be some fancy picnic,' Harvey hummed, bringing out the wine in one hand and a tin of alcohol-free beer in the other.

'Wine, of course,' she scoffed with a laugh, tilting her head approvingly.

Harvey put out some treats for Max along with a bowl of water and let him wander off the lead.

'This is lovely, Rose, I can see why you like coming here,' he said, enjoying the peaceful vibe.

'I can't tell you how many people thought I was crazy to come to this part of the world, but then I realised that not one of them had ever been here, and their assumption was that it was a quiet backwater with nothing to do,' she countered.

'Well, amen to that, let's hope it stays that way. The last thing we want is everyone coming to see what the fuss is about, eh? I like the peace and quiet, and I now know that it is certainly not boring here,' he agreed.

'So, tell me, how are things going with your side hustle?' she asked.

'Side hustle? By that you mean solving murders and finding lost treasures?' he laughed.

'I wouldn't know, you're keeping it all to yourself, remember?'

'Well, I can tell you that the murders *have* been solved, the treasure *has* been found, justice *is* being dispensed, and the world is a better place for it,' he replied, raising a glass of wine for them to toast.

They clinked glasses together and they both smiled, enjoying the moment.

'This is nice, Harvey, I do like moments like this. Simple, but somehow you never forget them, do you?'

She reached over and kissed Harvey gently on the lips. The kiss lingered for several seconds before she pulled away. He noticed that her eyes were still closed, and she was smiling blissfully, before her eyes opened and she laughed softly.

'Well now, that was nicer than I'd anticipated,' she whispered.

'Would you believe it, I just realised that I haven't turned bright red or passed out, I think I'm cured!' he exclaimed with glee before they both burst into laughter.

'Are you sure? I thought I saw a hint of crimson... let's make sure, eh?' she leaned back in for another kiss as the words left her lips.

This time it was Harvey who kept his eyes closed and smiled.

'Yep, I think you're cured,' she confirmed. 'Now, before you do anything else, and I apologise for ruining this special moment, but you need to go and see to Max.'

'What? Why? Oh...' he trailed off in defeat, reaching for a bag.

THE DAY PASSED TOO QUICKLY for them both as they exchanged more stories about their earlier lives, compared places they'd both visited and wanted to visit, and generally found out more about each other. It was during the leisurely drive back to Sheringham that Harvey's phone rang. He glanced at it to see who was calling and quickly decided to pull over and take the call.

'Is everything alright, Evelyn?' he asked, dreading that something had happened to Millie or her.

'Everything is fine, Harvey. I'm so sorry to disturb you but my mother insisted that I call you. Can you pop over any time soon?' Evelyn asked.

'Yes, of course. Can you give me an hour? I have a valuable package that I need to deliver first,' he grinned in Rose's direction as she gave him a sharp dig to the ribs.

'Yes, that will be fine, see you then,' Evelyn replied.

'So, I'm relegated to a package now, am I?' Rose demanded in mock offence.

'A valuable one, you heard me say it,' Harvey defended.

'Okay, well, you are forgiven, but only seeing as it has been a wonderful day,' she said, smiling.

'It has, hasn't it? Even Max enjoyed himself, didn't you, boy?' he asked, to which Max, who lay comfortably harnessed on the small parcel shelf behind them, barked twice.

'I think it's safe to say that I'd like to see you again, Harvey,' Rose established, reaching over and placing her hand on his arm. 'I've enjoyed spending time with you much more than I'd expected.'

'I'd be devastated if you didn't, Rose,' he replied, keeping his eyes firmly on the road but not in any way attempting to hide the enormous grin on his face. 'I guess playing the bumbling fool and unexpectedly dropping my trousers worked its charm, eh?'

'I miss that man,' she replied, laughing at the memory. 'He was so refreshing and funny.'

––––––––

Harvey took Rose back home and then took Max back to the cottage to feed him before leaving to go and see Millie and Evelyn.

'What's happened then, Evelyn?' he asked in a rush as she let him into the house.

'I'll leave it to Mum to explain, she has a small surprise for you,' Evelyn waved him into the lounge.

'Hello, Millie,' Harvey greeted, leaning down to kiss his friend on the cheek. 'What's this about a surprise?'

'You once mentioned that your aunt's name was Agatha,' Millie trailed off, waiting for Harvey's agreement or disagreement. 'Did I hear that correctly?'

'You did, yes, Agatha Ross. She was my father's sister,' he replied.

'Well, I was looking through my memory box as I wanted to read some of the letters that Percy had sent me. I keep things like that in the box, you know, flower pressings from a precious day out, a ticket stub from the theatre, that sort of thing. And I came across this photograph,' she indicated to a photograph on the table, picking it up from the table next to her and passing it to Harvey.

Harvey looked at the small, six-by-four-inch, black-and-white photograph. It was in surprisingly good condition for its age, and the resolution was nice and sharp. The photograph was of a group of seven young women, four seated and three standing behind them, all wearing the same outfits of a dark-coloured skirt and white tops. There was a small trophy on the floor in front of them.

'That's the Norfolk County Netball team from 1960. Do you recognise anyone?' she asked, grinning mischievously.

Harvey looked closely and noticed that the lady seated on the end looked familiar.

'Is that you?' he pointed out.

'Yes, it is. Evelyn was just two years old at the time and netball was the way I used to relax back then. It helped keep my body and soul grounded.'

'You look lovely, Millie, and that looks like a smile I can see too,' he added.

'I did smile occasionally, Harvey!' she exclaimed.

Harvey chuckled. 'Just teasing you.'

'But that's not who I was asking about. Do you recognise anyone else?' Millie asked, winking at Evelyn.

'Hm... let me see,' he replied, looking closely at each woman in turn.

'Wait, is that...'

'Yes, Harvey, it is,' she confirmed.

'Aunt Agatha,' he whispered.

His beloved aunt was one of the three standing, the furthest away from Millie. She had a beaming smile on her face, which was why he hadn't immediately recognised her, but there was no mistake, it was Agatha.

'We'd just won the South-East finals, so we were all ecstatic. Agatha went off to work after that, so we hardly ever saw her. She was a wonderful player and a lovely lady,' Millie praised.

'Wow, what a small world it is that we live in, eh?' he remarked. 'It's a fabulous picture, she looks so happy.'

'You take that, Harvey. Evelyn took a scan of it for me, so I'll always have a copy for myself.'

'That's very kind, Millie, thank you. But couldn't this have waited until tomorrow?' he asked.

'I suppose it could have, but I wanted to share it with you while it's just the three of us,' Millie replied.

'Why, is there more coming for lunch tomorrow?'

'Yes,' Evelyn said. 'We decided the whole family should be here and we'd like you to meet them all, including my artist daughter and grandchildren that I mentioned, along with their two dogs, and my two sons, their wives, and another five grandchildren. It will be a very full house.'

·'Wow, so that's...'

'Sixteen of us... and three dogs,' Evelyn cut him off.

'That's a decent sized party,' Harvey replied, raising his eyebrows.

'I hope that's okay, Harvey. I want to tell them all what's happened and it's important to me that they meet the person responsible for it all,' Evelyn spoke softly.

'Of course it is. I look forward to seeing their faces when you tell them,' he replied. 'And hopefully, Max will make new friends too.'

'They'll love him to bits, I'm sure.'

'It looks like you're tied to us for life now, young man,' Millie grinned. 'That'll teach you to get involved in other people's business,' she laughed.

Harvey turned to Evelyn and said, 'You know, you'll have plenty of money when you sell everything, more than enough to put your mum in a half-decent home for a couple of decades.'

Millie laughed just as loudly as they did.

35

FAMILY GATHERING

As Harvey had expected, Max had no problems making friends with the visiting dogs the following day. The large garden was the perfect playground for the trio to run after each other and go exploring amongst the bushes at the end.

'I told you they'd love him,' Evelyn announced as they watched from the kitchen window.

'It was nice to meet your family, Evelyn. Have you or Millie told them anything yet?'

'I think she's about to do that now,' Evelyn replied, ushering him out of the door and into the garden, where the rest of the family were now joining them. Harvey saw Millie being led to the decking area where the table and chairs were, by her granddaughter Amy, Evelyn's artist daughter. When they reached the table, Millie kissed Amy on the cheek and stood, leaning against the table for support, to speak.

'Thank you so much for coming at such short notice, it is always lovely to see the family gathered like this. I know most of you are champing at the bit to find out what's going on, so

I'll keep it short and sweet, and maybe Evelyn can help me. Come and stand here with me, darling,' she waved Evelyn over.

Some of the family looked worried, expecting bad news, while others looked perplexed.

'Don't worry, everyone, Mum is just fine, everyone is fine, it's actually exciting news,' Evelyn interjected.

'Yes, it is, but also with some news that will surprise a few of you. As you know, your mother and grandmother here, is my only child. What you don't know, however, is that Reg wasn't her father,' Millie announced.

There was a stunned silence for several seconds before she continued.

'Don't look so upset; Reg was aware, and he was a wonderful dad to Evelyn, a wonderful husband to me, and a wonderful grandfather to you all. Evelyn's father, Percy Flynn, was someone I loved dearly and who I wanted to marry and share my life with. I was pregnant with Evelyn when he was murdered, and Reg stepped in and took care of me... of us... a few months after Percy's death,' she continued.

'Nana, why have you kept all this a secret?' one of Evelyn's sons asked.

'Roger, it was because I didn't want to upset the man that I suspected had killed poor Percy. I kept quiet to make sure we weren't harmed in any way.'

'So, why now?' Roger challenged in confusion.

'Harvey, would you mind stepping up here with me?' Millie welcomed the man up with her.

Harvey joined them both. He could see there was a lot of confusion amongst the family members, wondering where this was all going and what this man was doing here.

'This is our amazing friend, Harvey Ross, who found us

just a few weeks ago and told us an unbelievable story that has led to this announcement,' Millie explained. 'Harvey is an ex-detective from London. Thanks to his dog, Max, who you have all met, they found something on the beach that led Harvey to believe that Percy had been murdered. Percy had left a note for me and some evidence that suggested he'd been poisoned. Anyway, because of Harvey's determination to see justice served, Evelyn is about to inherit a small fortune,' she added, cutting it short and indicating to her daughter.

There was a lot of confusion and chatter amongst the family.

'Fortune?'

'Is this for real?'

'What's going on?'

'Well, do you want me to tell you or not?' Evelyn teased, 'because I can't if you're all jabbering away like that.'

'Sorry, Mum, please tell us,' Roger said.

'My real father, Percy, was the son of a wealthy landowner —a hero from the great war who sadly died in action. Percy and his mother were both murdered so that her second husband would inherit the estate, but what he didn't know was that Percy found out and hid all the documents and family valuables to deny him. There was also a declaration that some land that was gifted to the family would be returned to the Crown when the family line ended. The murderer knew none of this, and so he couldn't sell anything off after Percy and his mother were killed.'

'Wait, Mum, how is it that you're inheriting it after all this time?' her other son, Ian, asked.

'The police did a DNA test and matched it to Percy's, so I am the only surviving family member,' she answered.

'What did you inherit, Mum?' Roger piped up.

Evelyn glanced over at her mother and Harvey before replying.

'As far as I know, there is one hotel close to the beach, eight cottages, and around five hundred acres of farmland. Oh, and a couple of very valuable paintings, some jewellery, and my grandfather's Victoria Cross. Did I forget anything, Harvey?' she turned to the man to confirm.

Harvey leaned over and whispered in her ear.

'Apparently, there are some very valuable cars that have been seized from the murderer's son that will be sold, with the proceeds coming to me also,' she added.

'What will you do, Mum?' Ian asked.

'I'll need to take some time to figure a few things out, but what I will tell you is that our lives will be better for it,' she declared. 'Harvey has introduced us to his solicitor, who will be dealing with the whole thing, so that it is done properly.'

The chatter turned to cheers and hugs amongst the family, many of whom came and embraced Harvey in thanks.

'It looks like your list of friends and admirers is growing, doesn't it?' Millie asked cheerfully, giving him a gentle nudge. She looked very happy to see the family reaction and Harvey saw her wiping away the odd tear when she thought nobody was looking.

'Thank you for allowing me to be a part of this,' he told her. 'You have a lovely family, and I am over the moon for you and Evelyn both,' he said, giving her a peck on the cheek.

'Well, you are now part of this family, whether you like it or not, so I expect to be kept out of that home you joked about yesterday, okay?' she warned with a playful serious face.

EVELYN AND HER DAUGHTER, Amy, joined Harvey as he watched Max continue to play happily in the garden.

'Amy here wanted to thank you in person, Harvey. I've told her that I'll be helping her out sooner rather than later. I've already asked the solicitor to investigate what I can do now,' she mentioned.

'Thank you, Mr Ross, I can't tell you how grateful I am. The last few years have been a struggle since the kids' father bailed on us,' Amy shook his hand warmly in thanks.

'Please, call me Harvey. According to your mum and grandmother, I am part of your family now,' he replied.

'Yes, you are, Harvey. Max too,' she replied, laughing as he playfully jumped clear over one of the other dogs.

'I have an idea of how you can raise some money quite soon,' Harvey suggested.

'How?' Evelyn asked.

'I told you about the hotel, Cambourne House, didn't I? Well, I know for a fact that the current tenants have tried many times in the past to buy it from Franklin, but of course, he couldn't legally sell it. I'm sure you can come to an amicable agreement with them quickly; they're good people. If not, then you still have the rent that will come in from it, because it will all be transferred to you and away from Franklin,' he informed the pair.

'That's good news, I'll ask the solicitor to chase that up tomorrow,' Evelyn nodded.

'Also, I know the police have a signed disclaimer from Bradley Franklin that avails him of ownership of the cars. I reckon they'll fetch around three hundred thousand pounds when they sell, and you will have a solid claim to that money

as compensation for what has happened. You'll get no opposition and support from Norfolk Constabulary,' he added.

'Wow, Harvey, that all sounds amazing,' Amy replied
in awe.

'That's not all. I know your mum can't sell some of the
land, but from all accounts, I think at least two hundred acres
of it is owned by the Flynn family. The rest is Crown land
that you will continue to receive good rent on, if you decide to
sell the rest. And don't forget the two paintings, that's a cool
million or two if ever I saw,' he laughed.

'It's a little overwhelming, that's for sure,' Evelyn
remarked.

'You know, you'll need someone to manage it all, so why
not make it a family business and have Amy do it? There will
be plenty of time to paint. All you need to do is liaise with the
estate management company a couple of times a week and
the rest of the time is yours,' Harvey countered.

'You've thought of everything, haven't you?' Evelyn
laughed in shock.

'I haven't been retired long, Evelyn; the efficient
managing of things is still running through my veins,' he
joked.

'What a wonderful day it has turned out to be,' Evelyn
hummed, hugging her daughter.

'I'm going to start saying my goodbyes to everyone, I need
to get back home. Call me if you need anything else, okay?'
he gave both ladies a peck on the cheek before turning away.

'Thanks again, Harvey, you are an angel sent from heav-
en,' Evelyn praised.

'I've not been called that before,' he grinned. 'But thank
you. I'll pop in soon for a cuppa.'

It took an age to make his farewells, but eventually,

Harvey and Max were able to leave. The night sky was clear of clouds, and the stars were gleaming in the dark sky, the air fresh with a gentle breeze blowing—a perfect evening for a walk as they made their way back to the cottage.

'They were right, Max. Home *is* where the heart is.'

———

36

THE JOB OFFER

Harvey was enjoying a bowl of cinnamon porridge when he received an unexpected phone call from his old boss from London, Chief Superintendent Marvin Russell.

'Good morning, Guvnor, it's good to hear from you,' Harvey greeted.

'Hello there, Harvey. I thought I'd check in and see how retirement is suiting you? Got any regrets yet?' Russell asked.

'Not at all. The first few weeks were a little tricky, and I must confess, I thought I'd made a huge mistake. But things have changed and I'm enjoying life here now,' Harvey replied.

'I bumped into Steve McGarry, and he told me that you'd gotten involved in some sort of investigation?'

'I suppose you can call it that, yes. Norfolk Constabulary are dealing with it; I handed over what I'd found and left them to it,' Harvey responded, unsure of where the conversation was heading.

'You can't take the investigator out of a retired detective, can you?' Russell jested.

'I have enjoyed working with them, to be honest, it wasn't difficult to do at all.'

'So, is it all done and dusted now?' Russell probed.

'Yes, the paperwork is all but done according to my contact there, and it looks very much like justice will be served,' Harvey announced, the pride and contentedness evident in his voice.

'So, what are your plans now that it's all finished, Harvey?' Russell urged.

'I'm not sure, other than having some reading to do, and a few follow-up enquiries on some unrelated matters,' Harvey replied, purposely keeping his response vague.

'That doesn't sound as exciting as what I thought you were after, are you sure that's enough for you?'

Harvey paused, hesitating slightly before responding.

'I won't know until I try it, will I?' he replied.

'Maybe I can help you with that,' his old boss countered.

'What are you saying, Guvnor?' Harvey asked.

'I want you to come back to London and get your old job back,' Russell pleaded.

Harvey's pause was much longer this time.

'Excuse me?'

'I think you heard me, Harvey. Come back and oversee the expansion of the department, they're doubling the size,' Russell explained.

'Wow, firstly, that's great news, there's more than enough unsolved murders in London and I asked for more staff more times than I could remember. Secondly, you already have someone to do that, my replacement, remember?' Harvey reminded the man.

'The new DI is very good, I'm not denying that, but your

experience in all aspects of the job make you the ideal person for the new role,' Russell explained.

'I've got to hand it to you, Guv, it's thrown me a bit,' Harvey countered honestly.

'Well, the fact that you paused suggests that you are interested. Is that the case?'

'You taught me never to make snap decisions when it comes to career moves, remember? Can you give me a few days to think about it?' Harvey offered.

'I'll give you until tomorrow close of play. It's a great opportunity, Harvey, don't let it pass you by,' his old boss advised, hanging up.

'Well now, that's a hell of a way to start the day,' he uttered out loud.

HARVEY LOST TRACK of time as he thought about the offer that Marvin Russell had made. He was somewhat conflicted; the job offer was a great one... one that he would have accepted instantly during his first few weeks on the coast. But now? The last few weeks had been nothing short of great, and he wanted more of that, but was it too much to ask?

'I need to think fast, Max,' he muttered. He picked up his phone and called Rose.

'Good timing, Harvey, I'm just about finishing at work. How are you doing?' she greeted, the smile on her face showing in her tone.

'Do you fancy meeting up for a coffee and a chat? Something interesting has happened and I think talking about it will help,' he admitted.

'Sure, I can meet you. Why don't you come over in about

an hour. I'll make us some spaghetti Bolognese if you're up to taking a chance on my cooking,' she warned.

'Perfect, see you then,' he replied.

He took Max for a walk and fed him before driving over to Rose's apartment.

'I brought another bottle of red,' he said, handing it over.

'You know me so well, and it's been just a few short weeks,' she cheered, planting a kiss on his lips. 'Come through, I'll pour us a couple of glasses and you can spill the beans. Dinner will be ready in the time it takes for me to boil the spaghetti, so whenever you're ready for it,' she offered.

A few minutes later, they were sat next to each other on her comfortable sofa, wine glass in hand.

'So, what's this interesting thing that's happened?' she asked, taking a sip.

'My ex-boss rang me and offered me my old job back in London,' he replied.

Rose stopped mid-sip for a second before putting the glass down.

'I didn't expect that,' she stuttered.

Harvey could see that she was slightly disappointed but trying not to show it and impact on his emotions in any way.

'I just wanted to talk to someone, because if I'm being honest, I don't want to go, but I also don't know whether it's the right decision,' he explained, surprising her.

'You don't want to go? Why not?' she asked, playing Devil's advocate.

'Well, I'm starting to enjoy life very much here. I've found something that I enjoy doing, I've made friends, the sea air is wonderful, the town is wonderful... and I met someone I really like. Why should I go?'

'So, you've made your mind up?' she probed.

'Yes, but do you think it's the right decision? I wanted to ask you because you're switched on about things like this, and your situation isn't too dissimilar to mine. You know, coming from a busy city, leaving that stress behind, you know what I mean,' he added.

'I do. Ultimately, only you can make that decision, Harvey, but I will tell you this. If you go, I'd like to hope that you'd keep in touch and visit regularly,' she confessed, holding his hand. 'I know it's only been a few weeks but I... I've become very fond of you.'

She leaned over and kissed him gently on the lips.

'You think I should go?' he asked.

'I didn't say that. I just want to reassure you that whatever decision you make, I'll support it, and I'll support you,' she replied.

'That sounds very much like girlfriend talk, Rose. Am I your... boyfriend?'

Rose grinned and tilted her head to one side.

'What do you think, Detective?'

They kissed again, this time taking longer, savouring the moment.

'I'm not a detective anymore, Rose, I'm a civilian, remember?'

37

CELEBRATION

Harvey offered to pick everything up from the police and take it to Evelyn, now that the investigation had been concluded. He met Emily at the station and joined her for a coffee.

'You did a good thing, Harvey, we're very grateful for your part in this,' she expressed her appreciation.

'It was my pleasure, Emily. Millie and Evelyn are wonderful people, and they deserve to see justice done after all these years,' he replied.

'You really care about them, don't you?' she wondered.

'They've become good friends, which is good, as I'm still relatively new to the area, remember?'

'Well, don't forget me, Akira and the kids, otherwise you'll get the same treatment as McGarry,' she warned with a laugh.

'I wouldn't dare. In fact, I insist that you come round for dinner one night, I'd like you to meet Rose,' he insisted.

'Ooh, sounds interesting, we wouldn't miss it for the world. Just get me some dates and I'll let you know,' Emily replied.

'So, is everything ready for me to take?'

'Hold your horses, Mr. There's someone who wants to have a word with you before you leave,' she stood briefly before continuing. 'Wait here while I get her.'

'Get who?'

'My boss, Chief Superintendent Susan Wilkins.'

'Why does she want to talk to me?' he questioned.

'Who knows, maybe she wants to thank you?' Emily grinned. 'Wait here.'

Harvey saw her return with a tall woman wearing a grey suit and light blue shirt.

'Harvey, this is Detective Superintendent Susan Wilkins, my boss, just like I told you,' Emily introduced the pair.

'It's good to finally meet you, Harvey. I wanted to thank you for your assistance in bringing this matter to our attention,' Wilkins stated as they shook hands.

'No need to thank me, ma'am, I was just doing what any other... retired detective would've done,' he shrugged.

'Yes, but you did it particularly well. I was impressed with the way that you handled it, and yourself, throughout the investigation.'

'I was happy to help,' he reassured.

'Is it something you'd be interested in doing a little more often?' Wilkins asked, raising an eyebrow.

'I'm sorry, what do you mean?'

'I think you'd be a great asset to us, Harvey. With your experience in London, we could do with someone to help us with the backlog of unsolved major crimes. I'm offering you a consultancy role, if it's something you'd be interested in. It would be part-time, but the hours would be flexible to suit your requirements,' she explained.

'Wow, two job offers in the space of two days, I must be doing something right,' he laughed.

'You have another offer on the table?' Emily asked.

'My ex-boss wants me back to oversee the expansion of the team,' Harvey replied. 'And I have to respond by five o'clock.'

'That's a shame, it would've been great working with you on more cases,' Emily hummed in defeat.

'I'm going to turn him down,' Harvey announced.

'Really? Why?' Emily asked.

'I like my new life, and I want to make the most of it,' he shrugged.

'Does that mean you'll be turning me down also?' Wilkins asked.

'No, ma'am, I think it suits me perfectly. I'd like to accept your offer,' Harvey declared contentedly. 'With one condition, if I may?'

'What's that?' Wilkins pressed.

'My aunt left a binder with some interesting unsolved mysteries that I'd like to delve into. I'm keen to investigate them where I can and hope that you'll allow me to do so; I can assure you there will be no conflict of interest.'

'Harvey, as long as you don't break the law, you'll have no objection from me,' she assured, holding out her hand.

Harvey nodded in thanks and shook hands with his new boss.

'WE ABSOLUTELY HAVE TO CELEBRATE,' Rose exclaimed with glee when Harvey called to let her know. 'That's great news!'

'What do you fancy doing?' he asked.

'I think it's time for another visit to North at Burlington, don't you?' she encouraged. 'I'll call and book a table for tonight. Have you told your old boss yet?'

'No, I'll do that later today, I have to drop some things off to Millie and Evelyn first. Drop me a message when you have a time for the table and I'll pick you up,' he smiled.

'Okay, see you later.'

Harvey shook his head in disbelief at the day's events, and now here he was with the things that he and Max had found, about to be returned to their rightful owners.

'Thank you so much for this, Harvey,' Evelyn expressed her gratitude as she led him through to where Millie was sitting in the kitchen.

'There's my hero,' Millie announced, holding her arms out for her now familiar hug and kiss.

'I brought you some goodies,' he told them both, taking a number of items out of a large holdall.

He laid out the documents, including deeds to properties and land, along with the proclamation and other letters.

'Some of these are badly water damaged, but there's enough for you to get replacements, the solicitor will help with that,' he informed them.

Next came the engraved tin that Harvey opened and took out the pendant with the picture of the young family and the lock of Percy's hair.

'Bless him,' Millie murmured, stroking the toddler's face.

'These are amazing, Evelyn... your grandfather's medals. This one in particular,' he held out the Victoria Cross.

'I know it's weird to say this, as I didn't even know about him until a few weeks ago, but I feel somewhat proud, of both of them,' she indicated to the picture of Percy.

'This is your grandfather's pocket watch,' he handed that to Evelyn as he spoke.

'And this, Millie, is the original letter from Percy to you,' he then handed the envelope to Millie.

Harvey watched as Millie slowly took the letter out and read it, seeing her instantly clutch it to her chest the moment she finished reading, a bright smile on her face.

He then took the empty arsenic bottle and showed them both.

'I doubt you'll want this, so I'm happy to dispose of it for you,' he said.

'Please do,' Millie pleaded.

Harvey then took out another two bags carefully.

'Don't be upset, but these did not end up with the police. I didn't want to take any chances with them being held up if there wasn't a positive conclusion to the investigation,' he explained.

He carefully unwrapped the two small paintings and laid them side by side on the table before taking out the two jewellery boxes. Those, he opened and placed next to the paintings.

'I can tell you now, Evelyn, that these have enormous value,' he started, pointing to the paintings. 'And it would surprise me if the jewellery didn't fetch six figures.'

Evelyn gasped at the treasure laid out before her. She darted her eyes back and forth between her mother and Harvey, seemingly helpless, her emotions running high.

'What am I supposed to do now?' she stuttered out, her hands trembling.

'Don't you worry, Evelyn. I'll speak to the solicitor so that he can oversee their sale, if that's what you want to do. There will be some fees, but I'm confident you'll be left with enough money to take care of your family,' he soothed.

Evelyn shook her head in disbelief before going back to her mother for an embrace. Harvey watched as tears flowed freely from both women as the tension and unsettling memories started to leave and turn into something more positive.

'I'll leave you to it, ladies, I have a dinner date that I don't want to be late for,' he said, waving as he left.

'Thank you. Harvey, thank you.'

EPILOGUE

Sheringham, one month later

Harvey let Max off the lead as they approached Millie's front door. Since starting his new role as a part-time consultant with the Major Investigations team, Harvey was delighted that Millie and Evelyn had offered to look after him while he was away working. Max loved going there as Evelyn regularly arranged for Amy's dogs to be there to keep him company, so it was a win-win scenario for all involved.

'There's my little man,' Evelyn greeted, reaching down and ruffling his head.

Max let out a small bark before rushing past her to run to his waiting friends.

'How's it going, Evelyn? Any update from the solicitor?' he wondered.

'As it happens, it's all going very well; he's just finalising the deeds, and we've exchanged contracts on the hotel with the new owners. It's all starting to happen, Harvey, just like you said,' she welcomed him in with a kiss on the cheek once she had answered his question.

'I spoke with Emily Leclerc, and she tells me that the confiscation paperwork is almost done; it just takes time when it comes to police matters, as you know. On a positive note, the cars are all now safely in storage and out of reach of anyone who thinks they can grab them back,' he added.

'That's good to know. Please, come in. Amy is here and she has a little surprise for you.'

Harvey followed her to the lounge where her daughter and mother were both sat with their customary cup of tea.

Harvey embraced them both and sat facing them.

'You both look very happy with yourselves, what's going on?' he asked.

'Do you remember that photo I showed you of the netball team... the one with your Aunt Agatha in it?' Millie asked.

'Yes, of course I do. It's already framed on the mantelpiece, back at the cottage,' he replied.

'Well, you may have to move it and make space for something much better,' she grinned mischievously.

'What's going on, Millie? I know that cheeky look, what are you up to?' he urged, furrowing his eyebrows in confusion.

'Evelyn, why don't you tell him, love?' Millie replied.

'It was a joint decision, and there's nothing you can do about it, Harvey,' Evelyn prefaced.

'What on earth are you talking about?' he asked.

'As you know, Amy here is a very talented artist. Well, in light of everything that's happened these past couple of months, we wanted to show you how much we appreciated everything that you've done for us,' Evelyn grinned. 'So I asked Amy to paint a nice picture for you.'

'Oh, wow, that's very kind of you. Is it of Max?'

'Not quite,' Amy piped in, standing. She walked back towards the door to the lounge and from behind it pulled out a large, three feet by three feet painting that was covered by a sheet. She lifted it and placed it on the side table, leaning it against the wall.

'Wow, that's a big painting!' he exclaimed.

'Are you ready?' Amy teased.

'Go for it.'

Amy pulled the sheet away to reveal a vibrant painting of Aunt Agatha, from the shoulders up, as she had looked in the photograph. It was painted in a contemporary style, the vivid colours emphasising her wonderful smile. Harvey was stunned at the beauty of it and couldn't stop staring at it.

'That is incredible, Amy, just incredible. That's the welcoming smile I remember when I was a kid, from all the happy summers I spent with her,' he reminisced. 'She was an incredible woman, my aunt.'

'When I told Amy about the photograph, she instantly suggested a painting as a gift, and I think it was a perfect choice, don't you?' Millie questioned. She had walked over to him and stood next to him, her arm entwined with his, the pair admiring the painting and the woman that it portrayed.

Max wandered into the room and watched, perplexed as the four humans stood in front of the painting, motionless. He trotted up next to Harvey and looked up at his best friend, noticing something different about him. The terrier stood on his hind legs and leaned against Harvey before barking once to reassure his friend.

'I know, Max, thank you.'

'She would have been very proud of you, you know,'

Millie praised, 'with everything you've done since you've arrived back in Sheringham.'

'Not as proud as I am of her, Millie, not as much as I am of her.'

THE END

TO THE READER

I'm truly grateful for your support, and it would mean a lot to me if you could share your thoughts by leaving a review on Amazon. Your feedback is invaluable, as it helps other readers find books they might enjoy. Also, if you enjoyed this story, please help me spread the word by telling a friend about it.

Thank you for being a precious part of my writing journey.

Click here for the review link.

Gratefully yours

Theo

ACKNOWLEDGMENTS

Thank you, first of all, for taking a chance on the first book of the new series. I hope that you enjoyed it enough to want more!

There are many people I'd like to thank who graciously helped me with this book and the research required for it to be as accurate as possible.

I'd like to start with many thanks to the folks at the Sheringham Museum, especially Lisa, Ken and Lynne, without whose help I would have struggled to make sense of the history. If you are lucky enough to visit Sheringham, I highly recommend a visit to the museum, it is a jewel that will surprise you.

My thanks to Scott Eltringham for his historical knowledge that supplemented the information I was able to glean from the museum. Malcolm Stiles did a great job with the cover and Clare Stagg's help with Norfolk Constabulary information was invaluable, my thanks to you both. My partner Alison has been an invaluable source of local information and also helped tweak the cover to the final version, for which I am truly grateful.

Thank you also to the wonderful ARC readers who helped with the final version of the book. Maureen, Marc, Doris and Michele, I appreciate you all and am very grateful indeed.

A huge thank you to the super-talented Alexia Markos, the wonderful editor that helped me through this new venture with minimum fuss. I look forward to working with you on many, many more books.

Finally, I should add that I have changed the name of some locations and can assure you that this is a work of fiction and the slight changes will reflect this.

Again, my thanks to you all.

Theo

ABOUT THE AUTHOR

Theo Harris is an emerging author of crime action novels. He was born in London, raised in London, and became a cop in London.

He now lives on the North Norfolk coast.

Having served as a police officer in the Metropolitan Police service for thirty years, he witnessed and experienced the underbelly of a capital city that you are never supposed to see. As a result of the Official Secrets Act which he signed upon starting his career, he is unable to tell all!

Theo was a specialist officer for twenty-seven of the thirty years and went on to work in departments that dealt with serious crimes of all types. His experience, knowledge and connections within the organisation have helped him with his storytelling, with a style of writing that readers can associate with.

Theo has many stories to tell, including the *'Harvey Ross Coastal Mystery'* series along with the *'Summary Justice'* series featuring DC Kendra March, and will follow with many more innovative, interesting, and fast-paced stories for many years to come.

For more information about upcoming books please visit theoharris.co.uk

Printed in Dunstable, United Kingdom